THE
WAVE

THE
WAVE

LOCHLAN BLOOM

DEADINK

DEADINK

First published in Great Britain in 2016 by Dead Ink.
An imprint of Cinder House

ISBN 978-0-9576985-6-7

Cover art by Lola Dupre.
Cover design by FiST

*Printed and bound by CPI Group (UK) Ltd, Croydon,
CR0 4YY*

WWW.DEADINKBOOKS.COM

Made possible by support from Arts Council England.

LOTTERY FUNDED | Supported using public funding by
**ARTS COUNCIL
ENGLAND**

Books are made not like children but like pyramids, with a premeditated intention, and by stacking large blocks on top of each other, back-breaking, sweaty, time-consuming work and they serve no purpose! And they stay in the desert! Jackals piss at their foot and the bourgeois climb up on them.

Gustave Flaubert

In the end, who can say whether it is all one big coincidence or not? The story, if you call it that, starts with μ but where it leads and what it all adds up to is another matter. There are apparent links, sure, but do they amount to anything important? Do the various events and connections, described in such detail, form part of a bigger picture? You could waste a lifetime poring over these sorts of questions, burying your nose in a book, looking for some underlying structure, but these questions are never for the story itself to answer and, in any case, there are far better ways to spend your time than sitting around reading a novel.

1

The Post Arrives

μ opened the front door and there it was. It struck him as unusual. There was never normally post for him – some bills perhaps – but even that was less now that he had moved flats.

He turned the envelope over, feeling its weight. The heavy-duty manila suggested its contents might be valuable. His name was written on the front in thick marker pen. Brightly coloured stamps and postmarks crowded together – wavy lines of red ink. One mark looked like it read: 'Brasil' and another: 'Airmail'. μ didn't know anyone in Brazil.

He pulled at the thick glue that held the envelope shut. Inside lay a sheaf of typed sheets. Names and descriptions of locations were interspersed with clips of dialogue, as if someone had been following people, noting down their actions. It made no sense. Had some confidential dossier been sent to him by mistake? He looked closer.

It appeared to be some sort of film script. He didn't read these sorts of things and he struggled to grasp the layout. Most of each page was white space, broken only by small regular clumps of text floating in the centre. Why had it been sent to him?

He leafed quickly through. Page after page was covered in light grey font reminiscent of old-fashioned manual typewriters. He ran his finger over one of the pages but it was smooth and appeared to have been printed rather than hand typed. Who would send him this? He checked the envelope again; it definitely looked like one of the stamps read 'Brasil'. There was no letter of explanation enclosed.

μ threw his bag on the couch and placed the script on the table, orbiting around it. The flat took up two floors of a draughty old building that had been half-heartedly renovated in order to rent out. The landlord was never there and his flatmates weren't back by so he had the place to himself.

He flicked through the first few pages. What a disappointment! Twelve pages in and it was clear that this was no 'Citizen Kane'. Instead there was a confused story about a character named Ddunsel, who seemed to be the main suspect in a case involving several abductions, child molestation and murder. In several places graphic descriptions of his crimes were included. He seemed to be some sort of all-powerful psychopath. The action jumped around at random and the dialogue was uniformly poor. Who had sent him this drivel?

The few sections that contained anything approaching a decent plot were ill-thought-out and μ felt a dislike for the writing. There was no narrative line, only a haphazard collection of scenes, and it was obviously written by someone with little love of language.

Despite the clumsy phrasing, μ felt it was all written for a purpose, as if by some malevolent intelligence. He was in the middle of reading one repulsive section, describing the brutal rape and murder of a young boy by Ddunsel, when the sound of the front door made him jump.

They would all be returning for dinner. μ put the manuscript down and then, on impulse, covered it with a magazine. He had nothing to hide, but still, child murder was not what he wanted them to think he usually read.

He was sharing the house with foreigners. They entered, talking amongst themselves, and threw a nod in μ's direction. He nodded back and they busied themselves preparing their evening meal. There were only three others that actually lived there – Georgi, Ivan and Katarina – but often their friends would come around in the evenings and as many as ten or twelve of them would sit in the shared space eating and talking.

μ had not stayed in the flat for long but it already felt a lot better than the place he had been before. It was hard to believe that he had stayed in that old house for so long. Now he was sure his problems were behind him.

'All those people living on top of each other, rubbing against each other every day,' he thought. 'It's just as well that I moved out.'

The foreigners kept themselves to themselves and were pleasant, and tidy, which made living there that bit easier. He had no problems with them and would almost have said he liked it there.

That evening the script played on his thoughts. Its arrival seemed purposefully designed to disrupt his peace of mind. What a shitty present to receive. What kind of spiteful bastard had sent him this? From the little he had read, it did not seem to have been written for entertainment.

It was possible that it had been sent by some person quite separate from the original author, but somehow that seemed unlikely. μ felt sure that the writing and subsequent delivery of the package was the result of some invisible intellect tangling with a not quite realisable issue.

Georgi, Ivan and Katarina always arrived home at about

the same time and prepared a meal in the same communal way, amongst themselves in their own language. They spoke too fast for μ to understand and he would normally just wait until someone addressed him directly or else nod along, pretending he got the gist of what they were saying.

When they spoke directly to μ in English it was in broken, stuttering sentences and μ sensed that he was holding them up. He tried to imagine what it would be like to be from their country and speak their language. To be able to walk down the street there and understand what everyone was saying.

It was only the three of them that evening and μ felt relief that there wouldn't be a huge crowd for dinner. If truth be told μ had something of a crush on Katarina. She was light and elfin with eyes that seemed to permanently flicker with laughter.

When, sometimes, μ tried to laugh along to a joke of hers, Georgi and Ivan would give him a look that suggested they knew he was a faker, but something about Katarina always made him believe she was sharing a true part of herself with him.

As they cleared the table μ slipped the script up to his room, unseen behind the magazine. When he returned the food was ready and he helped set out the dishes of fried meat they had prepared as Georgi opened some cornershop wine.

It was good food, fatty and simple. μ ate in silence preoccupied by the script and who could have sent it to him.

After dinner they carried on talking and drinking. μ waited, unready to brave the solitude of his room. They talked louder now amongst themselves. μ was thinking of bidding them good night and finally going up to his room when out of nowhere he blurted:

'Do you know anyone in Brazil?'

They looked at him surprised. Katarina's eyes twinkled.

'Brazil?'

'It's nothing,' he said, embarrassed to have raised it. 'Forget about it, I should get up to bed.'

Awkwardly, he lifted himself from the table and shuffled to the door. They smiled back at him and he nodded his head as he ducked out the door. Going up the stairs he heard Georgi pronounce something loudly and they laughed. Katarina loudest of all.

Walking up the threadbare staircase, μ felt his emotions shift and the awkwardness of social contact was replaced by a vacuum. It was strange how quickly convictions could be replaced, trodden on, negated.

'How fickle I must be,' μ pondered. 'It's clear I was just feeling a bit down in that old place, nothing more than that and yet I was so certain… now it seems like nothing more than a passing cloud…'

μ thought of Jesus' disciple Peter. How he must have felt sitting at the Last Supper when Christ told him:

'Verily I say unto thee, that this night before the cock crow, thou shalt deny me thrice.'

When Peter had heard those words, the wine whipping his thoughts to grander heights, he must have refused to believe it could happen. What solid, unshakeable ground he must have felt he was on. His master earnest and innocent in front of him, he had replied:

'Though I should die with thee, yet will I not deny thee.'

At that point, there in the presence of his lord, conviction had driven him to tears. The idea that he, Peter, would deny his friend, the holy ghost made flesh, the true manifestation of pure love, that he should deny all that was sacred, not once but three times, was preposterous.

And yet, a few short hours later, and his conviction was gone. He would curse and rail against those that claimed he was with Christ and publicly denounce his lord. If that – the conviction of the deepest, metaphysical love – could prove to be nothing more than a passing sensation, then what after all could be true? If life was no more than a series of sensations linked together by chance, then what weight could any of it carry?

Safely in his room, μ closed the door, although he might equally have left it open for all the privacy it afforded. Through the floor he could make out the laughs of his flatmates and outside screaming devils shouted in the school playground across from his window. A constant rabble of children, baying at one another, bashing dissonantly on musical instruments. What were they still doing on the school grounds at this time of night? He found it hard to concentrate.

He decided to make a list. He wrote:

Find out who sent script
Leaving drinks
Strings
Look for job

He made these little lists frequently but seldom referred back to them. It might have made sense to tick items off once they were finished or even compare his progress against some timeline but he never did. He only wrote the lists to reassure himself that while some tasks might seem impossible everything could in fact be broken down into smaller components. The whole was just a series of simple steps that could easily be achieved. People talked about the big picture but μ had the feeling that the 'big picture', if it were ever to be revealed, would be a terrifying vision.

He started to read the script again, but the wine he had drunk with dinner made him woozy and he couldn't concentrate. It was difficult to keep his attention on the page and something buzzed at the back of his mind. He needed to find out more about where this had come from. Could there actually be a real-life Ddunsel out there?

Unearthing his battered laptop from a pile of papers, he powered it up and waited while it chugged to open the browser. He couldn't find anything about any Ddunsel that appeared to be related – the few places the name cropped up were clearly not relevant and there was no obvious connection with Brazil. Instead, he tried searching for some of the phrases in the script, but that produced far too many results to make sense of.

Having yawned twice, he decided to continue reading in bed

and as he lay down he noticed three small red lumps, close to each other on his upper left arm. He must have been scratching them idly throughout dinner. They looked inflamed.

'A mosquito,' he thought, 'or perhaps three mosquitos.'

An image came to his mind of three identical mosquitos, wearing bowler hats, travelling everywhere together, leaving these three red marks as a form of symbol. It was a strange kind of symbol, if that were the case. His arm itched like hell. No – perhaps it was a symptom of something.

Opening another tab, he searched for any information about his affliction, but the results were ambiguous. Most of the pages he found seemed to suggest that it was just a mosquito bite, but then, as he read more, he discovered that it could also be a sign of early stage Pemphigus vulgaris. Some of the images of blistered skin were particularly disturbing. He searched various reference sites and forums, feeling slightly nauseous, all the while telling himself it wasn't productive to look at such things.

At the side of one of the pages an advert read: 'Meet hot girls in your area'. It was accompanied by a picture of a young Latino teen in a bikini bending toward the camera. It was quite bizarre, he thought, that they should have this advert on a page about skin diseases, but he opened a private tab and searched for pornshute anyway.

The site was one of his favourites. It contained a seemingly endless stream of content all filmed with a certain realist style. He flicked from one clip to the next, rapidly opening new tabs – a lesbian couple who discovered each other's pleasure 'for the first time', a horny wife who wanted to 'swallow hot cum fast', a lusty blonde who wanted 'to be pounded'. He chose the clips impulsively, scanning the thumbnails for a shot that looked enticing or some glance that suggested a human connection.

Although the clips were short he watched each one for only a moment, some addiction making him flick on, wanting more. The greater the humiliation or discomfort on the face of the actress, the more he felt, the more he wanted. It was like falling into a hole.

A Filipina girl cried beneath the weight of a potbellied white man with greying pubic hair. Her little body looked so fragile under this old letch. A prick of excitement mixed with guilt. She looked very young but it was only a performance, wasn't it? He couldn't be blamed just for looking at it? Even if it was realistic. She whimpered loudly as the weight of the man forced her face into the pillow.

Apart from the thin walls, the other problem with his room was the bed, which made a terrible squeaking noise every time he lay on it. As a result he had to stay as still as possible, the volume turned down low, as his forearm moved quickly back and forth. He was not able to hear as much as he would have liked, but the headphones were downstairs.

He was enjoying one artfully shot clip when the battery on his laptop died. It was a real piece of shit and he generally had to keep it plugged in, otherwise the battery barely lasted twenty minutes. To make matters worse, the charger was downstairs as well, so obviously he would have to carry on without it.

He closed his eyes trying to conjure up the image of the young girl again, but he couldn't concentrate. Instead he tried to picture Katarina, her eyes twinkling mischievously as she went down on him, struggling to fit him entirely into her mouth. He let out a groan as he felt himself getting close. She played with him, sucking him deeper and deeper into her mouth, the corners of a teasing smile tempting him cruelly. He was very close. He focused on her eyes, making him harder. One moment they gleamed wicked, the next they were innocent. He ignored the squeak of the bed. She goaded him on; complicit. He was very close. He tried to avoid breathing. Out of nowhere an image of Alberta came into his mind.

He wiped it up with a pair of old underpants. He was empty. Empty and irritated. Why had he pictured Alberta all of a sudden? He pulled the duvet over and switched off the bedside lamp waiting to drift off. Normally he would fall asleep straight away, but that night he lay awake.

He had not thought about her in ages. It meant nothing, surely, but still, it was strange that he should think of her just at that moment. His rash burned, the bites red and angry. What was she doing in his head? He didn't care, he told himself. Anyway he was in the city now.

He was far too awake. His brain raced and the emptiness that had once promised to lull him into sleep now expanded, engulfing his thoughts. His whole position seemed ludicrous in this state of mind.

Forty minutes later he got up and turned on the light. He paced around the room a couple of times before finally picking up the script from the edge of the table.

INT. PUBLISHER'S OFFICE - DAY

A cramped, book-lined office overlooking the River Thames.
UP, a woman in her fifties, sits attentively in front of an oak desk. She wears a thick woollen skirt.

On the other side of the desk a corpulent man, DOWN, sits scratching the side of his face nervously. Also in his late fifties, he wears a crumpled suit and sports several days' stubble. On the polished table top lies a manuscript, titled μ.

DOWN places his hand on top of the manuscript.

      DOWN:
 It's not going to work.

      UP:
 No?

      DOWN:
 No, it's weak, this character, μ, far too passive.

UP looks horrified.

      UP:
 Passive?

      DOWN:
 Horribly passive.

      UP:
 You think so?

THE WAVE

                DOWN:
But that's not the issue.

                UP:
Look, Tob, you don't need to decide
anything now. Let me leave it with you...

                DOWN:
Yes, but it's not about that anymore...
I wanted to talk to you about something.
This... it's just not something I can do
anything with. I mean nobody wants to read
about someone wanking into a sock. They're
out to get us...

DOWN stands and moves to the window, fidgeting.
He glances about as if seeking out the faceless
agitators responsible for his plight somewhere
on the streets far below.

            DOWN: (CONT'D)
New York is very unhappy with the numbers.

                UP:
Unhappy?

                DOWN:
They've been unhappy for a long time.

                UP:
So, just to get you straight, you're not
considering it at the moment?

DOWN turns briefly to look at the manuscript.

                DOWN:
I don't blame them you know. For being
unhappy.

UP:
Frankly, Tob, I don't know why I bothered coming all the way down here if you're not even considering it.

DOWN:
There's something I need to talk to you about.

UP:
I've got mountains of work. It's a long way to come.

DOWN:
We're too old for this. When did it all get so impossible?

DOWN's shoulders go limp. UP walks over to the table and places her hand on the top of the manuscript.

UP:
I should go. I'll leave this...

UP lifts the manuscript towards DOWN, but he ignores it and continues staring out the window.

UP: (CONT'D)
So tell me then, what is it?

DOWN:
They're making cuts, big cuts.

UP:
Is that all? Aren't they always? Well, people will always read new books.

DOWN:
New books? It's all cookery these days.

12

THE WAVE

Celebrity Chefs.

DOWN spits out the last two words as if choking on a badly prepared langoustine.

> DOWN: (CONT'D)
> They're going digital.

> UP:
> Digital?

> DOWN:
> Yes, they're closing nearly all the imprints.

> UP:
> You don't know that.

DOWN turns away from the window and considers UP.

> DOWN:
> You and me, we're relics.

> UP:
> You cheeky sod. Speak for yourself.

> DOWN:
> All except two.

> UP:
> Jesus. Do you know who the lucky ones are?

> DOWN:
> Lucky?

> UP:
> Who they're saving?

DOWN:
There are no lucky ones. Just what's left.
They're splitting the spoils - between us
and Vintam.

UP:
Well, there you go. That's got to be a
win. You'll need to sign some new authors.

UP moves toward the table and picks up the
manuscript again, offering it vaguely in the
direction of the window. DOWN ignores her.

DOWN:
I wonder, sometimes, what will people
think of us in a hundred years? Two hundred
years?

UP:
Come on. I'm sure they'll be far too busy
to think about us.

DOWN:
They'll sneer at the stupidity of our
lives. That's what they'll do.

UP looks uncomfortable, quickly darting a glance
at the closed door before putting the manuscript
back on the table.

DOWN: (CONT'D)
Greed.

DOWN motions out of the window at the shimmering
glass towers lining the river.

DOWN: (CONT'D)
You know they used to believe an invisible
being was going to make life better in the

The Wave

future. They built towers, spent years building spires of worship, in the hope of a better life to come. Now what do we believe? We build even taller spires in the belief that an invisible hand will make our life better in the future. Nothing changes – we sneer at our ancestors and repeat their mistakes evermore ineptly.

UP motions to the bookcase lining one wall.

> UP:
> Hopefully we've helped to contribute something.

DOWN snorts derisively and marches over to the bookcase as if looking for evidence of a contribution to literature. Finding none, he turns despondently away and slumps back in front of his desk.

> DOWN:
> No. Celebrity Chefs – that's where the market is.

> UP:
> These things change.

> DOWN:
> Nothing changes. Whatever our nature is, we won't escape it. All we can do is exacerbate the situation, repeat the same mistakes like worn out machines. God, I don't know how people manage to convince themselves to keep on going.

> UP:
> Well, what's the choice?

DOWN:

What's the choice? There is only one choice. That's what all these books should be about, not fucking cookery. There is only one fucking choice – whether to shoot ourselves in the head or not.

UP:

Jesus, Tobs, you are feeling sorry for yourself today. Most people can make that choice quite quickly.

DOWN:

Most people are idiots.

UP looks apprehensive.

UP:

Look, maybe I should get going.

DOWN:

Get going? No, stay.

UP:

Really I should go. It's not a good day... I'll come back another time.

DOWN:

No, stay. I wanted to speak to you.

UP:

About what? You seem all on edge today.

DOWN:

I felt like you would understand. We were close.

UP:

Tob, that was a very long time ago.

THE WAVE

DOWN:

Many moons...

UP:

What's got into you today?

DOWN:

No. Nothing. Just ignore me. Maybe you should go.

UP stands to leave but doesn't move immediately. Instead she eyes DOWN worriedly. He toys nervously with his ring - a gold band emblazoned with a green stripe.

DOWN: (CONT'D)

I just couldn't bear to write any more justification, I had to leave something that wasn't just another page of scribbles.

UP:

What are you talking about? Look, I'm going. Why don't we get a breath of fresh air, grab a coffee?

DOWN:

I just need to explain. It's a case of looking at things rationally, that's all.

UP:

What? What is?

DOWN:

Eventually all the reasons run out.

UP:

What reasons? What are you talking about, Tob?

DOWN is silent for a long moment then reaches into the top drawer of his desk and pulls out an antique Webley Mk II hand pistol. He fumbles unfamiliarly with the gun.

UP leaps back in shock.

>   UP:
>   Jesus Christ! Where did you get that from?

>   DOWN:
>   I had some news last week and it helped me
>   reach a decision.

>   UP:
>   Shit, is it loaded?

>   DOWN:
>   It's reached a certain point and I thought,
>   you know what, I can do this.

UP looks at the decrepit handgun with a look of incredulity and horror.

>   UP:
>   Decided what?

>   DOWN:
>   There's no point trying to change my mind,
>   all this. It's nothing much to leave
>   behind in any case.

DOWN motions around the room with his gun hand as if to illustrate the emptiness of his office, and existence in general. UP flinches as the barrel swings past her.

>   UP:
>   Ok, how about you put the gun down, eh? We

can talk, it's just… it makes me a little nervous.

DOWN:

I thought of writing a note you know? I even started writing down my... explanation, an apology if you will, but I couldn't do it, I couldn't bear the thought of adding any more crap to the pile. The world is clogged enough already with mountains of words.

UP:

Put it down for a moment.

DOWN:

We rake through them, regurgitated splodges of letters, but there aren't any new thoughts any more, just recycled phrases, readable clichés and clever fucking plot devices that just leave you... cold.

UP:

How long have we known each other, Tob? You're not going to do this.

DOWN:

Yes.

UP sinks back into her seat in horror.

DOWN: (CONT'D)

Don't worry, I cleared my diary for the rest of the afternoon. I'll wait till you've gone.

UP:

My God, you're serious? You expect me to walk out and let you shoot yourself?

DOWN:

I told you I've reached a decision. This isn't some madness. I'm going to do it in any case, and from what I've read it's probably better not to hang around to watch – but I can't stop you.

UP:

From what you've read?

DOWN:

We actually publish several different titles on the subject.

UP:

You're joking?

DOWN:

Would you believe one of them is written by an expert. He made seventeen unsuccessful attempts before turning to writing. What does that tell you?

UP:

That's not even funny.

DOWN:

It had very good sales in France.

UP:

Give me the gun, you're not going to do this.

DOWN:

We've become separated from Nature, you know. It all becomes one big abstraction. It's too late now to find a way back.

UP takes a couple of steps towards the desk

more confidently.

>   UP:
>   What is this talk? You don't want to do
>   this. It's been a bad month, that's all,
>   no reason for this.

>   DOWN:
>   It's nothing to do with that. You think
>   it's just a bad month?

>   UP:
>   It's a stressful time just now.

>   DOWN:
>   That's the point. It's always a stressful
>   time. Everyone is always stressed. We
>   live in a world that is full of stress.
>   We're not designed to live without stress.
>   Our bodies are built for it. That is the
>   problem.

>   UP:
>   Stop it.

>   DOWN:
>   That's what I didn't realise – what stopped
>   me from doing this for so long. I knew I
>   wasn't the only one.

>   UP:
>   The only what?

>   DOWN:
>   You just have to look at the world around
>   us; everyone is unhappy, but I told myself
>   there was something we were missing.

UP:

What are you talking about?

DOWN:

I thought there could be some misunderstanding, a cosmic misunderstanding, if you will. That there was some sort of divine truth that we had all forgotten. Now I see how naive that is.

UP:

Look, Tob, stop this now. You're scaring me.

DOWN:

We're designed this way from the moment we're born. There is no salvation, no spiritual redemption. We cannot raise ourselves up higher any more than a rock can roll itself up a hill. These half real notions we have, these books, they only torment us further. The deadlock is 'an error in the original fettering.'

DOWN lets out a sobbing laugh and slumps against the window frame.

DOWN: (CONT'D)

What a joke.

UP:

Come on, this isn't you. Pull your socks up.

UP takes a step towards the intercom on the desk.

UP: (CONT'D)

I'm going to call through, ok?

The Wave

DOWN looks confused for a second and then swings the gun to point at UP.

                    DOWN:
   Don't touch that.

Slowly UP raises her hands from the intercom.

                    UP:
   What are you doing?

                    DOWN:
   I've got two bullets in here. So no more
   ideas.

                    UP:
   What? You'd shoot me as well?

                    DOWN:
   It's not like I'll have long to feel
   guilty about it.

                    UP:
   This isn't you speaking. You've got so
   much in your life.

                    DOWN:
   So much! Don't make me laugh. You of all
   people trying to convince me of that. You
   have about as many reasons to go on as I
   do.

                    UP:
   Why would you say that?

                    DOWN:
   Because I'm fed up of lying to myself and
   I can see you pretending that your life
   isn't empty as well.

UP crumples back in the seat, the stain of a tear in her eye.

                    UP:
    That's cruel.

                    DOWN:
    It's the truth.

                    UP:
    You're not going to shoot me. You think you're the only person who feels low. Fine, if you have to, go ahead, do it. I'm not getting in the way of a bullet. There'll be someone else here next week with better taste.

                    DOWN:
    I'm sorry I asked you here. Just leave me.

UP struggles to swallow some painful emotion.

                    UP:
                (sarcastically)
    I'm sorry if I've disrupted your grand exit.

                    DOWN:
    You think I'm not going to do it while you're still here?

                    UP:
    I told you I don't care either way.

DOWN raises the gun and puts the muzzle in his mouth.

                UP: (CONT'D)
    For Christ's sake, stop this, stop it,

stop it.

DOWN steadies the tremor in his hand but does not pull the trigger. He tilts his head slightly, his eyes closed.

>   UP: (CONT'D)
>   What was the news?

DOWN opens his eyes and looks sideways at UP. Slowly he withdraws the muzzle from his mouth.

>   DOWN:
>   I was at the hospital. Last Wednesday.
>   They say it's spread now.

>   UP:
>   It's spread?

>   DOWN:
>   The cancer. It's eating me out.

>   UP:
>   Cancer?

>   DOWN:
>   They called me in for a scan three months
>   ago.

>   UP:
>   Jesus, Tob. I didn't know.

>   DOWN:
>   They said it was routine - they always
>   say that, I guess - to check my liver
>   function.

>   UP:
>   Jesus. Can't they treat it?

>DOWN:

Maybe. No. Does it matter? We're all headed to the same place. An extra year or two vomiting into a bucket? No thanks. I'm just saving a little time.

>UP:

How little?

>DOWN:

It's nothing to do with that anyway. It's not like I'm really doing anything that wouldn't happen anyway. I've had time to think.

>UP:

To think about what? Shooting yourself here? In the middle of your office? Out of spite?

>DOWN:

I'm not going to hide in a hole. But you should leave. Please. Tell Rosie I won't be taking any calls.

>UP:

I won't leave you to do this.

>DOWN:

You're not going to stop me.

DOWN lifts the gun and mouths the barrel again. There is a long silence as neither of them move. DOWN has his eyes closed and his finger on the trigger.

The room is silent and UP stands up warily to approach him.

THE WAVE

                    UP:
                 (in horror)
    TOB!

DOWN squeezes his eyes tightly and pulls the
trigger.

In the silence there is a loud click as the gun
misfires.

Down looks around, uncomprehending. A look of
astonished disillusionment breaks across his
face and he staggers as if under a great weight.

                    DOWN:
    What happened?

                    UP:
    Tob, give me the gun.

DOWN remains with the gun in his hand. Both Agent
and Publisher stand in silence.
The silence is broken by the sound of the door
opening.

ROSIE, nineteen years old and fresh faced, rushes
in. She gasps, shocked.

                    ROSIE:
    Sorry. I didn't...

DOWN lowers the gun, avoiding eye contact with
Rosie.

                    UP:
    That's fine. Thank you.

                    ROSIE:
    I'm sorry, I didn't realise. There was a

shout. I just came to...

DOWN, starting to shake, places the gun on the desk, trying to hide it behind the manuscript.

                    UP:
    Thank you, Rosie.

Rosie looks between the two friends, clearly terrified and confused.

                   ROSIE:
    Should I… bring the coffee?

                    UP:
    No. No, thank you, Rosie. That's all.

DOWN lets out a low moan and starts to quiver. Rosie hesitates for a moment before retreating out the door.

DOWN sinks to the ground, his head in his hands.

                   DOWN:
    Oh God.

UP walks to the table and moves the gun gingerly out of DOWN's reach. She places a hand, maternally, around DOWN's shaking shoulder.

                    UP:
    Come on. It's over Tobs. It's going to be
    ok.

                   DOWN:
    What luck.

                    UP:
    Yes.

THE WAVE

> DOWN:
> What shitty luck.

> UP:
> Yes, but it's ok now.

> DOWN:
> I did it. I really tried to do it. That
> piece of shit.

DOWN starts to sob louder and UP draws him closer,
helping him up into the seat.

> UP:
> There, come on, sit up, it's ok.

DOWN pulls himself up into his seat.

> DOWN:
> I can't believe it. What utter shitty
> luck.

> UP:
> Let's get out of here.

> DOWN:
> Yes. No. I don't know. God, just leave me.

DOWN recovers his composure a little.

> UP:
> I'll get Margo to come over. Let's go and
> wait somewhere more comfortable, get some
> fresh air?

UP supports DOWN on one side and together they
limp out of the room.

On the desk lie the gun and the manuscript.

LOCHLAN BLOOM

A Local Entanglement

μ must have fallen asleep. He awoke from an uneasy dream to find he had been bitten again. The bites were starting to transform into a rash that spread along his upper left arm. It looked red and angry but there was no particular sensation. Perhaps there was something in his bed. He took a close look at the mattress but couldn't see anything. The thought of some monstrous vermin living in there made him shudder.

The pages of the script lay scattered by his bed. How far had he got through it? Images from the night before rose up in his head. Had he read about the gruesome rape of a young boy by the character called Ddunsel , or had he dreamt it? As he remembered the details he felt a slow nausea. He was still half asleep. Another image, of the girl in the pornshute video, her buttocks spread, face down in the carpet, half-real, followed again by a thought of Alberta. He tried to clear his head.

His arm itched and he thought again of the bugs that must have eaten him in the night. Why did the idea of one creature preying on another seem so disturbing? Living matter was what the body was designed to consume, after all. Eating the flesh of another organism was the most natural thing in the world. There were precious few animals that could survive eating sand or rock.

The clock glowered at him as he forced the last of his toast down his throat. Was Katarina still in the house? Normally they all left much earlier than he did, but he was suddenly mindful of being nearly naked, sitting there in his pants.

Back in his room he slipped on a shirt and felt the fabric rubbing against his left arm. He didn't bother with a tie. Collecting the scattered pages of the script, he was about to place them on the desk when he changed his mind and slipped the script into his satchel.

The underground was relatively quiet as he made his way through the lengths of connecting tunnels. He was self-conscious about his arm, even though it was hidden from view, and tried to avoid passing near anyone on his left side. Luckily his station was never too busy. The route he took went from one undesirable part of town to another, hence not too many people got on or off at his station. Other lines, like those feeding the financial district, would be packed at this time with brand new shining trains appearing every minute to whisk workers in and out of their offices. The stations on those lines were lavished with attention.

As μ walked along the platform he spotted a man sitting begging next to one of the entranceways.

'Any spare change?' the tramp mumbled as μ passed.

μ carried on as quickly as possible. He didn't remember seeing anyone begging in this station before. Who had let him in? Had he bought a ticket purely to beg down here? The tramp was dressed in a three-piece suit that was two sizes two big and covered in stains. Perhaps someone had mistaken him for a commuter.

'I didn't always do this you know,' the tramp hissed after him. 'Fascists. I've got my rights the same as anyone else.'

He walked a little way past his usual spot, to put some distance between himself and the man. From the other end of the platform he watched the tramp standing in his piss-stained suit shouting 'DIGNITY'.

μ was used to the rhythm of the daily commute. He knew where to stand to find an empty carriage, he recognised other commuters and knew the spots where they stood, he could even pick out the new advertising signs from the old.

The train was delayed and he thought of the script. Who had sent it to him? He searched for any connection with Brazil. He considered pulling it out to examine but he never liked reading on the train. In fact he rarely read at all these days. Not since he had finished university. How long ago was that? It was like another world. He stared down the platform looking for the train. The tunnel was dark.

How long he had been in this city already?

'It's only a temporary job,' he told himself.

He worked in the Customer Billing Services department, on the phone all day, answering calls from bored, angry or irate customers. The products that they spoke to him about all had vague, meaningless names conjured up by the marketing department to inspire feelings of desire or inadequacy in the paying customer, but μ knew them only as numbers on his screen. He had next to no knowledge of exactly what they did. That was not required.

He had been told at the start that it was better if staff in his department didn't worry themselves overly about the operation of the company. There had been some problems in the past. Staff in the Customer Billing Services department had offered advice to customers on how to save money and this had impacted the company's profit margins.

It had been explained that this sort of behaviour wasn't in the best interest of the shareholders – it was better if customer billing agents didn't know anything at all about the nitty-gritty of operations or indeed the company in general.

If there was a question that he couldn't answer μ was told to forward the call to the sales department, where staff were a lot more knowledgeable about the shareholder's needs. μ could see the logic in this and had never bothered to find out any more about the company or the products they were selling.

'In any case,' he said to himself, 'this is just a temporary job. There's no point getting too involved.'

Compared to most of the cretins doing the job he was more than capable, but the managers all felt that he was too unreliable to promote to any position of authority. He was only on a temporary contract after all. They tolerated him. This was fine with μ. He had been there more or less since he arrived in the city.

He had initially planned to transfer from his old job in Sygeton, but there had been some miscommunication and when he arrived at their headquarters it was only to interview and not for a job. Eventually they had decided he was 'not the right fit for the role requirements'. What an idiot they had made him look. What had he been thinking?

Not that μ blamed Allan, his old boss; he had taken a liking to μ

from the outset. Allan seemed to see some similarity to himself in
µ. He would sometimes take him aside for a chat and, once, after µ
had been there only a couple of weeks, he had said:

'It might be good for you to move to the city – try it for a couple
of years. Get some experience there and then you can always come
back. Look at me. I let things just happen to me and here I am. I'm
never going to get anywhere now. I guess you don't notice these
things until they've passed you by but it's different when you start to
realise that not all the doors are open to you anymore. In fact, you
realise most of the doors have been locked all along and you never
even had the guts to try and open them.'

At that point, Allan had looked morosely up and down the office
as if looking for confirmation of this statement. There were no
doors in the open plan office. He had brightened up and with a grin
finished the conversation by saying, 'Part of getting old I suppose.'

µ had muttered some vague acknowledgement with no intention
of moving to the city. It was only after some time had passed, and
he did not receive so much as a postcard from Alberta that he
approached his boss to discuss a transfer. A week later he was on a
train heading east to the city.

The day at work passed quickly enough, as µ's job didn't allow
him time to entertain anything other than the most mundane of
thoughts. He sometimes felt his days were a solid mass of cloud
drifting past the ground below, although what precisely the 'ground'
was and whether it was he or that something else that 'drifted' he
couldn't say.

That evening a few of his colleagues were going for a drink
after work. The bar was a frequent haunt of the employees at his
company, and the place was normally packed out with the after-
work crowd. As he walked down the steps to the basement he found
a few of his colleagues at a table near the entrance. They laughed
and slapped him on the back. The rest of the office was at the back
bar, they told him.

The room was done up to look like some foreign cantina; brightly coloured stools and fake wicker leaves lined the walls. The bar staff all wore flamboyant shirts and clattering jewellery, and one of them had even gone as far as to sport a moustache, although μ couldn't tell if it was real.

The central area was lit by a bright overhead light and was a crush of suits, just out of work. They jostled and gabbled loudly and μ had to push past them to reach the passage that led to the back bar.

It was a lot quieter and dimmer there, with candles providing most of the light. A mix of hard leather sofas and upright seats accommodated around thirty of his work colleagues. They looked like they were having a great time and μ started to think what a terrible idea it had been to come. Nobody turned as he approached and now he felt sluggish and out of place. The conversations buzzed around him.

Laughter broke out in waves, like a disease, from each little huddled group and then died away into the crowd. As far as μ could tell there was no particular reason for any of the hilarity and there were no apparent punch lines. Awkwardly he positioned himself at the edge of a group standing by a pillar. They talked mostly about people he didn't like or didn't know.

'God', he thought, his head starting to swim from the beer. 'Why did I decide to come here?'

He sat in the midst of everyone without really saying anything beyond a yes or no. He didn't want to go home but he was uncomfortable standing there. He swigged back his beer intending to leave once he had finished. As he reached the bottom of the bottle he found he needed to piss and made his way to the toilets.

The evening crowd had got busier and he had to shove his way through the dense crush in the centre of the front bar. The lights had been turned down and the music turned up. With a few drinks in them people were now trying to dance. This had the effect of turning the entire floor in to a swaying, jostling sea of suits.

The route to the toilets led past a small outside smoking area, enclosed on all sides by concrete walls that went up to street level. The space was really nothing more than a storage area that had been converted with a few tables, umbrellas and a gas heater, but the desire for nicotine evidently enticed people out into the rain.

On his way back, μ paused at the entrance to this smoking area, thinking he heard someone shout his name. He scanned the group to see if anyone was speaking to him. Although the space was small, the comparative silence and emptiness made it seem quite spacious. Several people waved and motioned in his direction but he didn't recognise any of them. He hesitated a moment too long at the doorway and it was obvious that he had seen them. There was no way he could walk off now and so he stepped outside to see what they wanted.

Even in the low light he could see that the man who had been shouting his name was far from sober. He was trying to stand up, but he was extremely drunk and had his leg caught in-between the bench and the table. It was only as the man reached out a hand that he recognised him as somebody he knew from Sygeton. A man by the name of Simmonds.

They had never been particularly close but seeing Simmonds suddenly brought back memories. What was Simmonds doing here? μ had been apprehensive before he knew who it was calling out, but he knew Simmonds; he was tolerable.

Relieved, μ shook his hand and they exchanged some pleasantries, but the man was so drunk that he seemed to be muddling μ up with someone else. μ tried to continue the conversation as best he could, but Simmonds soon lost his track and lapsed into drunken silence. Sensing this pause in proceedings, one of Simmonds' companions collared μ, proffering a full pint of beer.

'Join us. Have a drink,' he shouted, 'ideal afternoon for it.'

This was met with riotous laughter from around the table.

μ was trying to think of an excuse, but before he could make an escape he was dragged towards a spare seat, the beer set down in front of him. Reluctantly he took his place, setting his bag down under the table.

Apparently it was Simmonds' birthday and the ragtag group that had assembled mostly hadn't known each other before that evening.

Empty shot glasses cluttered the table and a stream of new orders kept arriving from the bar as friends brought in rounds. μ was still aware of his colleagues upstairs and as the conversation sped back and forth he gripped his drink, sipping slowly.

Simmonds had obviously not shown any such restraint and was by now roaringly drunk. Some of his comrades appeared to be intent on following him into that special oblivion of the holy drinker, but Simmonds had a substantial lead. His head flopped uncontrollably left and right as he tried to form each sentence and then, sensing he was incapable, he burst out laughing uncontrollably. He would fall silent and then wake loudly with some cry; he would gesticulate wildly one moment and then, sensing where he was, would suddenly straighten up.

'Right,' he screamed, 'what we need is something a bit stronger.'

He flung himself up out of his seat, evidently intent on going inside. In the process his flailing arm caught several of the drinks on the table and sent them smashing on the cobbles. Alcohol and glass mixed in a rush towards the open drain, disappearing amongst a muddy wedge of leaves.

The other drunkards in the group found Simmonds' antics hysterical and in a roar of noise they rose as one, slapping Simmonds on the back and propelling him towards the bar. Huddled together they limped forwards, like an injured squad of soldiers heading for friendly cover, and left an audible vacuum behind them.

The rest of the group were all more or less sober and, not knowing one another, resorted to hesitant small talk. Evidently most of those remaining were keen to escape as soon as possible. μ was trying to decide whether to wait for the others to return from the bar or just leave when a flinty looking man to his right spoke.

'So, you made it?' he said speaking deliberately and slowly, as if reiterating something that everyone around the table already knew. It took a moment for μ to realise that the man was speaking to him. There was something unsettling in his demeanour, something hard and unpleasant. He looked familiar. Had he not seen this man somewhere? μ searched his face for some recognition, but the man was emotionless.

'Hearst,' the man said extending a hand. 'My employer has been interested in your case.'

'Your employer?' μ asked. 'What case?'

Was this a joke? Looking around μ looked for help, but nobody else appeared to be listening to this corner of the table. Was this man from the office? Human resources?

'My employer has a very unique perspective on it.'

Hearst gave a lopsided grin that was entirely out of place and reached into his jacket pocket. He produced a small card, bright green in colour and about half the size of a business card.

'He wants me to pass this on to you.' Hearst put the piece of paper, for it was actually surprisingly flimsy, into μ's hand. On it was written a number: 324-52-867. It didn't look as if it was the correct format or enough digits to be a phone number. But it was the name below the number that caught μ's attention. In a crisp dark green font was the name Ddunsel. μ's heart jumped at the sight of the name. He was about to ask Hearst what it meant when the drunks returned from the bar.

They came bearing a tray of drinks and lurching gaily across the wet paving stones. Simmonds was no longer with the group and, when one of those who had remained outside asked where he was, they were told:

'Simmonds was cunted.'

He was sleeping it off in the toilets. That seemed to be the impetus needed to split up the little party.

Now that their host was no longer present, those friends of Simmonds who had only turned up to be polite started to make their excuses and leave. Many of them looked as though they had already stayed longer than they would have liked, and seized this opportunity in case Simmonds should miraculously wake up and corral them into further festivities.

Meanwhile, the contingent freshly returned from the bar seemed determined to get drunk with or without Simmonds and were quite oblivious to anything but their own inebriation. They laughed and shouted across each other as the rest left. There was a short flurry of activity as everybody disentangled from the table, putting on scarves and coats and shaking hands. It was only after this commotion subsided that μ noticed his mysterious companion, Hearst, had disappeared.

μ had been hoping for an opportunity to restart the conversation and speak to this man further, but in the confusion he had somehow slipped away. What had he meant by his 'case'? Was he really employed by someone called Ddunsel? The way he had handed the card over had suggested he was serious, but then what, if anything, did that have to do with the script? Was Hearst responsible for sending it from Brazil?

It was dark by now and he had no desire to stay with the dregs of the party. Grabbing his coat he walked inside and up to street level. He didn't bother to stop at the back bar and say goodbye to his work colleagues.

On the tube ride home his itching had started to reappear and as he looked around his room he wondered again if there might be bugs. The crystalline yellow light lit up the uneven paintwork on the wall, highlighting every grain of dirt. He hated this room, the detritus of possessions that cluttered the place. He had already thrown away a good deal of junk, but still there were too many things. Each object seemed to weigh on him as if exacting some price for its existence there. He had to get rid of everything save for the essentials.

There, next to the bed, lay the sprawled pages of the script. Reaching in his pocket he pulled out the card and turned it over in his hand. Who was Hearst? What was the connection to Ddunsel and the script? He felt a tingle of excitement. He wished he had had the presence of mind to corner Hearst while he had the chance and question him some more. Why had they not included any other information besides a solitary name?

Pulling out his phone he dialled the number.

The Dead Boy

The phone clicked twice as if connecting, but all μ could hear was a background hiss. It sounded alive. Was there something on the other end? After twenty seconds he presumed it wasn't working and tried dialling again. The second time there was a 'number not recognised' message.

There weren't enough digits, so μ wasn't sure why it surprised him that the number did not connect. Looking angrily at his room it struck him again how untidy it was; he was disgusted by the state of it. No wonder there were creatures living in his bed.

Although familiar objects lay all around, μ's brain refused to recognise them in the chaos. In a frenzy he started cleaning. He had been concentrating on other things for too long. Half of his belongings he still hadn't unpacked. This room just needed a good clean. He was ruthless in his scourge.

Eventually four black bags of crap were ready to be cleared out. He took them down to the back door for collection and when he saw the room afresh, without all the junk cluttering the space, it was actually a lot bigger than he remembered. He thought about the belongings he had just thrown away and was elated that they were gone. He would get some new lighting or maybe a small armchair for the evenings.

He had space to think. He would be able to sit down and read this script more closely. Work out who had written it.

It was getting late and he still hadn't eaten. He had forgotten to get anything in and downstairs in the fridge he found he only had a little rotten cheese. He needed some cleaning products anyway so resolved to walk to the corner shop.

The neighbourhood was quiet at this time of night. There weren't many bars around there and the odd restaurants that survived all shut early. The local corner shop was closed for renovations so he walked down to the main road to try the off-licence there. It was shut as well, but it had stopped raining by then and he didn't mind walking since it was a pleasant enough night.

Having gone several blocks beyond his usual patch he noticed a shop with its lights on down a side street.

It had a sign above the door that read: 'Value Suprmarket'.

It was strange that it was open so late.

'Must be immigrants,' he thought. 'They can't even spell.'

It looked like it had just opened recently and evidently little effort had been spent creating the frontage. It was the sort of shop that stocked whatever plastic junk could be imported cheaply. Labels printed in a foreign language because they couldn't be sold elsewhere. A sign in the window announced a 'Super Value Sale'.

'Cheap imports from abroad, the economy dribbling down the drain – does everything get reduced to a cheap copy in the end?' μ thought, starting to cross the road towards the shop.

He needed to get his thoughts in check. He was only too aware of his 'moods' and he didn't want to slip backwards again. Nonetheless he felt something akin to that stark, shimmering mental state that signified a 'change' was coming.

The door pushed open easily, eliciting a cheap ring from the bell attached to the frame. He couldn't see anyone inside but the sheer amount of junk made it hard to make out the rear of the shop. Rows of plastic items filled the space, each slightly imperfect, different from the next, churned out by some low-quality manufacturing process in an overseas factory. Assorted household goods, mops, power adaptors, light fittings, cables, cooking utensils, door mats, bottles, replica ornaments, plastic containers, jars, rope, electronic thermometers, tools, gadgets and toys crowded out the shelves.

Stepping across the boundary he was somewhere foreign. The shop had an indefinable otherworldly feel, as if the piles of plastic and tin were arranged along ancient ley lines, the product of some greater organising principle; beyond his understanding, yet obvious and powerful.

Again he felt that stark shimmering.

Careful not to disturb the teetering goods, he browsed through the shelves until he came across a section of bottles and sprays that looked like they might be what he needed. The labels were all in

Arabic or some other script he didn't understand so, picking up a bottle and spray that looked the most promising – one with an image of an evil looking black bug covered in a cross, he made his way deeper into the shop to find whoever worked in this place.

The shopkeeper, if that's who it was, lay next to a doorway at the back of the shop next to a small pile of receipts. He was no more than a boy, perhaps only eleven or twelve but handsome. He wore a patterned djellaba made of rough cotton that was open and loose about his breast. His face was turned slightly downward, but the glow of the shop's light emphasised his light olive skin and boyish good looks. His lower half was covered by some sort of blanket and he lay there unmoving, supported by a couple of cushions with his back to the wall.

At first he presumed the boy was sleeping for, even though he was lying on the dirty floor, he looked comfortable amongst the cushions. For all he knew the boy lived and worked in the shop. It didn't seem unreasonable that he might take a rest there.

'Goodness knows what hours he's forced to work here,' μ thought.

The boy looked peaceful. His hand curled on his belly as if he had just fallen asleep after a good meal. μ took one step closer, and it was only then that he noticed the dark sticky stain, spread out on the ground behind the boy.

The boy's shirt was torn, leaving his shoulder and bicep exposed, and with shock μ now noticed a black bruise standing starkly on his upper arm. He couldn't move. The atmosphere of the shop had been shattered and a simple, chilling chaos crept over him. Everything was still.

Up close he could see that the blanket covering the boy was a thick, heavy material more like a rug or carpet. It had been placed over the body in a hurry and in places was black with blood. It was hard to see exactly where the wound had been inflicted and μ was reluctant to disturb the body. A sticky pool covered the uneven floor.

It was only as his hand touched the rug that it occurred to him that he may not be alone. Looking around, the exit was an unbearable distance away and the air inside stifling.

Without another thought for the wounded boy he struggled towards the door, but the instant he tried to move there was a great pressure on his shoulders as if he were deep underwater. Each footstep became an effort, as if he were walking through thick treacle, and his movement towards the door seemed interminable. His nerves tingled, infusing him with a desperate need for action but his legs barely responded. He was trapped in a gelatinous sliver of time. The stark shimmering rose to fever pitch.

The instant he stepped out onto the pavement he felt a rush of blood to his head.

'I'm going to be sick,' he thought and promptly, there on the pavement, he was sick.

It was as if he had been holding his breath the entire time he was in the shop and had only just realised it. His head swam with a hundred impulses and he had to stop himself shaking by gulping down breaths of air and focussing intently on his shoes.

He looked back inside confused. He wasn't sure how long he had been in there. He tried to remember why he had gone into the shop. What he had been doing beforehand? With an effort he recalled his room, his job, Sygeton, his life. Looking down at his arm he was almost surprised to discover the red inflamed bite marks were still there. He felt normal. It was late, he should be getting back. He set off at a pace.

It was two blocks away that he remembered the boy and stopped thunderstruck. What had he been thinking? How had he forgotten? Had he been hypnotised, his mind taken over for those instants? A boy was dead back there. What was he doing idly walking home when the boy still lay there? Was there something wrong with him? He rushed back the two blocks, but at the shop's entrance he hesitated. It was if some force repelled him from entering.

He collected himself – he had to phone the police. His fingers started to tremble as he hurriedly dialled the number. There was a crackling pause and then the phone started ringing. The hoarse noise from the handset sounded as if it was coming from a great distance away and so he pressed his ear closer to the receiver. It rang five times and then stopped. The crackling on the line had disappeared and was replaced by silence.

'Hello,' μ said.

'Hello,' a woman's voice replied. 'Can I help you?'

She sounded well educated and impatient.

'Is this the emergency services?' μ continued. The woman was most unprofessional if it was.

He could hear a distorted version of his own voice echoing back a moment after each word left his mouth.

'Emergency, which service?' the woman asked.

'There's a boy, I think he's dead.'

'Sir, you will need to speak up, which service do you require?'

'Ambulance.' μ shouted.

'Sir, I can barely hear you can you tell me your location please.'

'I need an ambulance at...' he realised he didn't know the address.

The woman read out an address. How did she know where he was?

'Hello sir, can you confirm that is your address.'

The woman continued asking questions and μ wasn't sure how much she could hear. Finally she seemed to understand that an ambulance was needed and, unable to communicate any further, μ hung up.

It was not an ambulance but a police car that turned the corner and pulled up outside the shop. A tall officer stepped out and scanned up and down the road, clearly checking for any signs of danger or criminal activity. Spotting μ lingering at the shop front he came over to question him. μ answered the policeman's questions as briefly as he could and, motioning in the direction of the shop, explained what little he knew. The policeman took this at face value and asked μ to accompany him inside to find the boy. μ took several leaden steps towards the door but once again found it was as if a force field prevented him entering. He stopped weakly and the policeman looked him up and down, then ducked inside the door.

It was five minutes before the policeman returned, ashen faced. One minute he started asking difficult unpleasant questions and the next he was on his radio barking orders in a curious half-whisper half-shout. All the time the policeman didn't take his eyes off μ, and it was only when an ambulance and a police van arrived that he seemed to relax.

With the addition of the extra crew the scene turned into a blur of activity. Medical equipment was rushed inside. Hazard tape was draped across the exterior of the shop. Notes and photographs were taken. μ felt forgotten in all the rush, even though one police officer, a burly lump, always seemed to be by his side.

He heard snippets of conversation whip past him – male, twelve years old, witness, 112 Rokforth Avenue, bleeding. The world seemed to reel. One of the policemen took μ to the side. He was a thickset man with a bushy moustache that looked like a prop from a bad detective film. He wasn't smiling.

'Your name sir?' he asked.

μ told him.

'And what were you doing in the shop at the time of the incident?'

μ was agog. He explained that he had been looking for cleaning products to kill some bugs in his room. The policeman noted this down intently and, confused, μ started to show him the red bites all along his arm.

'You live alone then sir?'

'No.'

And so the questions continued.

Was he a regular at the shop?

How long had he known the boy?

Why had he chosen to go into that shop for the first time that evening?

Did he have any previous convictions?

Was he sure there was no previous relationship with the child?

Did he have proof of address with him?

Who else was there when he came across the boy?

What was his relation to a Mr Ddunsel?

Who had sodomised the boy?

His head spun. Odious images arose in his mind. Why did he feel somehow complicit in what had happened?

They asked more questions and took his address and ID. The moustachioed man retired to the police van and spoke into his radio in a hushed tone. He kept his eyes on µ the entire time. Eventually, receiving some sort of confirmation from the radio, he returned with the documents in his hand.

'You're free to go,' he said, standing uncomfortably close to µ. 'We may need to call you in for additional questioning so don't make any plans in the next few days.'

Where would he go in any case? µ's left arm was shaking and he noticed he was still clutching the cleaning products.

'I didn't pay for these yet.'

The policeman eyed him suspiciously.

'Keep them,' he said, waving µ away.

Back in his room he started spraying every surface, cleaning in all the gaps, scrubbing at the dust and grime. What had happened in that shop tonight? Why had he never seen that place until now? Why could he not shake the feeling that it had been prearranged? He felt sick again.

He carried on scrubbing, cutting through the dirt effortlessly. It was only after half an hour that he realised he had a splitting headache. The spray was doing its trick, but it did smell terrible, filling the air with a thick chemical perfume. What was in it? No wonder he was so ill. His pulse was pounding in the side of his head.

He pushed the window wide open and sat down to survey the room. It did look a lot better.

'Tomorrow', he thought, 'I might even decorate.'

As he glanced around, his eye caught the pile of papers on his desk. The script! Had it not described a scene almost exactly like the shop with the dead boy he had just found? He looked at the pages, afraid now to touch them.

Words from the previous night awoke in his head. The description of the boy's body being discovered, the back of a dollar shop, rectal bleeding, a torn djellaba. In his mind it sounded like an exact description of what he had seen. Who was at the bottom of all this? Was the script a description of the dead boy or had the body been placed there to mirror the script?

His head pounded with the chemical smell. There were similarities, possible connections, but was that all? Most of the script was nothing to do with him. He filled one more bin bag with items, still afraid to confirm his fears by double checking the pages on the desk. It was well after midnight by now. He crawled over to the bed and climbed under the covers.

He was almost safe there for a moment, tucked up in his cocoon. The new place wasn't paradise, but Georgi, Ivan and Katarina were all decent people – certainly nothing like his previous flatmates.

An Implicit Order

The next morning it was μ's day off and he awoke early. Earlier than he needed to. Having breathed the chemicals all night his head hurt and, as he coughed, the inside of his lungs tightened.

'I should have read the instructions,' μ thought 'it probably isn't even safe for humans.'

The chemical didn't seem to have deterred the bugs as he was now bitten up and down his right arm. He tried to see where they could be coming from but there was no sign. This wasn't a good start to the day.

The room was empty; he remembered packing everything frantically the night before. The last black bin bag he had filled still sat in the corner. What was he trying to prove? Did he really need to throw this all away? Was he trying to avoid something?

He lay there for a long time trying not to scratch, staying as still as possible, in the belief that sleep would eventually return. It was no use; the bright morning sun constantly invaded his thoughts. He recalled his encounter with Hearst and the dead boy.

He finally got up and sifted through the papers on his table, but the script wasn't there. Had it not been on the top of the pile? He was sure he had seen it last night. Had he inadvertently thrown it into one of the black bags?

Opening the bin bag he raked through it but couldn't find anything.

'It must be here,' he thought. 'How did I manage to throw it out?'

Where had it gone? His frustration slowly turned to panic. He needed to find it. He tipped the bag onto the floor to better search through the contents. Old magazines, a set of bike lights, mismatched socks, broken CD cases all fell out on the floor. He sifted through the dusty piles but it wasn't there.

He struggled to remember when he had seen it last. Had he definitely seen it there the previous night? Had he thrown it out the previous morning? Or somehow left it in the pub? He couldn't be sure now. Shit. The room was an utter mess again.

He rushed downstairs to check if the bins had been collected, but the slot outside the back door was bare. It was a cold morning and although the sun had streamed in his windows it was actually surprisingly dull outside. Grey clouds hung above the street and the only sounds were those of the early morning deliveries.

Could someone have taken the script? Georgi? Ivan? Katarina? They seemed trustworthy, but then what did he really know about them? They could have easily just walked in and taken it. Christ, he didn't even have a lock on his door.

He considered going downstairs to confront them but it seemed too fantastical. What did they have to gain from stealing some incomprehensible script? Who, then? The original author? Again the thought occurred to μ that it had been sent to him by mistake. Perhaps whoever had sent it needed it back and rather than confront him had merely broken in to his room. It couldn't have been that hard.

The chemicals still made him feel sick and his stomach bubbled from lack of food. He had to get out. He didn't have anything to eat in the flat in any case. Taking his bag and coat from the hall he pulled the front door shut.

Walking cleared his lungs and after a few blocks he already had less of a headache. The early morning streets were crisp and orderly. The day had barely begun and he had it to to himself; he could do anything with it. He grimaced. How little he had in his life.

That stranger, Hearst, couldn't possibly have known he was going to that bar the previous evening. μ didn't even know he was going himself. He had never seen the man before and yet his 'employer' had apparently asked him to pass on the note. Hearst had pulled out the slip of paper already written, already prepared. μ felt in his pocket – it was still there.

He decided to try the number again. Perhaps the number was blocked from his phone? He found a phone box on the next block and searched in his pocket for change. He only had three coins. The booth smelled strongly of urine so µ left the door slightly ajar as he dialled. There was a pause, and µ was about to replace the handset when he heard the line connect and an electronic dialling noise. It rang twice.

µ waited to hear who was there. An automated voice spoke.

'If you know the extension of the party you are trying to reach, please enter it now. If not, please hold for an operator.'

µ waited, expecting to hear some holding tone, but there was no sound. He stood for almost half a minute but nothing happened. Finally, he replaced the handset. Searching in his pocket he found another coin and tried again. The same message played, but this time he tried entering an extension. He didn't know where it might be so he simply tried 1-1-1- pausing in between each press to see if he was still connected. Without ringing once the phone was answered by a woman.

'Amanda Peck's phone, can I help?'

'Amanda Peck,' µ repeated, surprised by the rapidity of her answer.

'Yes, Amanda won't be in the office until 8.30 this morning. This is her PA speaking.'

Thinking on his feet, µ said 'I'm looking for Hearst. Is it possible to transfer me?'

'I'm afraid I don't know anyone of that name, does he work in this office?'

µ didn't want to ask her where exactly it was he was phoning, so he simply said, 'I believe so.' He could hear typing in the background.

'No, I don't have any record here. If you want to phone back after 8.30 Amanda may help you.'

She rang off and µ replaced the handset, perplexed. He tried the number a third time, planning to find out the name of the organisation at least. This time he tried the extension 1 - 3 - 5.

There was no automated voice this time; instead µ was greeted with a cacophony of noise. At first it sounded like static or loud distortion, but as he listened he could make out a voice all but drowned out by music and laughter. It sounded like a party was going on in the background. The voice shouted above the din.

'Hello.'

'Hello, who's there?' μ was sure he had dialled the same digits but this was clearly not the same office.

The man on the other end moved somewhere slightly quieter.

'You got my message?'

μ waited, silent. Whoever was on the other end of the line was clearly drunk. The voice continued.

'Come around here!' There was a loud banging in the background and a drunken laugh. 'No, no, later. Come at... four. You have the address?'

'No.' μ could barely manage a whisper.

The voice gave an address on the east side of the city, repeating the street number several times and adding some directions. μ struggled to grasp his slurred speech. There was a pause as he evidently fumbled with something and then the sound of a woman's voice.

'Am I speaking to Ddunsel?' μ asked.

'Yes, yes,' the voice replied impatiently, 'you got my message... be here at four.'

There were more sounds of hilarity from the other end of the phone, the woman laughing flirtatiously in the background. μ listened for a while but could not make out any clear words.

The receiver went dead.

μ hung up the phone.

Had that really been Ddunsel? He couldn't believe it. Was that the same person who had supposedly sent him the script? He had been sure that it was this Ddunsel who was behind it all, but now it seemed unbelievable that this drunk, a joker, was in any way involved.

μ walked back the way that he had come. He had hours to kill before four.

μ's rash was growing more intolerable and he decided to take a detour past the bookshop to see if he could find something that might explain the cause of his affliction. He liked the quiet, calm of the bookshop. It was a large chain store and he preferred it to the smaller second hand shops in the area. In those shops there was always a sense of serious bookishness which μ found off-putting, whereas here one could wander up and down freely and buy any old rubbish without anyone asking a question.

In the smaller shops everything from the latest potboiler to the oldest leather bound first-edition carried the same musky smell, but here each section displayed its own character. Each floor had a different atmosphere, almost as if the books themselves emanated their own character.

In the children's section mothers and kids bounced around the brightly coloured scenery while upstairs in the classics section beaten old leather sofas and standing lamps were disturbed only by the occasional cough.

The medical reference section was on the top floor, furthest away from the entrance. Up here there were no decorative flourishes. This area was a serious, academic zone. No comfortable sofas or life-size cut outs of authors. The customers of medical reference books were mainly students or researchers.

It must once have been an attic and work was evidently still ongoing to convert it. In-between the shelves some wires were still exposed and in one section the carpet had been ripped up, leaving bare floor boards that were uneven and loose. There were signs that staff had tried to disguise this work in progress with some thin scraps of mismatched carpet, laid over the gaps, but in general there was little sign of any visual merchandising. It didn't look like many people came up here.

In fact, the place was empty save for two other customers standing in the section marked tropical diseases. They were clearly twins for they had identical thin physiques with long bony limbs, wiry black hair, and pale skin. One of them was poring over a weighty looking tome while the other was lounging as best he could on a metal folding chair. They looked like medical students. μ browsed through several different books that looked like they might be relevant, but couldn't shake the feeling they were looking at him. He tried his best to ignore them and leaf through a text called A Treatise on the Cimex Lectularius; Or, Bed Bug, but the older one – for µ felt sure the one on the seat was older – was definitely gawping at him.

He had an intense stare as if trying to understand something about µ, something very complex, and yet at the same time this was at odds with his simple, almost imbecilic demeanour. He sat close to the other one.

µ found a couple of entries that talked about bed bug infestations, but there was nothing that said how to get rid of them. He was thinking of going to find a clerk to ask him what other books they might have when he saw the older twin tug on his companion's sleeve.

The younger one who had been engrossed in his book until that point, only occasionally pausing to look up in µ's direction, started whispering in the other's ear. The other listened carefully and then, when he was finished, grinned broadly and nodded, all the while looking at µ. It was quite obvious they were talking about µ for there was no one else on the same floor. They pointed directly at him but there was little he could say.

Something about their appearance and their attitude infuriated him. They looked like two schoolchildren with a secret from the rest of the class. As they talked back and forth in hushed tones, their long pointy limbs moved awkwardly and they continued to steal furtive glances in µ's direction.

Did he overhear the words 'manuscript' and 'Ddunsel' whispered hurriedly? Was he imagining that? They seemed oblivious that µ could see them and at one point the younger one started gesticulating towards µ, his index finger extended. Annoyed by this childish behaviour, µ stomped over to their little encampment, but the moment they saw him coming they fell silent. Normally µ would have been uneasy approaching two complete strangers like this, but these two looked so ineffectual. As he approached, the older one got to his feet and they both looked nervously this way and that, as if looking for an exit.

'What have you got to say?' μ demanded.

'Nothing,' said the older one somewhat rebelliously.

'That's right, we weren't talking about anything,' said the other.

'Yes, you were, I could see you talking and pointing at me just now,' said μ. 'What have you got to say?'

The pair looked at each other as if to check their twin's reaction to this allegation.

'Oh, earlier?' said the older one as if only now realising what μ was talking about. 'Yes, we were just talking about books.'

'Books?' repeated μ.

'Yes, books,' said the older one, evidently getting into his lie. 'Books and art and things. Why not? We are in a bookshop.'

His glib response only infuriated μ more.

'We're in the medical section of a bookshop. One might suppose you would be talking about medicine, not literature.'

'You're right,' said the younger one, as if conceding a well-argued point. 'We should be going.'

With that he closed his still-open medical book and put his hand on his brother's shoulder, steering him away.

'What does he pay us in any case?'

μ was about to make some other comment, but in an instant they were gone, scurrying towards the stairs, sneaking the briefest of glances at μ before they disappeared.

The whole incident and their stupid infantile behaviour had disturbed μ's train of thought and he couldn't be bothered looking for any more information now. On the way out he asked a clerk if they had any books about the removal of bed bugs, but the clerk just shrugged and suggested trying the bigger store out of town.

No sooner had he left than he realised how ridiculous it was looking for a cure in a bookshop; he needed a pharmacy. A couple of blocks and he stumbled upon one. Inside, everything was deathly quiet and μ stalked the aisles waiting for some assistance. He was examining a display with odourising insoles when a withered old woman emerged behind the counter. She exuded a cloud of annoyance and disappointment.

'Yes,' she squawked. 'Can I help you?'

'It's uh, it's my arm.'

µ rolled his sleeve slightly to show her his ailment and she wrinkled her nose in disgust.

'You'll need to see a doctor.'

'A doctor?'

'Yes, you want Xypribol, dear. Can't give you that without a prescription.'

'I do? Is there nothing… a cream maybe? I don't think it's that bad?'

'Don't think it's that bad?' The woman shrugged grumpily. 'What do I know?'

'Well, I thought, maybe bed bugs.'

The woman was evidently bored of the conversation and wanted µ out of her shop. Sharply, she whacked a packet down on the table.

'Take this if you want but it won't do any good. You'll need to see a doctor.'

µ hesitated. Did she expect him to buy it? Even though she had just told him it wouldn't work?

'Well I'll just leave it in that case.'

The woman ignored his statement and pushed the package towards µ while ringing it up on the till. Confused and embarrassed, µ paid for the cream and thanked the woman. He heard her tutting loudly as he left.

He was ravenous and it was still hours until four. Was he really going to go all the way across town to that address? He wanted to sit down after the brusque encounter with the woman in the pharmacy and so he stopped in to a small cafe off the main road to eat.

µ chose a seat near the back and surreptitiously pulled the packet of cream out of his pocket as he examined the menu. Slowly he worked a globule out of the nozzle and rubbed it into his arm, trying to keep it hidden from the waiter and two girls at the bar. His rash was starting to annoy him again and he rolled back his sleeve to scratch his arm better.

The street was getting busy as the rush hour traffic arrived. He watched commuters marching along the pavement, looking neither left nor right. They nearly all wore suits. None of them looked inside the cafe and μ felt free to examine them at will.

Amongst the crowds, his eye fell on one woman. She looked like a secretary or a receptionist and walked along the pavement in a decided way. There was nothing exceptional about her, but she was pleasant enough to watch nonetheless.

Just as she was drawing level with the café window, her handbag fell, dropping its contents on the ground. It looked like the strap may have snapped. Seeing her possessions scatter, she scrabbled to pick them up and an elderly gentleman walking the other way bent to help her. It was a perfectly ordinary looking incident and none of the other commuters seemed to notice. Seamlessly, they adjusted their paths to avoid the debris and continue on their way.

It was only as she straightened that she looked directly into the café. In that instant something in her eyes caught μ unaware. Her eyes conveyed some dark feeling in him, almost as if coming from somewhere outside her, some deeper reality. He had a powerful desire to rush outside. It was not a sexual urge per se, but an element of sex was undeniably there. It was as if the intensity of the connection somehow overpowered the more ordinary, basic sexual desire.

It took her no more than a moment to collect her few items and continue along the pavement, clutching the bag in her hand. She did not look in μ's direction again, but he was left with an unmistakeable impression of having had an encounter. The outcome of the 'meeting' was unclear to him, but his instinct told him it was not good.

He thought again of the dead boy he had discovered the night before. What vile deeds had happened in that shop? A wave of disgust washed over him. He was sure he had done the right thing in reporting it to the police, but then why did he feel so guilty?

All the secret recollections that μ held indelibly in his brain – secret, shameful memories hidden at the back of his head – now seemed to bubble up in front of him unbidden. The time he had been jeered at in school and hadn't had the courage to answer back, the time much later when he had the courage to answer back and the consequences he then suffered, this girl he ignored, that girl that he chased, the night of his first kiss. All these thoughts picked at him like ghostly mosquitoes.

Remembering each one it seemed to him that these guilt-ridden memories, these shamed episodes were somehow sharper than other remembrances. Sharper even than everyday life. He tried to focus on remembering a single moment of triumph or achievement, but every memory he recalled was unreal compared to the more dishonourable episodes of his life.

When he tried to recall passing an important exam, the image would crumble and fade away, to be replaced by the reminder that here was the very same person who also cheated in a different exam the year later.

If he remembered a happy afternoon with a girl, a moment of sexual pleasure, even happiness, it was only to be surpassed by the recollection that she was the same person he later treated so cruelly.

Those memories, the most disgraceful, the guiltiest, were the only ones that seemed to form sharply, acutely in his mind. Although they rang through his mind with an unpleasant shriek they were also the ones that resonated the loudest. If the aim of life was to remember things clearly, to look back and recall every experience one had, then, he wondered, was it not worth living one's life as badly as possible for those memories to stick?

Surely a man who did everything right, if such a man could exist, would come across old age with nothing but indistinct and blurry recollections of who or what he was. A man, on the other hand, who took every opportunity to lie and cheat and steal from his neighbours, would no doubt reach old age with any number of demons pursuing him, but with each episode etched unforgettably in his mind.

He let these thoughts rumble around. It took him another few minutes to realise that the woman had reminded him of Alberta.

THE WAVE

INT. EDMONTON AIRPORT, ALBERTA PROVENCE, CANADA
- NIGHT

An airport departure lounge filled with crowds
of passengers, all well wrapped up in winter
clothes. The split-flap departure boards clatter
noisily, displaying cancelled flights.

The glass wall facing the runways is illuminated
by the light from the air-traffic tower. A vicious
snowstorm rages.

Everywhere people are huddling down trying to
find a corner to sleep. A young man, DOWN, in a
business suit sits on the end of a line of hard
metal seats.

                    TANNOY:
    Edmonton International Airport would like
    to apologise for any inconvenience caused
    by the inclement weather conditions.

                    DOWN:
                    Shit.

                    TANNOY:
    Unfortunately, all flights from this
    airport are grounded until further notice.
    Passengers are advised to remain in the
    terminal building for the time being until
    alternative arrangements can be made. We
    repeat, all flights from this...

                    DOWN:
    Shitting hell.

A young organised-looking woman, UP, emerges from
the ladies toilets. She wears a long black skirt
and a jacket with shoulder pads. Her short black

fringe hangs over an eager face. She approaches
DOWN.

> UP:
> Thank you for watching my case.

> DOWN:
> No problem.

> UP:
> Nothing moving?

> DOWN:
> Only back to the hangars.

> UP:
> Looks like it's going to be a long night.

> DOWN:
> Too bloody long.

> UP:
> Well at least we're safe here.

> DOWN:
> Safe. Great. How the hell did they miss
> the fact there was a huge bloody snowstorm
> coming.

> UP:
> The steward said these weather systems
> move fast.

> DOWN:
> Did he indeed.

> UP:
> You were on the London flight? That was
> diverted?

THE WAVE

DOWN:
I had just ordered a drink. Can you believe
it?

UP:
You are unlucky.

DOWN smiles slightly.

DOWN:
Is that sarcasm?

UP:
I'm going back to London too. Or trying
to.

DOWN:
What a disaster. I thought these Americans
were meant to be organised.

UP:
Well they are, but this is Canada now.

DOWN:
From sea to shining sea.

UP:
I suppose they will find us a hotel
eventually.

DOWN:
In this tin-pot town?

They both lapse into silence and UP smiles
awkwardly.

UP:
What were you doing in Seattle, if you
don't mind me asking?

DOWN:
A trade show. Publishing.

UP:
Really? I've always wanted to work in publishing. It sounds so… glamorous.

DOWN:
Don't, it'll drive you to shoot yourself.

UP:
It's that fun? You really must be keen to get back to London then. I have to say I love it over here.

DOWN:
It's all so uncivilised out here.

UP:
Really? Uncivilised? It's the future.

DOWN:
My God, then we're all screwed. What brought you over to Seattle?

UP:
I wasn't in Seattle. A little place just outside – Redmond.

DOWN:
Never heard of it.

UP:
No one has, but it's got this feel there, like it's all just about to happen.

DOWN:
Like what's just about to happen?

THE WAVE

UP:
Oh I don't know, something, anything.

DOWN:
And it was that that enticed you all the way over here?

UP:
No, my job. I'm a Relationship Manager. I work for a company there. They're not that big yet but they're growing really fast. They've got big plans for the personal computer.

DOWN snorts derisively

DOWN:
Computers!

UP:
Well, we call it the PC.

DOWN:
PC, not even Superintendent?

UP:
Well, I just work there, I have no idea how they actually work.

DOWN:
They're never going to take off.

UP:
You'll see, one day books might even be published on them.

A family with six children blunders past and once they have gone UP and DOWN watch the snow flung in the wind outside.

> UP: (CONT'D)
> I would love to get into publishing,
> really. It must be such a lot of fun.

DOWN smiles briefly.

> DOWN:
> You're a funny character. Are you
> perpetually so cheerful?

> UP:
> Oh God no. Not when I'm in Britain.

DOWN smiles mischievously.

> DOWN:
> What say we get a drink?

> UP:
> Oh I don't know. A strange man I've never
> met, in a foreign airport lounge bar.

> DOWN:
> Sounds the recipe for trouble.

> UP:
> Maybe I like trouble.

DOWN stands up and lifts UP's bag

> DOWN:
> Well don't hang around then. We've got a
> long night ahead of us.

DOWN walks off in the direction of the bar, taking
the bag with him. UP watches him for a moment,
hand on hip, a smile forming at the corner of her
mouth. Finally, she hurries after him.

THE WAVE

UP:
You never even told me your name.

CUT TO:

INT. AIRPORT BAR - NIGHT
In the background, the airport departure lounge
is quiet as passengers sleep next to each other
on the ground. Outside the window the snowstorm
has died down slightly.

Everyone still awake appears to have crammed
into the small bar area.

In the far corner UP and DOWN are nestled
together at a small table. DOWN is a little drunk
and holds UP's hand, examining her fingers with
pretend earnestness.

DOWN:
I would insure these fingers for... let me
see... $5.

UP:
Oh really, is that all?

UP pretends to snatch her hand away in mock
annoyance.

DOWN:
But... but... your wrists...

DOWN slips his hand along to hold UP's wrist.

DOWN: (CONT'D)
... your wrist must be worth...

DOWN pauses and, in that split second, their
eyes lock, their lips pulled towards each other

by magnetic forces. They kiss hard.

UP suddenly pulls away.

> UP:
> I shouldn't, we shouldn't.

> DOWN:
> We shouldn't why?

UP lifts DOWN's left hand and looks pointedly at the ring finger. A gold ring sits there, emblazoned with a slash of green emerald.

> DOWN: (CONT'D)
> This? It's not. We're separated.

> UP:
> Separated?

> DOWN:
> Separating… It's over. Come on, forget it.

> UP:
> But you are married?

DOWN struggles to squeeze the ring off his finger and slips it into his inside suit pocket.
After a moment's thought he takes the ring out of his pocket and puts it in UP's hand.

> UP: (CONT'D)
> (sarcastically)
> Really?

> DOWN:
> Really. It means nothing to me.

THE WAVE

DOWN reaches across the table and takes UP by the wrists again, drawing her towards him. She hesitates initially, but finally relents and lets herself be moved. DOWN kisses her again, more slowly this time.

> DOWN: (CONT'D)
> Do you know, you have the most mesmerising eyes?

> UP:
> Did you know that you have the cheesiest of chat-up lines?

> DOWN:
> What do you say we get out of this bar and try to find a hotel in this godforsaken blizzard town?

UP bites her lip and looks at him thoughtfully.

Sygeton

The room contained a single bed, a sink, a chipboard writing desk and a small wardrobe built into one wall. He settled into it quite easily; he didn't have many things in any case. The building was made up of identical rooms on the outside of each corridor, with communal showers, toilet and kitchen areas in the centre, shared between every four or five rooms. All the fixtures and fittings were the cheapest possible and it was far from luxurious living, but the other students were all welcoming and μ soon got used to university life.

The campus buzzed with exciting people, full of interesting ideas. For μ everything was new; he was only just starting and he had all the time in the world. Unlike those students doing professional degrees such as medicine or law, his timetable in the Social Sciences was undemanding. The first term he had to choose ten modules and, besides two core classes, he had pretty much free rein in picking subjects.

μ liked the esoteric feel of these older university departments and the crabbit, eccentric professors that stalked the corridors. Inside, the buildings were confusing mazes of corridors, linked by seemingly random flights of stairs and doorways that sprung out here and there. Signposts, where they existed, were invariably incorrect or pointed to departments that had long ceased to exist. Nearly every piece of flooring was uneven or hastily repaired.

He had chosen his course because it seemed the sensible option, something that offered a number of credible career paths, but now he was actually there he was inundated with new ideas of topics to study. He could barely decipher half the complicated sounding course titles, so instead he picked courses based on what his newfound friends suggested or what suited his schedule.

It was in taking one of these outside courses that μ came to meet Professor Wijklawski. He taught an undergraduate course entitled 'The Logic Of Narrative: The Incomprehensibility Of Multiple Narratives'. His lectures were held on Tuesday afternoons in a small meeting room on the third floor of the Morgan building. It was barely big enough for ten people to sit in, but that didn't prove to be a problem as there were only eight people taking the course.

The first day, μ arrived late after getting lost in the maze of buildings and found the professor writing on a chalkboard that was so thick with half rubbed out equations and notes from past lectures that he could barely make out what was written there.

'...indicating that it is our psychological flaws as readers that entirely determines...' the professor paused in mid-sentence, noticing μ who was still standing silently by the door. The other students turned to follow his gaze.

μ had entered at the back of the room, and with dismay realised that the only three empty seats were at the front, directly facing the professor. He edged his way in front of the other students as the professor stood with pursed lips, still paused mid-sentence. With a few hushed apologies, μ stumbled forward and sat down.

The professor was an impassioned but largely incoherent talker. He would start on a particular idea and then quickly change tack onto some unrelated topic. Sentences were unfinished. Concepts flashed and fizzled. He was entirely captivating, but his arguments never appeared to quite finish. Not that he left questions hanging for his students to deliberate on – if anything it was quite the opposite: no sooner was an idea put forward than it was conjured away as if under some sleight of hand.

Each new thought appeared to consume the professor's entire attention, but as soon as the next one entered his mind the last was made meaningless. He talked as if puzzling over the meaning of each statement for the first time.

μ found the lecture exhilarating. Professor Wijklawski didn't bother with tedious explanations but dashed from one thought to the next. It felt to μ like he was striking a flint and sparks were jumping across the lecture room.

'There is a body, an entity we refer to as literature, and every story however long or short is a part of it, an element of this great shape. In the same way as the human body is made of molecules and cells, muscles and bone, so the body of literature is composed of countless parts: Stories, ideas, threads, themes – even down to single words, letters.

'These constituents can join together in different arrangements, in the same way as the body can stretch and jump, but each part is always dependent on the whole to exist, in order to function. In the human body the muscle needs the stomach to provide nutrients to grow, the stomach needs the muscle to move the body and find food; every part is symbiotic, dependant on the rest to continue.

'Some parts are more vital than others of course – the foot needs the heart to keep pumping blood or it will wither and die, but the heart can function well enough without the foot.'

The professor paused to stare lengthily at his own foot.

'Is it just an idle obsession of academics to classify and straightjacket literature? No. Every story itself has a need to connect, to relate to the wider family of literature. It is a natural desire of the written word itself. Every story is entangled with every other, entangled in the mesh of literature.

'No piece of work, however short, however ill-thought-out can be said to exist alone. Indeed no narrative can survive on its own, any more than a human can.

'In the same way that man needs company, can only exist with others to reinforce his beliefs, to stand beside, to procreate, to question his purpose, to argue, to discuss, to love or hate – so too can a story exist only in relation to literature.

'There are oxbows and meanders of course. Some book or oeuvre may seem far removed from the mainstream, unrelated to the body of literature as a whole, but there is no such thing as complete isolation.

'This "entanglement", if I can call it that, is a universal concept. Interconnectedness is fundamental to mankind. Interconnectedness is fundamental to literature. It doesn't matter if a person chooses to live a hundred miles away or on the other side of the sun, they are forever bound to the rest of humanity by the fact they are human. They live in the human bubble. Similarly, it makes no difference what the story may be about – it is part of literature by the very fact it is a story.

'What is more, there is a link between these two grand families – literature and humanity – for the one reflects the other. Logically, we all know that the world surrounding us is empty; intrinsically we are aware of this truth. Our deepest scientific reasoning even backs up this view. We are surrounded by a frictionless arrangement and re-arrangement of atoms that achieve nothing. We are ourselves nothing more than a section of empty vacuum criss-crossed by fleeting electric charges.

'Our so called friends, our families, the houses we live in, everything from the ground we stand on to the stars above us, is nothing more than a temporary, fleeting configuration of electronic charges, dust turning and swelling, briefly, before disappearing forever. This is the truth that everyone knows inside them. In the darkest hours mankind even comes close to admitting this fact.

'However,' at this he raised a finger combatively, 'this is not the reality in which we live, this is not the reality elected for us. Instead for whatever reasons, we LIVE. We recognise amongst this mud and rock and flesh that fills up the world something other, something that we know in our core does not even truly exist, should not even have a name, and yet we name it.

'We go further; we bring not only names for the world around us but stories to decorate it with. Yes, how well we decorate this empty, hall of a world with stories. We are inexorably drawn to do this, as to contemplate it in its bare form is unthinkable. That is our social nature, the universal principal of which I spoke, the desire to negate, to deny the reality of our existence through elaborate word games.

'And what is a word other than some scratches on the surface of nothingness. Does the written word feel the need to justify its existence? The word games of an author are only desperate attempts to disguise the flimsiness of the constituent parts, the flimsiness of every word's existence. An attempt which can be sustained only so long as all the other balls are also flying in the air. This is literature.'

*   *   *

μ looked around at the other students expecting to see them as enthralled as he was, but they mostly looked bored or hungover. The boy next to him was taking notes furiously, evidently trying to write down every word the professor said, but failing to keep up. It didn't look like he had any concern at all for the subject matter but was simply concentrating on transcribing as fast as possible. He could as easily have been copying mathematical formulae.

μ meanwhile was unable to write a single point, engrossed as he was in the professor's ramblings. It was over before μ knew it and although he had decided early on that he must speak to the professor directly after the lecture, to pick his brain and clear up some of his confusions, one of the other students got in first.

Next to μ on the front row sat a group of piggish boys. They all looked identical – podgy, superior, well-fed cheeks, sons of land owners no doubt. One of them was even wearing tweed.

'Why is there no reading list?' one of them smirked. 'The course administrator told us we would get a reading list with every course.'

This seemed to flummox the professor and he stopped and scratched his head.

'A reading list,' he asked distractedly, 'but, no, you see... of what?'

The professor appeared wholly different now that he was no longer in motion.

'Well that's what you're getting paid for, isn't it? To tell us what we should read?'

'Yes, well, if you speak... with the syllabus, you see... the administrator.' The professor was having difficulty getting his words out.

'Some of us are paying a lot for our education, and the course syllabus says there should be a reading list.' The boy clearly enjoyed showing off to the rest of the class. 'We are paying your wages after all. We demand customer service.'

There were titters from the back of the room.

'Well... technically... I think... customer service... if you.'

It was hard to tell if the professor was exasperated or nervous.

After a moment huffing and puffing he simply turned around and walked out of the room. The moment he was gone the class broke into roars of laughter. The fat boy crowed loudest of all.

'It's our rights, student rights! Student rights!' he repeated several times.

μ felt ashamed he had not said anything. He had wanted to defend the professor but his nerve failed him. The piggish boys didn't look like they had read a book between them as they pushed past μ to get out of the room, laughing and showing each other around.

Despite the ignominious entrance and exit from the class, μ found his mind racing over the professor's words the rest of that day and the next. For the first time he went to the library and took out books that he didn't specifically need, to try and glean some further information about the topics Wijklawski had raised. The germ of an idea was building in him. He waited anxiously for the next lecture.

His days were full to bursting, making friends, impromptu parties, invitations to student events. He got to know a few other students that lived near him in halls and would hang out with them, discussing anything and everything under the sun in a garbled rush of ideas.

Term

'Are you going to Bee's on Friday?' Juls asked over lunch. They were sitting with Franko and Bull in the student union café at Balthesam Square.

Balthesam Square was a small cobbled plaza near the centre of town that housed the oldest buildings at the University, including the faculties of Divinity and Art. The university had long since outgrown these few crumbling buildings and was now mainly housed in more modern sites throughout the town: brand new science blocks housing laboratories, a sports academy, an institute of business psychology, a geochemical institute and so on, all with shiny glass buildings and off-street parking. The heart of the university still remained around the original Balthesam Square.

'It should be great. Bee said they'll have a band playing,' μ replied, pleased that he was able to provide the inside track. Everything moved so fast – he had only met Bee the week before. She shared a lecture with him once a week and had invited him to the party the day before. Juls lived two doors down the corridor from μ and the five of them often hung out together between classes.

'They are not,' Franko said disinterestedly. 'It's going to be the same old people. There's a deconstructionist film night at The Bunker on Friday and then they're setting up a sound system in a disused warehouse. We need to go.'

μ barely had an idea what these events entailed but they all promised something new.

'Yeah, could do,' he said casually, unsure whether to ask what deconstructionism was. Instead, Juls started talking about a friend's recent meningitis scare and μ's gaze drifted out of the window at the ancient buildings that bounded Balthesam square.

Although the structures were formed in distinct sections, they somehow seemed to all merge together, causing a disturbance to the eye. The construction of each building, in contrast to the more classical granite elsewhere in the town, seemed to be entirely haphazard. Turrets appeared at random from walls that bent and buckled this way and that. Various materials were used with no clear continuity and windows of various heights and alignments burst forth from all sides.

The overall effect was that the square appeared to be surrounded by a single warped entity that had been carefully excavated and then repaired time and time again. It was unclear to what extent this disorder was something that had been created by the architects or indeed if there ever had been any design in the first place.

'I've got Logic of Narrative tomorrow. It's pretty interesting stuff,' μ said at a lull in the conversation.

His thoughts had been returning to the topic of Wijklawski's lecture ever since the previous week. He talked eagerly about the last lecture but his friends looked uninterested.

'He's nuts,' Bull said. 'Everyone in the faculty knows Wijklawski's a joke. The only reason to do the course is because his exams are so easy. No one's failed his course in the whole time he's run it, but all the other professors say he's crazy.'

'I don't think he's crazy,' replied μ. 'A little eccentric maybe.'

Bull just snorted.

It didn't seem possible to μ that the professor's reputation was so poor, but he began to hear the same opinion again and again.

'He's only here because he used to be a friend of Professor Von Hoer,' they would say, or 'did you not know he's on the bottle?'

The next lecture arrived and μ felt trepidation in case some of their accusations should prove true, but he was delighted to find the professor continued in the same vein as before, talking with great appetite. It was true that his lecture was unfocused and, from a certain perspective, disjointed, but μ found each point resonated with him. This time there were only half as many students attending.

As the term progressed attendance dropped significantly and at most lectures μ was one of only two or three students there, but this did nothing to stop the professor's flow. The presence of students, or lack thereof, appeared to have little impact upon him. He talked as if animated by some greater desire than simply educating those around him.

As time went by, μ found opportunities to speak to the professor and in some way built up a rapport with the old man. μ would arrive early for lectures armed with questions and the professor would spare him some time, never making eye contact and speaking somewhat brusquely, but nonetheless pleased to have an interested student. He never directly answered any of μ's questions, but only because his responses made μ understand how each question was inadequate.

'You mentioned imbroglios in the lecture last week?' μ asked as Wijklawski stood with typically distant expression. It often looked as if the professor were not listening and μ would continue trying to jog him into awareness.

'You said they were overly complicated plots, often damaging the power of the narrative. I was wondering how you know when a plot is overly complicated and when it is just complicated?'

'Imbroglios, yes, hmm,' the professor would reply, as if coming to the concept for the first time, 'an interesting question. From the Italian imbrogliare "to tangle", cognate with, and probably from an earlier form of the French embrouiller "to muddle or embroil". I presume by asking this you are seeking to imply that literature itself might be said to have a purpose? And that perhaps the plot goes some way to further this purpose? An interesting hypothesis....'

Of course, this was not a question that had occurred to μ up until that moment, but he was eager to hear the professor's response in any case.

'I have asked myself a similar question but, mmmh, perhaps we can reformulate your interposition with the supposition that "literature" is in itself a device to drive forward "plot" in a grander sense.

'Is it not possible that the idea of "literature", an idea that has been largely invented, that supposes an abstract whole composed of many written works, is greater than its parts, mmmh, yes indeed that is an interesting concept you have raised. Could literature itself be a narrative that governs the development of writers?

'These great writers we all admire, the work they produce, their daring, their passion – is it not governed by an idea of "literature" that exists beyond them – above them if you will – that drives the plot of their own history...'

Wijklawski would continue talking to himself like this until some distraction carried him back to the real world and μ had completely forgotten his original question. Despite the professor's eccentric behaviour and constant digression there always seemed to be some point to his arguments. μ had an unmistakeable feeling that he was touching on important issues, but when talking to other students who asked him what the wacky Wijklawski's lectures were like, he could never find the words to describe each topic adequately.

Alberta

As the term passed, μ found himself spending more and more of his time concentrating on the lectures. He harboured thoughts of becoming a writer himself and studied, not out of any need to pass exams, but some quite different need altogether – almost discipleship. Slowly, Wijklawski acknowledged μ's presence and conversation developed between the two of them to the stage that they might discuss the finer points of language. Wijklawski took an interest in μ and when no other students turned up for the lecture they would move to his office instead.

Wijklawski's office was even more cramped than the designated lecture room but, amongst the monstrous piles of paper and filing, he had somehow squeezed in two threadbare armchairs. In this chaos an espresso machine was hidden and the professor would make thick cups of coffee. Since the lectures never really followed any strict pattern, the dynamic was essentially unaltered by the shift of location.

It was here, however, that μ first met the professor's assistant, Alberta Mqoy. The professor referred to her, jokingly, as his apprentice, but the role she played seemed to entail that of carer, assistant and student all rolled into one. She brought him coffee, found his glasses, searched for buried submission papers, photocopied, took dictation, filed umpteen unrelated notes and messages and so on.

'I am sorry to disturb you, professor,' she would always say, before edging into the room to give him some update on her administrative duties. She treated the old man with the utmost deference and it took μ a while to realise that he even registered on her radar.

Alberta's appearance was plump and youthful, but μ found it hard to gauge her exact age. She seemed naive and let herself be ordered around, which led μ to initially imagine she was much younger than he was. She went hither and thither on the most menial tasks without the least complaint, accepting the professor's every whim with the unquestioning attitude of a child.

'She is probably still at school,' he thought. 'She's been sent here on some form of work experience.' But, as he saw more of her, he changed his mind, deciding that she must after all be several years older than him.

She had what μ came to see as a certain solidity, in so much as she lacked slyness that would have made her in any way devious. She took every sentence quite literally and seemed oblivious that any utterance could represent anything more than its simple meaning. To μ, the professor's language was filled with allusions and each sentence resonated with numerous different meanings, but these never appeared to impact on Alberta, who went about her work with the utmost practicality.

At first μ took this as dull wittedness, but as he observed her and the professor working together more clearly, and as he came to realise that she was with him far more than the few hours per week that would constitute work experience, he understood that her solid, unquestioning character was something quite necessary for the professor.

At moments μ caught a glimpse of Alberta as a mother dealing patiently with Wijklawski as one might with a young child, interested in his outpourings but ultimately too mature to take them seriously.

She seemed different from the other girls that studied with him. The fact that she wasn't a student but had a full time job was one huge gulf, but at times it was almost as though he couldn't quite attribute her with feelings of her own. She existed in another lane, scurrying about and occasionally moving into view.

One Thursday, well into the second term, the lecture was busier than normal. Six students were attending, and in the corner sat Alberta. For some reason Thursdays were always the busiest, and even though μ was well used to her presence by then, he noticed her specifically because she never normally sat in the professor's lectures.

The professor was speaking.

'...and therefore all analysis is essentially an arbitrary measure, there is no absolute length in literature, a chapter does not need to end at the finish of a scene or mark some turning point in the story, quite simply it can lie anywhere...but what does this tell us? Well, nothing.

'There is no way to tell a correct structure from an incorrect structure, a finished chapter from an unfinished chapter, a complete scene from an incomplete scene. Put simply, there is always something that could be added to any story, as much as there is always something that could be taken away.

'When we read a great piece of literature, we have the feeling that each section leads on from the last seamlessly, each section fits together perfectly so that not one word could be changed or taken away, but this is nothing more than fallacy. Even in the finest writing there are multitudes of perfectly fitting options, all existing equally, true in themselves.

'In essence the pages on paper are part of an infinite series of unwritten books – a superposition of ghostly books. We never see these in a literal sense, but great writing can make these reverberations appear almost within grasp. Even the author can only glimpse these unwritten books, but they are there as surely as the solid hardbound copy that lies in your hand.

'This is why we can only appreciate or understand a great work in retrospect. The actual process of reading, the continuous process, so to speak, is separate from the contemplative process. When we close the cover of the book only then do we sit down to consider its true meaning and only then because we believe the story is over. But we can never know that any story is truly complete, only surmise it from the fact that we have reached the last page.

'We may presume the author has put down their pen, content that they have conveyed their message or, if they are of a more gloomy persuasion, convinced that their talents have been exhausted and there was no sense in writing any more. In either case the presumption is that the book in our hands is the full extent of the story.

'But this is never the whole truth. There are always chapters the author left out, different ways they could have written each paragraph, sentence, or word. Any book is only a part of the infinite unwritten book....'

The other students had all filed out and μ was speaking to Wijklawski when Alberta came over. She was wearing a green dress.

'I'm going for my lunch,' she said.

The professor looked at her questioningly.

'Very well,' he said, clearly waiting for some explanation, but she merely lingered.

'I thought I might take the afternoon off.'

'Very well.'

Despite the professors reassuring words he seemed suspicious at this, and in fact shifted position slightly to put himself in Alberta's way. There was some definite tension, but μ could not decipher the exact causes.

'It's sunny so I thought we might go for a walk together.' She looked at μ directly as she said this and he had an uncomfortable feeling that she was issuing some order. The professor made no reply but was clearly displeased.

'Would either of you like to accompany me?' she said.

Although the question was open to both of them, it was clear that it was directed at μ only. He said nothing, but she still lingered as if waiting for some word before adding, 'If you can take the afternoon off?'

A sudden shyness swamped him – in front of the professor he was unsure how to react. The thought of the two of them together; what would they talk about? He remained silent. Eventually the professor made the slightest of movements towards the blackboard and Alberta left on her own.

From then on μ started to take more notice of Alberta, and in particular her appearance. He wasn't sure how he had missed it before, but she was an incredibly sensual person. Perhaps she had new clothes, but he found his eyes drawn to her body whenever she entered the room, fantasies bubbling under the surface.

Her definite mannerisms and no nonsense attitude slowly

dissolved in μ's mind as he started to feel he could discern a certain subtlety to her. She was a constant presence around Wijklawski and on occasion he would observe her quietly as the professor spoke. When the professor was absent from time to time the two of them would chat and it seemed to μ that she liked him.

Exams

μ found Wijklawski's class the only stimulus in the syllabus, but it was essentially an outside course. As he concentrated more on the professor's subject, at the expense of other classes, his grades suffered. Wijklawski gave him good marks, as he did all his other students, but that was not enough in itself to help μ pass the year.

When the end of year exams came around, μ was therefore far behind his fellow students and, realising that he may be kicked out of his course, he knuckled down. Instead of spending his time discussing theories or spending time with Alberta he dedicated himself to rote learning and practice.

He still had little interest in learning the other subjects, but as a student he was capable enough to learn the answers that were needed. This approach was taken by the majority of students and for two months prior to exams the entire campus was silent, save for the few nihilists who really did not care if they passed or failed.

During these months μ saw nothing of Wijklawski or Alberta, as the professor's module had officially ended in the second trimester and there was no real reason for μ to visit the faculty. It was a week after the last exam when she arrived.

He was in his room and had just declined an offer to go to the pub with Franko and Juls. Despite it only being five o'clock, they were already quite drunk, enjoying their freedom from study. They tried their best to persuade μ but he refused, saying that he might join them later.

He then returned to read his book when the door was knocked again. He assumed it was one of his friends coming back to persuade him, but instead there was Alberta.

'Can I come in?' she said.

She wore a clumsy outfit with long socks, a skirt and blouse.

'Is anything wrong? Did Wijklawski send you?'

She made no reply but stepped forward, brushing her thigh

close against μ as she did. She stood in the centre of the room. Uninterested.

'I've been reading,' μ said.

Alberta made no reply but sat on the bed. μ stood by the door feeling uncomfortable. From her action he presumed that she intended to stay.

'Maybe you have something to drink?' she said.

'There is something in the kitchen.'

He found a bottle in the fridge, It was a cheap white wine and had already been opened, but he didn't want to return empty handed. He had to wash two wine glasses before returning.

Walking along the corridor he wondered about Alberta again. It seemed evident that she wanted to sleep with him. He had certainly fantasised about this situation enough, but it seemed unreal that she should turn up at his door.

She was not cold or distant by any means, but he was at a loss to understand her interaction with others. It was as if she were coming at things from an oblique angle; some basic fundamental aspect of her character was quite different to his and this made it hard for him to imagine light-hearted foreplay.

While their conversation until then had always been friendly, it had tended to be rather matter of fact, and he always felt there was a chance that they were misunderstanding each other. He would have been hard-pressed to define the difference between them, but he had a sense that she was strangely hollow, somatic. She didn't appear to be driven by any of the normal urges that drove other people. He got the impression that she equally had no concept of his own rationale.

When he arrived back at the room Alberta was unbuttoning her blouse. She took the glass he proffered and swallowed a mouthful. She drank as though it were only intended for her stomach, rather than her palate. μ took a sip.

'I could have been waiting years for you to ask me out,' she said. 'I thought I'd take things into my own hands.'

Alberta was naked. The thought of sex and childbirth and blood all existed in her. She was undeniably alluring, but at the same time he had a flicker of detachment, as if he was watching animals fucking, aware of the carnal nature of the scene but not involved.

A certain weight built up over him. She had not said a word, but µ felt a strange sense of duty that his action was not determined by either her or him but simply by the situation. He drew the curtains and undressed.

She moved on top of him, hydraulic, machine-like, sucking strength from the motion, focussed on the action and only peripherally aware of µ. It was not that she didn't seem to enjoy the movement, her belly pushing up and down on top of him, but more that it was something entirely non-frivolous to her. She was quite concentrated, pragmatic, on the action.

µ put these thoughts out of his mind and finally came, breathing heavily underneath her. She rolled off him and picked up one of µ's jumpers from the floor. For a moment he thought she was going to get dressed and leave immediately, but she put on the jumper and climbed back into bed beside him.

She grabbed his wrist and brought his arm around her so that they were curled tightly together with µ against her back. He felt he couldn't move from this position without disturbing Alberta. He wanted to speak but couldn't talk to the back of her head. She seemed extremely happy lying there with his arm around her, and after a moment µ drifted off to sleep.

When he awoke, Alberta was standing over him fully dressed.

'I have to go,' she said.

µ mumbled in response.

'I had fun,' she continued. 'We can see each other again.'

She gave him a kiss on the cheek and left.

Closer

It was a week before μ saw her again and in the interim his thoughts had not dwelt on their encounter a great deal. While it had been pleasant, it was not something he could see any future in and since Alberta had not been in touch the next day he had presumed she saw things the same way.

He stopped in at the professor's office to return some books, unsure if Alberta would acknowledge their tryst or not. The professor was not there and μ was unprepared for the force of her greeting. As soon as he came through the door she all but threw him into a chair, straddling him, pulling at his trousers, pulling him inside her, moving him, teasing him on until they both shuddered to an orgastic halt.

He had no time to think whether he was enjoying it or not, but as she stepped off him he felt a huge weight had lifted. He wanted to say something but she was already straightening herself out.

'The professor will be back soon,' she said.

μ felt he had to leave.

From then on they fucked regularly. It was good. For μ it was always accompanied by the same relief, both psychological and physical, as if eased of some burden. However, though he grew to depend on their regular meetings, he had a growing frustration that Alberta was essentially indifferent to him.

She was unadventurous sexually, yet whenever he suggested something she accepted it without hesitation. She could be incredibly passionate one moment and then intensely worried or secretive as if she were afraid of being seen with him. He wondered if they were any closer than the first day they had met. She regularly told μ that she loved him, but he got the impression there was something else going on.

This shouldn't have bothered μ. He told himself he didn't love Alberta. When she did occasionally speak about topics that interested him he generally found her thoughts dull.

'It's fun for now,' μ thought to himself. 'What we talk about isn't important anyway.'

But it was important, and μ found himself becoming obsessed with 'having' Alberta. Quite what he wanted by this he didn't understand fully, for she gave her body to him wholeheartedly. To begin with he mistook his feelings for lust and increased the frequency of their encounters.

Though Alberta was evidently happy with this arrangement it did nothing to satiate his feeling. If it had been some other girl he might have said he wanted to 'have' her emotionally, but it was clear that Alberta gave her emotions to him just as freely. The problem was that what she gave only left μ wanting more.

Their relationship carried on like this over the rest of the summer. They met either in μ's room or else would go out for walks. They rarely walked far, though. It normally just meant finding a secluded corner of a park or some unused lecture room. Once they had found a few suitable locations they simply alternated between them. She never took any interest in repeating their encounter in the professor's office.

Frustratingly, Alberta never suggested going to her place or even indicated whereabouts she might live. μ started to wonder if she wasn't hiding something at her home.

'We always meet at mine,' μ said one afternoon as they lay in bed. 'Why don't we go to yours one day?'

Alberta's wide eyes were on him.

'It wouldn't be good there. My paps lives there too,' she replied, a tone of worry in her voice.

'Does he not like visitors?' asked μ.

'No, it's not that.' Alberta hugged him closer. 'It doesn't bother you, does it? You know I love you, it's just better here, that's all.'

'No, it's fine,' replied μ, unsure what to make of this. Was she ashamed of her house? Was her father violent? Was he jealous of her boyfriends?

With the academic year over, μ rarely saw Wijklawski. The professor had little reason to contact a first year student, even if he had made vague mention during the final term that μ might help him with his research. There had even been the suggestion of a small amount of pay, but frustratingly the professor never mentioned the role again once the term ended.

A few times, μ visited the professor's office, hoping to surprise Alberta, but on each occasion Wijklawski seemed almost standoffish. At first μ put it down to the professor's eccentricity, but after one visit, about a month after his exams, he started to think it might be something more personal.

'We weren't expecting you,' said the professor, speaking for both himself and Alberta, who was also present.

'I thought I would come by and see if there was any work I could help you with.'

'No, I don't think there is anything needing done,' said Wijklawski, as if ruling out any further discussion.

'Maybe I could help Alberta,' μ suggested, trying to continue the conversation.

'I think she has everything under control,' said the Professor, shooting a sharp look at Alberta, then adding, 'I don't see that your contribution is likely to be particularly useful.'

μ left without speaking to Alberta, but he had an uncomfortable feeling that the Professor's attitude had something to do with their relationship, or lack of it. He came back a few days later, hoping to talk to the Professor alone and find out if there was indeed some problem, but as he entered the corridor he saw Wijklawski was locking his door, preparing to leave.

Unusually for the Morgan building, the corridor that housed Wijklawski's office was fairly long and straight. As a result the professor was a fair distance away when he caught sight of him. He considered shouting out to attract his attention, but the academic still of the place stopped him. Instead he quickened his pace.

He was a good way along the corridor when the professor looked up in his direction. At first μ was quite sure that Wijklawski had seen him – the professor looked directly at him – but he made absolutely no sign of recognition. It was as if the professor were staring straight through him, and for a moment he thought that some trick of the light had made him invisible to the professor's eyes. Wijklawski turned and scuttled in the opposite direction.

It was enough for μ to stop in his tracks. Until then he had assumed that Wijklawski was fond of him, at least to the extent that he was an eager student. Now it seemed that he must have done something to displease Wijklawski, but quite what he couldn't imagine.

It didn't take long for μ to find out what the problem was. The next day he called at Wijklawski's office again to see if Alberta was there. She was, and the Professor with her. He was in a foul mood and was berating her about some trivial matter of filing. When he saw μ had entered, his already bad temper noticeably worsened. His body stiffened up.

'I wonder that you should appear here; today of all days.' Wijklawski's convoluted phrasing was choked with anger.

'I didn't realise I was a fugitive,' replied μ, struggling to understand what was going on.

'I think that both of you know very well in what regard you stand.' The professor was evidently angered, but instead of becoming more animated his movements seemed even more restricted than usual.

'No, I don't think we do.' μ was needled that Wijklawski should suddenly treat him like this. 'Personally, I can't say I've done anything to be ashamed of.'

Alberta gave him a look that suggested he had somehow gone too far, but if she had some inkling of what was going on her face imparted nothing to μ.

'I'm not going to spell this out for the two of you.' Wijklawski spoke slowly as if labouring with his breathing. 'That Alberta is an employee of the university is bad enough; that she is my assistant only compounds matters.

'Now although it is certainly within my rights to take a hard line with you both on this, seeing as it is in effect also a personal concern, I am prepared to put in a word for you in view of your possible naivety.' Here he looked at μ.

'Now, there is no doubt that this is going to negatively affect your academic career, but there is still a possibility that you can continue with your studies next year – provided, that is, that a clean break is made along with a suitable show of compunction. Obviously, it goes without saying, that all relations between the two off you must be completely broken off, and I would suggest that you provide something in the way of apology, in writing, to myself and the university authorities.'

μ was astonished. Was Wijklawski really suggesting that his relationship with Alberta was in some way illegal? He didn't know how to react. The idea that he should in some way apologise to the university authorities was utterly absurd, and yet both Wijklawski and Alberta appeared to be treating the situation with the utmost solemnity. He searched his memory for some indication of where this had come from, but he could find no reason.

'What is this about? I've done nothing wrong. I'm not writing any letter.' μ spoke curtly, and as he did so looked them both in the eye to show that he was not afraid of whatever they might have to say to him. Neither of them made any reply, however. The professor looked at him with barely concealed disappointment and aggravation, but it was Alberta's face that disturbed μ more.

While the professor had been speaking she had hung her head, avoiding eye contact, as if waiting for the lecture to be finished and the punishment to be handed out so that she could leave the room. Now that μ had challenged the professor she stared straight ahead with a look of unbridled anguish. Despite her evident distress at this situation her presence emboldened μ to continue.

'You have no authority to tell me what I should or shouldn't do. I'll do as I please. Alberta can do as she pleases too for that matter. As for my academic career, it is completely irrelevant to this. In any case I don't think you are one to decide on that score. Even if I am naïve, I know enough to know that you are hardly so well regarded in this university. I doubt even if you did put in a "good word" whether anyone would listen.'

μ had started his speech with a feeling of self-righteousness, but rather than coming up against a wall of opposition as he had expected, his words seemed to simply dissipate away into the corners of the room. Instead of provoking any counter argument from Wijklawski, his speech had the opposite affect, and once he had finished speaking the three of them stood entirely in silence.

The professor no longer seemed angered at all. He had lowered his eyes and was staring at the carpet with a gloomy countenance, as if all along the three of them had been attending a funeral. Alberta too had a melancholic expression and μ was suddenly struck by the impression that not just the professor but Alberta also was discomfited by his presence. If they wanted him to leave, then so be it – he wasn't going to stay around. Dismissively, he turned his back on them and stomped out of the room.

Hidden

Outside it was hot. µ marched away from the Morgan building under a dark cloud. He didn't understand exactly what had unfolded in the professor's study, but he couldn't shake the feeling that somehow he had transgressed. What he had done and what he was accused of remained obscure to him but nonetheless painfully real.

What was so terrible if they chose to have a relationship? Wijklawski had all but suggested it was immoral. What right did that old man have to make judgements? Indeed what right did anyone have to pass judgement on the sort of relationships he had? What did he care?

The other students infuriated him, carelessly lolling on the grass or engaged in lazy ball games, happy that the term was over and they were free to relax. He quickened his pace. What had any of this to do with that foolish old man? He could take her or leave her. That would show them both if he did just cut things off. But was that what they wanted?

He hated feeling like a naughty child. Why did he have to convince himself that he had done nothing wrong? Alberta was not Wijklawski's property.

He wanted to get as far away from the university and the campus as possible. The town was busy at this time of day and he thought of taking a bus to the countryside, but the idea of being trapped inside a vehicle with other passengers was repugnant.

He walked through the park in a rage. The sun was bright overhead and the stone buildings that lined its edges glistened keenly. µ took no notice. The dark shadows under the trees appeared somehow more luminous.

µ stomped away from the centre of town, following a path that ran parallel to the course of a small river. It was well into summer and the river, which was really more of a stream and was never particularly plentiful, had run dry. He looked at the banks in disgust, kicking a stone into the empty riverbed. It seemed to signify something, but again he was at a loss as to exactly what.

The park was fairly big and, although it was well kept near the centre, further out the grass had been allowed to overgrow. He walked on and the path led down a steep bank to run along the base of riverbed. At this point the banks were about three metres high and, standing in the dried-out channel, he was completely hidden from view.

There was no one around in any case, but it cheered him to think that he was safe here. Wijklawski may have tried to drive him out, but no one would find him here. He sat on a rock, contemplating the silt and detritus on the riverbed.

He had been there, immobile, for quite some time when a small chaffinch flew down and landed. It bobbed towards him.

'What a foolish creature,' μ thought.

He had the impression it was looking for the water that was no longer there and he let out a little laugh. The same sort of laugh that someone might make if they were told that with luck the firing squad might be ready for them five minutes ahead of time. At the sound of his voice the bird flew off.

Since leaving Alberta and the professor, something had been building inside of him; a knot of frustration that felt like it could only be released in an eruption, but now quite unexpectedly it had subsided. Whatever pressure had been pushing him down this path eased rapidly as if deflated rather than popped.

In exchange he had a sense of the real situation. Wijklawski was not as powerful as he pretended and there would be ways to present his case more eloquently. When μ thought about it he realised that very little had actually been said. He had probably over-reacted. In any case, once he was able to get to the bottom of things and explain everything that had happened clearly and logically he was sure they could work it out.

If the professor was so upset by the two of them seeing each other then it was no skin off μ's nose. He could take or leave Alberta in any case. Maybe that was the cause – that Wijklawski had a crush on her. That certainly would explain things. The old professor working next to her every day, fantasising about her, and then he finds out his student had usurped her, so to speak.

Well, if that was all then it was simple. He would end things with Alberta, reassure the old fellow and all would be fine. Alberta certainly wasn't worth risking his degree over. He could maybe even carry on with her further down the line if he felt like it. Provided they were discreet.

μ's mood lifted. He left the riverbed and climbed the bank. It really was hot. In the distance he could see a frisbee being thrown back and forth. He thought he might go straight back to Wijklawski's office but then changed his mind. He would try and catch Alberta first, let her down gently, and then speak to the professor later once he had composed his case. In the meantime he could enjoy the sunshine. The exams were over after all.

He sauntered back through the rough ground, happy to be outside. Maybe he might get a bus to the countryside after all. He knew the route that would take him out past the ring road. The river Vren, the river running through the centre of Sygeton, passed there. It would be flowing. There were some lovely cafés and bars along its banks. They were always packed with girls. He was meant to enjoy the time he had off.

As it was, he ran into some friends on the way back to the bus stop and, feeling far more sociable, decided to join them. They had a coolbox and were drinking beer and sporadically kicking a ball. μ took the can they offered him. As the afternoon wore into evening he knocked back many more. He followed the few stragglers to several bars they knew were open late and served drinks cheap. By the time he staggered back to his room he was quite, quite drunk.

He must have returned very late as it was four in the afternoon by the time he awoke. He hung around his room doing nothing and felt vague. The day after that was the weekend and he had arranged to go away with some friends. He had the suspicion that they only asked him to make up the numbers, as they were renting a car and needed to split the cost. He got on well enough with all of them and didn't see any reason that his altercation with the professor should change his plans.

Returning three days later μ was revitalised. They had visited the mountains and hiked a good distance. The weather had been excellent. The companionship too had been a surprise. They all got on well and by the time they returned had already planned another trip later in the year. He realised that he had not been away from Sygeton in months. He had spent too long on his own that term. He resolved to be more sociable the next year.

The fact that he didn't see Alberta again for over a week was therefore not down to any consideration of the professor's words. Quite the opposite, he had barely thought about the professor or Alberta since returning from his trip. When he did run into Alberta in the street it was something of a surprise to see her. She had already passed him by the time he called her name. She stopped where she was and waited for him to catch up.

Although she looked glad to see him, he got the impression that she was nervous speaking to him on the street. The professor's lecturing tone came back to him. He reminded himself of his course of action. He would play things cool. Let her down gently, then it would be easier to convince the professor.

'Nice afternoon,' he said, standing a little awkwardly.

'Yes, I thought...' she trailed off.

'I've been away,' μ spoke airily, as if his trip had been of major significance.

'Wijklawski asked me about you,' she spoke slowly, softly, as if afraid her words might do damage. μ tried to manage a smile.

'Really?'

'I didn't say anything, and then when I didn't hear, I thought...'

'Well there's nothing to tell. Is there?'

μ stared at her hard. He thought at first that she had understood his meaning and was upset that he wanted to finish things, but then it occurred to him that she was merely anxious that they might be seen in the street.

Perhaps she was quite happy to split up? Even eager to avoid

Wijklawski's anger? He had not considered whether Alberta would be upset before, but now that he found himself facing the question he was annoyed by the prospect that she might not be in the least bit worried. Surely she had deeper feelings for him?

'After all,' he continued, 'what does our relationship have to do with him?'

Alberta's face stiffened. She looked over her shoulder again and when she turned back μ could see her eyes had a nervous animal quality.

'But you heard what Wijklawski said.'

She said this submissively and yet with total conviction. μ was unsure how to gauge this reaction. It was clear that, whatever her true feelings, the guilt or fear or complicity she felt about their relationship was very powerful.

He had started the conversation planning to break things off, but Alberta seemed far too eager to accept the professor's words. Now, more than ever, the professor's ultimatum seemed completely ridiculous and the fact that Alberta should go along with it was downright insulting. He was utterly infuriated by her timidity. He wanted to snap her from whatever spell she was under. If they did break up it should be because of him, not due to Wijklawski's elliptical threats.

'I know what he said, but we don't need to listen to him. Let him do his worst. He's washed up.'

μ spoke brusquely and having spat this out was compelled to carry on.

'Why shouldn't we let everyone know we love each other? If anything we should be more open. I was just coming to tell you that.'

He paused, sure that Alberta would betray some sign of emotion, but there was no burst of enthusiasm. Quite the opposite. She looked thoroughly deflated. She said nothing. This only infuriated μ even further.

'Of course, if you don't want to carry on...' he said, trying to look nonchalant.

She shot him a dark, trapped look that seemed to suggest he had gone too far.

'You know I'm going to do whatever you say,' she spoke slowly, in a pleading tone.

For a moment he hesitated. It was clear that she was not pleading with him to stand up to Wijklawski but rather quite the opposite, to reconsider. He was confused. Did she want him or not? His pride was crushed by her submissiveness.

'Well there's no reason for us to hide, is there?' He knew he was speaking harshly and couldn't shake the horrible feeling that he was, at that moment, making a terrible decision, but she did not reply.

He tried to smile but the atmosphere was too tense. Alberta looked as if she were about to burst into tears. She was avoiding his eyes but he couldn't summon the strength to put his arm around her. Eventually he gave a slight nod before saying, 'We can tell him our decision tomorrow then.'

This was too much for Alberta and she turned, running down the street, hiding her face in her sleeve. μ stood for a minute, perplexed and uneasy. He was not sure what had just happened, but it left an unpleasant taste. He had a feeling that some indelible course had been chosen, but quite what importance it had he didn't know.

He was annoyed also that his initial plan of breaking things off had been so completely inverted and he couldn't help but hold this against her. The idea that she had done this on purpose was disproven by her sudden flight, but still he had a lingering sense of annoyance at what he saw as Alberta's weakness. If she wasn't going to say anything then she could jolly well follow him.

μ didn't tell the professor his decision the next day. Although he did go into the Morgan building he never made it as far as his office. Approaching across the courtyard he had seen Wijklawski standing by his window. The professor stood stiffly and was staring into the middle-distance. μ could not make out his expression, but there was something foreboding in his presence. He surveyed the square like some tyrannical landowner. μ imagined him standing with locked jaw and a black scowl high above the mortals.

He stopped in at the faculty office to ask after Alberta but was told that she was off work. The secretary didn't know the reason.

'She phoned first thing this morning to tell me she didn't feel well,' said the old woman, pausing to fix an accusing stare on μ. 'She was perfectly fine yesterday.'

μ tried to press her for more information, but the secretary simply said the university had a good policy regarding staff absence, whatever that meant. μ was convinced it had something to do with their conversation the previous day, but as he didn't know Alberta's address there was nothing he could do. He considered phoning her, but there seemed very little that they could say over the phone.

In any case there was no immediate rush. He didn't need to prove something to Wijklawski.

'I'll simply take things as they come,' he said to himself. 'She could well have a cold or some stomach bug.'

He needn't rush around in a panic just because she took the day off work. When she was back the two of them could speak to the professor and explain that, although he obviously had issues with their situation, they were going to continue their relationship and, while they didn't know exactly how they felt about each other or how things would ultimately pan out, that was for them, not Wijklawski, to decide.

The sun was bright outside, but amongst the old stone of the university buildings the air was cold. In the short time he had been inside, μ's eyes had adjusted to the shadow and now stepping outside he was dazzled by the light. He walked quickly, hoping not to bump in to anyone. At the far side of the courtyard he looked up and saw that the professor had left his window.

He didn't feel ready to go back to his room and so he called on some friends who lived nearby. They were in good spirits, lounging around, joking backwards and forwards between each other. They were a group of five who shared a spacious flat and they must have been smoking for some time as they all had large idiotic grins on their faces. He tried to tell them about his situation with Alberta, but they didn't know who she was and couldn't grasp the problem. They quickly seemed to lose interest and joked between themselves.

μ tried to put Alberta out of his mind, but the more his friends laughed the tighter he was wound up. Eventually he couldn't stand their monkeying and resolved to go and speak to Alberta once and for all.

With some persuasion he was able to get her address from the registry secretary, concocting a story that he had been sent to pick up some urgent files that Alberta had taken home with her. The pallid man behind the desk gave μ an excoriating look before handing him the address but evidently decided that μ didn't look like a stalker.

Alberta's address was on the far side of the town in an area that μ didn't know very well. It was a fairly poor neighbourhood dominated by a huge building that had once been a brewery but was now disused. It was only about thirty minutes' walk from the registry office but μ had never had any particular reason to go there. He took his time, thinking over what he would say when he got there.

As he walked, the buildings gradually became less and less grand. Brick and concrete replaced the stone and glass of the university departments. The heat had brought some people out into the street, but he avoided their stares and kept his head down. He wasn't sure whether or not Alberta would be angry at him for finding her home address.

In his mind's eye, she would at first be standoffish but once he talked to her she would see his point. He would convince her that the problems were all in Wijklawski's head.

Her flat was on the 6th floor of an ugly concrete block. The architect had tried to mitigate the harsh severity of the concrete walls with the addition of several copper embellishments jutting out at random intervals. These large blocks had weathered badly and gave the place a positively dilapidated appearance from the outside. μ was shocked. He had had no specific expectations as to Alberta's background, but this place looked like it housed the very dregs of society.

Inside it was at least clean and tidy. The corridors were lined with thick scuffed linoleum and the doorframes were painted a garish green, giving an impression of an institution rather than a block of flats. μ was curious to see Alberta's place.

On her door there were three brass numerals making up the number 116, but he could see no doorbell. He knocked twice confidently. There was no answer. He knocked again but less loudly. The door was eventually opened. However, it was not Alberta but a brittle old man that greeted him.

He was small and shrivelled and his features were set in what appeared a permanent squint. Strong brown hairs sprouted from his nostrils and eyebrows and yet the hair on the top of his head was thin and white. He sniffed at μ as if sizing up to him. This was almost comical considering that he was so small and fragile looking. For a moment μ forgot the reason he was there.

'I'm looking for Alberta.'

'She's in her room.' The man's voice was barely a croak.

μ was confused. He had half-expected the man to tell him that he had the wrong address. The man just eyed him inquisitively.

'I'm from the university,' μ said, hoping this would carry some weight.

'I thought as much.' The old man didn't want to give any ground. 'There's no trouble is there?'

'No, they sent me round to pick some things up,' μ lied. 'Are you her grandfather?'

'No, I'm her boyfriend.' The man's expression didn't change and it took μ a second to realise he was joking. He let out a polite laugh as the old man shuffled out of the way to let him in.

The flat inside was bare – austere even. A dark corridor led to a living room with a window, leading out onto a thin balcony. A kitchen was attached to the room via a hatch. The only furniture in the lounge was a sofa and a folding wooden table with two chairs. If there had been a cross on the wall or a copy of the bible it might have suggested a monk's cell. It was not what μ associated with Alberta. He did not think of her as particularly vivid or bohemian, but equally he struggled to picture her in such ascetic surroundings.

'Apologies it is so empty in here', the man said with a sigh. 'Ever since my wife passed away… Alberta tidies all my things away. Clutter, she calls it. I don't know what to do with that girl. I used to have the place done up just so. Yes, I worked in a printer's in my younger days so I had quite an eye for design you know, but since Alberta has been here it's all had to go. Bit by bit. 'It's all gone now.' He motioned above him with his cane and let out a wheeze.

He told μ to wait and, motioning to the sofa, left the room. μ heard a door open and a muffled conversation. He walked to the window and looked out. From the sixth floor the view took in much of the town and μ could see the outline of the university in the distance. He wondered what circumstances had brought Alberta to live here with her grandfather and why she had never mentioned it before. He heard footsteps behind him and turned to see Alberta.

'What are you doing here?' Her hair was untidy and she was wearing a dressing gown. She looked neither pleased nor unhappy to see him there but made no move to put him at his ease.

'I got your address from the university,' μ said, unsure how to start things.

'You've spoken to Wijklawski?'

'No. The registry office. I wanted to speak to you.'

'I thought we had already spoken?'

'Yes, but…' μ hesitated, 'Wijklawski can't tell us what to do.'

'No, you told me that.'

'But why should there be any consequences? By what right?'

Alberta gave μ a disparaging look that made him feel that his question was utterly juvenile, but she made no reply.

'Why are you off work today?'

'I'm feeling a little sick.'

μ could see she was lying.

'What are you going to do for money?' she asked.

'I have my grant.'

'And when you're not a student?'

'It won't come to that.'

Again she said nothing.
'I'll find a job.'
Alberta looked morose.
'It's all going to be fine,' he said finally.
'Yes.'
'You'll be at work tomorrow?'
'Yes.'

Together

The following day they told Wijklawski and, rather than the argument that µ had expected, he took the news very calmly. There were no fireworks or any sign of his previous barely controlled anger. That is not to say he looked pleased by the news. Both he and Alberta sat quietly for the most part as µ justified their relationship, but where Alberta listened to µ's every word the professor seemed distant and disengaged, as if he were already forgetting about his pupil and his assistant. When µ had finished speaking Wijklawski stood up and walked to the window.

'Well, I can see you have made a decision. I only wish you hadn't made the wrong one.' He let out a breath and shifted his gaze onto the horizon. 'But that is as maybe. Alberta will need to leave her position as my assistant of course.'

µ was about to protest this, but the professor continued.

'She will be given another role in the faculty of chemistry. As for you, I cannot comment, but it is sad to see a promising student's career cut short.'

This riled µ and he too stood up at this point.

'If you are trying to frighten us it's not going to work. Threaten us if you want, but if you try to sling either of us out we'll fight it.'

Wijklawski smiled sadly. 'Of course that is within your rights – there is the university appeals court – but believe me, I am not the enemy. I only want to stop you doing anything regrettable.'

This was more ominous than an outright threat and µ could summon no response. He walked up close to the old man intending to give him a piece of his mind, but as he approached Wijklawski shrank away. It was an almost imperceptible movement, but it was enough to tell µ that whatever strange logic was controlling his and Alberta's destiny it was not in the professor's hands but some larger agency.

'We'll take our chances,' he said finally. He left the office with Alberta, unsure if he had made the right decision or not but quite sure that their course was now set.

*   *   *

After this encounter with the professor μ expected to receive some formal notification of his reproach, but the two pieces of news that reached him a week later, and ultimately led to him moving in with Alberta, were both unrelated to Wijklawski.

The first piece of news was not entirely unexpected and came from the university examination board. It was a letter containing details of μ's exam results and those subjects he was expected to re-sit. At the time of the exams he had been far from confident, he had missed large amounts of most of the courses and despite his revision most of his answers had been guesswork. The only exam he thought he had done well in was Wijklawski's subject and after the professor's pronouncements μ had expected a summary fail.

He was surprised, therefore, to see that Wijklawski had in fact awarded him a high mark, far above what he deserved. It was the other subjects where he had fallen short and all except one he now had to resit.

The second piece of news was the death of Alberta's grandfather. She told him one afternoon while they lay naked in his bed. She spoke so off-handedly that μ didn't listen at first to what she was saying. It didn't appear to have had much impact on her. She talked about the funeral arrangements in detail but said very little about her grandfather himself. He had died peacefully, apparently.

μ went with her to the funeral two days later. The only others attending were two elderly ladies and the building attendant from Alberta's block. There was something comical about the two old ladies. They both wore identical thick glasses and bobbed up and down with the same motion when they walked. μ wasn't sure if they were relatives or not. Alberta spoke to them as if she knew them but with what μ felt was a touch of condescension. The building attendant was there, as he apparently used to share a cup of tea with Alberta's grandfather from time to time. The whole thing was over in about forty-five minutes.

That was the first night that μ stayed in Alberta's flat. He had been prepared to do the chivalrous thing and keep her company afterwards but had not expected her to suggest staying the night. Any time the issue had been raised previously she had been quite adamant that they went to his, but now she all but dragged him to her place.

'I don't want to stay there alone,' she had said.

On the way there, μ felt a slight trepidation Alberta's opinion had changed so radically, and so soon after the old man was buried. He didn't say anything. Alberta didn't seem to notice his concern and, if anything, was slightly freer than usual. The curtains were still drawn when they entered and she threw them wide.

After that first night it was some time before he stayed there again. He still had his place in the halls and it was closer to the university where he should study. As it was he got very little studying done. The few friends that had not gone elsewhere for the summer were intent on partying whenever possible. μ fell in easily with them and although he meant to get round to revising he somehow never found the time. When the re-sits came he had a faint dread, but that passed quickly enough once they were over and he was in the pub again. It was a month before the results came in anyway.

He had to leave halls around then as the rooms were reserved for first year students only and the intake for the following academic year were starting to arrive. He had vague plans of moving into a flat with some friends. They had a spare room and had offered him it, but told him they needed to check with another flatmate who was away travelling. The question of where to live didn't bother μ greatly. He was having fun.

With nothing else to do he quickly got into a routine of partying late and sleeping in. He split his time between Alberta's bed and various friend's sofas. As a result, he never got round to organising anywhere else to stay and so when Alberta suggested moving in with her, on a more permanent basis, it seemed the easiest thing to do.

Living together was superb at first. Alberta still worked at the university but her hours were reduced outside term time and at night she was all his. As the last weeks of the summer progressed, μ found he was relieved to have a place to call home again. The two of them redecorated the flat, taking their time to make the place feel tasteful, lived in. Things seemed simple and for a few weeks the concerns of exams and university life seemed far away.

There were some issues of course, but nothing μ thought that serious. After a few weeks he received a letter from the university authorities telling him he had failed to achieve the necessary marks in his re-sits. He was invited to attend an aural exam to ensure his place in the following year, but he left the letter on the table and somehow missed the appointment.

Alberta had barely any reaction when he mentioned it to her and it was surprising how easily he got used to his new status. He had enough funds to survive for the near future and soon found that idleness suited him well, despite the occasional argument with Alberta.

'You are here all day,' she might say. 'It wouldn't hurt to tidy up a little, would it?'

μ would nod in agreement. If he was sitting about on the sofa all day and Alberta came home after working eight hours it wasn't unreasonable that he might tidy a little or cook something for her, was it? She was out earning a wage after all, but then he was a student – was it right that she always expected him to foot the bill when they went out?

'Why don't we split the bill this time?' μ would say on occasion.

'I don't have my purse with me,' Alberta would reply.

'Well next time you can get it,' μ would try in a jokey tone.

Alberta would make no reply, looking a little uncomfortable, as if μ had asked something distasteful.

Although the start of the new term was nearing he gave scarcely a thought to either his course or his finances. There was no shortage of revelry still to be found on campus. The more studious of his fellow students had all found summer placements elsewhere which left only those interested in drinking and carousing. μ soon found he could fit in quite well.

As Wijklawski predicted, Alberta's position was moved to the chemistry department where she got a job with a grander sounding title that was nonetheless more of a demotion. She made no complaint but μ gradually got a creeping sense that she was displeased with him.

When, as increasingly happened, he returned in the small hours of the morning, filled with the joys of life, Alberta would seem ill-disposed or else would say nothing. The next day he sometimes got the impression that she was upset with him. She never said as much but to μ it seemed that Alberta developed an attitude of weary resignation to everything around them.

Whenever they were alone together in the flat μ found Alberta's thoughts depressing and unnecessarily gloomy. She foresaw only a steady decline in their position, now that she had lost her role with Wijklawski and he was no longer a student. He tried to argue that he could still reclaim his place on the course, but she could tell his heart wasn't in it. They repeated the same arguments over and over.

For such a long time it had been a foregone conclusion that he would study. It was something that always lay in the background – a degree, a certificate, a proper job, a justification for having moved to Sygeton and living there still. It was only now without any purpose at all he really started to consider his position for the first time.

Was he sinking into the same depression as Alberta? He spent most days alone in the flat, staring at the television or sometimes simply staring out of the window. Was there really a good reason to do anything? Surely the human consciousness could at best be viewed as a prototype, a badly designed attempt at being. A mis-formed ragbag of parts that was not designed for life. The optimists might talk about evolution, but who was to say it lead anywhere. Much more likely it was a dead end, like the dodo – an example of how not to create life.

He asked himself if there could really be some guiding principle, some hidden order to life, that he had so far failed to apprehend. The ideas of religion at school had always struck him as nonsensical, but then what was left in its absence? With time on his hands his thoughts were slowly unravelling.

It seemed clear to him that there could be no good reason for action, and without reason his existence was not just pointless but wearisome. He tried to talk to Alberta about his feelings but got nowhere. As their financial position worsened he grew frustrated at his dependence on her job, but at the same time was unable to think seriously about looking for employment himself.

With nothing to do all day he started to lose the urge to socialise. Alberta was out working and most of his erstwhile friends were focusing on their studies or else simply drifted away. He made little attempt to stay in touch, spending hour after hour in the house. He still drank, but when, occasionally, he did go out in a mood of optimism he always returned disheartened. Time slipped and juddered past him with a grim friction.

It was in this mood that he first started to grow suspicious of Alberta. Their conversation had by this stage deteriorated to such an extent that they barely talked, but still he could sense changes in her. If she was slightly more talkative it became a clear sign that she was covering something up and if slightly less then a sign of guilt. When she looked like she had made an extra effort with her appearance he would ask himself who the other man was. It was clear that she would not do it for his benefit. The flat became a cold, frigid box.

For a while, this doubt gnawed in the background unchecked, until one day, in a flash of inspiration, he realised that the other man must be none other than Wijklawski. The move of job had been a cunning ploy to distract attention, but it was evident that they had carried on their relationship through all of this. He plotted questions aimed at catching her out, but she was evasive and never swayed from her story – that it was μ she was in love with.

'You're back late,' he might say.

'Yes, the prospectuses are going to the printer this week.'

'The chemistry department?'

'Of course.'

'Why? Would you prefer to work somewhere else?'

'It's not so bad. It pays the bills.'

'You miss working with Wijklawski?'

'Why do you keep on with that? We're living together, aren't we?'

'Well I can move out any time if you're needing the space.'

'You're not going to move out.'

'Maybe I should.'

'That's ridiculous.'

His questions irritated her and she would normally end the conversation by going into the other room or leaving the flat. It was on one such occasion that she stormed out not five minutes after arriving back from work. She had just taken her shoes off when something he said infuriated her and she left, slamming the door behind her.

At first he was unperturbed by their row but as the hours passed Alberta's absence became more of an irritation. He imagined that she was simply staying away from the flat to demonstrate her annoyance with him. He pictured her angrily striding up and down the street outside, but as it grew darker he began to realise that she must, in fact, have gone somewhere else. He tried to imagine her sitting with some girlfriend, talking viciously about him, the friend nodding sympathetically and offering the occasional piece of advice, but the image seemed unbelievable.

Alberta didn't have many girlfriends that she was likely to have a heart to heart with. Not as far as µ knew in any case. Even if she did, he knew her well enough to know that in a foul mood she would never want to sit and chat. She would want to do something. The image of her in a bar sprang into his mind. A muscular, well-heeled guy in a suit, some marketing-type, talking to her indiscreetly. The two of them returning to his hotel room.

He imagined her and this businessman having sex, visualising it from every angle. One moment it was animal, pheromonal, compulsive, the next it was cold, powerful, almost mathematical. Their two bodies grinding together. Mechanical. Unstoppable.

The more images fell in his mind's eye, the greater his belief in their truth. There was nothing emotional about any of them. Whatever way he imagined the two of them was simple lust. No gentle caresses or warm smiles, no look of compassion or empathy, just hard cold sex. He felt nauseous. Why was he imagining these things?

It was two o'clock in the morning. She wasn't going to come back that night. He thought of going to sleep, but he had worked himself into a state of wakefulness. He was onto his second bottle and he noticed that he had already made quite a dent in it.

It was around seven thirty that she finally came back. μ had fallen asleep on the couch. His glass had spilt down his front leaving a damp, sticky trace. He heard her knocking at the door. She had forgotten her keys the day before in her haste to leave the flat. His brain clumsily recalled the darkness of the previous night. He was indignant. He didn't need to let her in straight away.

They argued through the thin plyboard door. He was still drunk. She was cold and angry. The both knew enough to know what would hurt. He said he wouldn't let her in until she admitted who she had been with. She told him she hadn't been with anyone. He shouted drunken names through the letterbox. He heard her crying. After a while she stopped.

He fell asleep against the doorframe.

Around lunch time he left the flat. He imagined that if he cooked a big meal there was a chance of reconciliation. He didn't have enough money for what he wanted and had to go to the cheaper supermarket that was further away.

On the way back he ran into an acquaintance and, explaining his woes, they stopped for a quick drink. With most of the ingredients for a good meal and a few drinks inside him he was sure everything could be worked out. He would make sure the meal was perfect and when she came in the door he would bowl her off her feet. He was sure there were candles in one of the drawers.

When he got back Alberta was already in the flat. She had already eaten. He had no idea how she could have got in and she made no mention of it. It was only later that he figured that she probably got the key from the building attendant. They sat in silence. Neither of them mentioned the previous night or the incident that morning. She went to bed early and he stayed up on the couch drinking the wine he had bought to go with dinner.

They carried on together for a while after that. There were some other arguments. μ had plenty of other opportunities to let his imagination run riot, but on the whole he found their existence more bearable. If anything, the sex was better than before.

The spring came around and μ's mood lifted a little. Prospects started to appear, indistinctly at first and far off on the horizon, but there was a sense that they might be attainable. μ thought seriously about finding a job and a couple of opportunities turned up. They would discuss plans for the future and go for the occasional walk together. He and Alberta even shared the odd joke.

'What is it you're looking for?' She asked him while he leafed through the job adverts.

All in all μ started to feel positive about the future and what it might bring. He drank less and started seeing some of his other friends. He stopped worrying about Alberta and his jealousy ebbed. It was a peaceful time between them, although curiously afterwards μ could remember very little of what they actually did. He sometimes thought they might have carried on like that indefinitely.

It was not to be, however. One day, returning mid-afternoon from a job interview, he sensed something in the flat was different. He was not expecting Alberta to be in, as she usually worked at that time, but the place felt empty.

There was no tangible sensation or any specific change he identified. There was no note or explanation and she had taken barely anything with her. It was just a feeling, something he remembered later when it became apparent that she had really left.

He was used to her staying away overnight by that point and he no longer questioned her about that. It was not uncommon she might be gone two or three nights out of a week.

When eventually, after a week, there was still no sign, he tried to make enquiries, but he got little real information. At first everyone claimed to know nothing, but bit by bit he caught rumours and hearsay and learnt that she had supposedly moved to the city. She had run off with someone from the university – nobody would say who it was. Later, when he checked her clothes, he reckoned she must have gone with only two or three changes at most.

Eventually he found a job and moved into a small flat in the centre of Sygeton. He did well enough and never really thought too much about the future, but the place never really suited him after that. It was only much later, once he had moved to the city, that he admitted, grudgingly, to himself that he might have been in love with Alberta.

THE WAVE

A Medical Verdict

The itching was driving him mad. μ was sure that everyone in the café was looking at him. He still had hours to kill before four. The lunchtime rush was starting so μ left the café and headed to the tube. To the doctor's. He needed to find something to stop the itching.

When he first moved to the city he had registered with a doctor and, although he now lived on the opposite side of town, he had never bothered finding somewhere closer. The place he had registered was really more of a drop-in centre than a typical medical practice, so each patient would be seen by whoever was available, rather than having a specific doctor assigned to them. This was fine with μ. He had never had to visit all that regularly so they were just names to him.

The receptionist on duty was young and bored looking. She took down his details disinterestedly and told him he would have to wait about half an hour before a Doctor Gllas would see him.

She pushed a slip of paper across the desk, circling a number on it.

'This is our phone number,' she said in a flat tone. 'What form of complaint are you expressing?' she mumbled as she tapped at the keyboard.

'Complaint?' μ was confused for a moment before he realised she meant his symptoms. 'I've got a rash, a skin rash.'

'Dermatological.' She typed each letter slowly as she spoke, a look of disdain on her face.

'It's got really bad.' For some reason μ felt that he had to justify his claim. Unbuttoning his cuff he peeled back the sleeve to the elbow, revealing his red blotchy forearm.

'It's been getting worse and I thought I should get it seen to.'

'Nasty, very nasty,' said the receptionist, suddenly shifting in her chair and brightening up. 'You'll need an antifungal at least for something like that.' She seemed to be immensely pleased by the sight of the arm.

She indicated a small opening that presumably led to the stairs and then turned back to her screen. μ nodded and ducked through the doorway, entering a steep, narrow staircase leading up. The steps were made of cheap plyboard and were stacked on top of each other nearly vertically. Each step he took seemed to rattle the entire staircase and he was out of breath by the time he was only half way up.

At the top, the stairs opened out on a tiny waiting room with moulded plastic chairs around the walls. μ wished he had thought to take a book, or been able to find the script. What was he going to say at four o'clock? He was no longer sure the voice on the phone had even been Ddunsel. At least if he had the script he could have looked for clues, had something to confront him with.

On the far side of the room a low table had a few well-thumbed magazines and in one of the chairs an old man was apparently asleep. He was hideously fat and seemed to ooze over the sides of the chair, his arms folded across his chest and his head rising and falling with each breath, lolling to one side.

The heating was on full and the air was dry and stifling. The stuffiness only aggravated μ's rash and he couldn't sit still. The itching was relentless. There was nothing worth reading on the table and he retired to a seat in the corner furthest away from the sleeping man.

On the wall opposite him were a number of signs designed to capture attention and promote a healthy lifestyle. Most of these detailed how to make good living part of your day to day routine. The largest poster was made up of four squares. Each square had a single word at the top in large colourful text. CHANGE, HELP, BEAT, FIGHT. Next to each word was a cheerful picture and beneath it a short paragraph describing the steps you could take to improve your health.

'Perhaps I have just been stressed recently,' he thought as he scratched his arm. 'Once I get rid of this rash I need to concentrate on getting some early nights.'

The heat, the waiting and the silence of the room all combined to exacerbate the itching. The clock on the wall crawled through twenty minutes, then another ten, and nothing moved. μ couldn't hear any sounds from the rest of the building and no other patients either came or went.

Eventually after sitting there for thirty-five minutes a tall brunette woman clad in a white coat appeared at the door. She held a clipboard stiffly in her long hands and glanced at it briefly to read out his name.

'Yes,' answered μ.

'I'm Doctor Ohlsson,' she said. 'This way please.'

μ rose from his seat and went to shake her hand, but she merely looked at his outstretched digits with distaste.

'I understood I was to see a Doctor Gllas,' said μ.

'Doctor Gllas is no longer with us,' she replied curtly and with that set off down the corridor. It wasn't clear whether she meant that Doctor Gllas had died or simply left the medical practice.

She led the way along a number of narrow corridors, never

stopping to check if μ was following or not. As they walked, her heels clicked on the creaky plywood floors and μ struggled to keep up with her. Finally, she stopped next to one of the doors and, pushing the handle, let the door swing open.

'This way,' she said impatiently, motioning with her free hand that μ should pass by and enter the room.

Inside it was bare, save for a large wooden desk with a screen on it, a bookcase-cum-filing-cabinet on the near wall and two chairs. The chair behind the desk was a comfortable looking reclining leather seat while the one in front, clearly for patients, was of the same type as those in the waiting room. μ squeezed past the doctor and sat down, putting his jacket across the back of the chair. She then entered the room, taking a quick glance up and down the corridor, as if, μ thought, to check whether they had been followed, before taking a seat behind the desk.

'You do know that we don't prescribe opiates to patients on their first visit,' she said as if to kick off proceedings.

'This isn't my first…'

She sat very correctly and pressed her fingers together into an arch. μ didn't know how to react to this.

'So,' she continued, 'what is the problem?'

'I have a rash. I think it's getting worse.'

'Hmm yes, a spreading rash,' she murmured, as if confirming some medical prognosis. 'And whereabouts has it spread?'

'My arms.'

'Right.' She paused again, as if tasting this fresh piece of information. 'We'd better have a look at you. If you could take off your shirt…'

μ had anticipated simply rolling back his sleeve. She watched him as he undid the buttons, as if looking for some clue as to the cause of his illness. Her room was a good deal cooler than the waiting room and as μ slipped the shirt off his back he felt goosebumps across his skin. He tensed his back. He was not used to getting undressed in the presence of strangers. He tended to stay covered up even when the weather got hot in the summer.

The doctor got up from her seat and walked over to where μ was standing. His shirt was draped over the chair now and he was acutely aware of her proximity. He tried his best to stand erect. Without a word she walked around behind him as if inspecting him for purchase.

'Have you had sex recently?' she said. By this point she was standing directly behind μ and he could not see her without craning his neck or shifting position. He wasn't sure if he should turn to answer her question or continue standing as he was. In the end he decided to stay.

'...unprotected sex,' she continued. 'Do you use contraceptives?'

'Normally, yes I guess so, yes,' μ said, feeling slightly uncomfortable.

'Hmm, yes, but not recently? No? Well I always ask. Sometimes it can be the cause of symptoms like this,' she said, coming round in front of μ again and giving him a long hard stare.

'Pent up frustration, stress levels, all that. Have you been feeling unusually stressed recently? We often find it's linked to obsessive behaviour. Personally, I never use contraception myself and never had a problem, clean as a whistle, but then you'd be surprised at some of the things people do get up to behind closed doors.'

She raised one eyebrow and tapped her pen on the desk as if thinking something over. μ was shocked. Was this the way she should be talking? Was she implying that he had some deep-seated sexual issues that were manifesting themselves as a rash? How long was it since he had had sex?

'Anyway, we can be sure that's not the cause in this case,' she said, and laying her pen on the table she reached out and gripped μ's upper arm. Taking a step forward she bent her head closer to examine the rash and brought his arm up into the light. He was surprised how soft and cool her touch was. For some reason, perhaps because of her brusque tone, he had expected her to be less than sensitive, but her hand felt smooth.

The top of her head was just below his eye level and he looked down at her thick brown hair as she carried out her inspection.

She drew slowly closer and closer to his body and he found himself holding his breath. Her body was alive at such close proximity and μ struggled with an urge to grapple her onto the table in front of him. He had no clear mental picture of this act, simply a desire that rose sharply inside him. His pulse increased and the harder he tried to stand still the tighter he felt his breathing.

She held him in that position for an uncomfortably long time. μ thought she was perhaps waiting on him to make a move and then, abruptly, she pulled away and strode back behind the desk.

'Ok, you can button up now,' she said.

μ awkwardly picked up his shirt and put it back on as she grabbed a pad of paper from one of the drawers and started scribbling busily.

'I'm going to tell you that you have psychosomatic rash related to certain existential issues.' As she said the last two words she motioned ersatz quotes in the air. What did that mean – existential issues? Why had she said 'I'm going to tell you', as if she were making up a story?

When he had done up his shirt completely she passed the piece of paper across the table to him. It was a prescription made out for three different medications.

'I'm prescribing you a course of xyhtolitol, xitolocol and bracebotol,' she said. 'Xyhtolitol is an anti-depressant. It's a new drug and very effective at alleviating certain symptoms, but one of the side effects can be a reduced libido. The xitolocol will counteract this by increasing your libido and may also reduce the itchiness. The bracebotol is simply a placebo but some patients do find that it helps.'

She patted the piece of paper before pushing it across the desk to μ.

'You may also find you become prone to episodes of mild narcolepsy.'

He took the paper, somewhat perplexed. The drugs she had prescribed seemed to have nothing to do with his affliction. He had been expecting to try some form of topical cream, perhaps a course of antibiotics.

'Is there not something a bit more...' μ searched for the right word, '...at reception, she suggested...'

'No,' Dr. Ohlsson cut in. 'As you were informed, we do not prescribe opiates on the first visit. In fact, we take a dim view of patients trying to score any sort of recreational drugs.'

She had clearly misinterpreted μ. Why did she seem convinced that he was trying to score drugs? Did he look like that sort?

'I mean, is there not something a little... simpler I could try... a cream or...'

'No, I'm afraid not. The best thing you can do is to take the medication and do your best to forget about it for just now.' She reached inside her breast pocket. As she felt around the pocket μ could see she wore a very low cut top beneath her white coat. As she rummaged around he got the impression she was deliberately taking longer than necessary in order that he might get a better view of her cleavage. She didn't make eye contact with him the whole time.

Eventually she produced a business card and put it on the table. Turning it over she started writing on the back. When she had finished she pushed the card, with her index and middle finger, across the desk towards μ.

'This, is my business card,' she said. 'Contact me any time, day or night. I've written my private number on the back, so feel free to call me at home if there is any change or you feel that you would like to talk to me. Any time day or night.'

She said all this in a very business-like tone that made μ unsure if she really was flirting with him. As she spoke, a brief, fleeting smile appeared to pass across her face but it disappeared so quickly, and seemed so out of character, that μ wondered whether he had imagined it. She was already standing to see him out. He was in the hallway a moment later.

'Please arrange another appointment with Diana for two weeks' time,' she said, rigidly shaking his hand.

μ presumed Diana was the glum receptionist downstairs. He muttered a goodbye and was alone in the corridor. The entire appointment had not gone as he had expected. He had the lingering sensation that the doctor had wanted something from him but her entire demeanour suggested the opposite. Confused, he folded the prescription into his pocket and walked back the way that he had come.

As he passed the waiting room he saw that the fat man was now awake. Two other men were struggling to get him out of his chair and the man was moaning and puffing loudly. They looked like nurses, but they were grappling with the man in the most bizarre manner.

They tugged and yanked at the seated man in an entirely uncoordinated way, neither of them seeming to take any notice of the other's efforts. Both of them simply grabbed at the fat man's limbs and pulled this way and that. It was evidently uncomfortable for the fat man as he rocked back and forward, groaning and cursing ever louder.

μ paused for a second to watch this spectacle and one of the nurses noticed him at the door. He frowned at μ and stopped what he was doing, before whispering something to the other nurse. The other then stopped as well and turned towards μ with an angry look. Dropping the oversized arm that he had been tugging on, he stomped across to the door and pulled it shut without so much as a word. μ hurried down the stairs and left the building.

Action at a distance

On his way home, μ went to a chemist's and picked up his prescription. They surely wouldn't do any good, but he ordered the pills nonetheless. To be on the safe side he also ordered a tube of antibiotic cream which the pharmacist said might help. Leaving the pharmacy, he popped open the three packets and took one of each of the pills. He walked aimlessly for a while, taking several detours through the streets, trying to keep his mind off his rash.

Within ten minutes he found that he was a good deal better. The itching had faded to a dull tingle as if some switch had been flicked off. Perhaps the pills really did work.

Seeing as it was such nice weather, and he had to kill time until four, he took the underground across the city to the Harnolt marshes. The marshes were a sort of mini nature reserve on the east side of the city. Several canals and reservoirs fed through them and while some of it was laid out like parkland with paths and roads, the majority of it was still unkempt. Sometimes he would go there and pretend he was out in the countryside. Since moving to the city he rarely got to see real Nature as often as when he lived in Sygeton.

The last time he had been to the marshes had been with a few acquaintances from work. It had been hot then too and they had all got on in an easy, relaxed way. He remembered it clearly because he had been dreading the usual dull questions about work, and conversations about people he barely knew, but instead he had ended up enjoying that afternoon.

Sitting on a bench μ started to wonder what side effects the medication he had taken might have. Every thought he started seemed to distend and fall apart before it fully formed, and his hands felt strangely heavy. The thick grey clouds above him were like a layer of insulation protecting him from the harsh, emptiness out in space. He tried rubbing them together but that produced an unpleasant sensation and so he let them flop heavily by his side.

He had once been taken to the mountains as a child, with a

group of other kids from the town where he lived. It had all been organised to let the children have a week of activities and outdoor pursuits away from home. They had travelled in two old minibuses for hour upon hour until they reached the remote spot where they were to stay. µ had instantly liked the place.

All the children slept in one wooden cabin and the instructors in another. They were nestled in the dense mountain forest, just like a scene from some fairy tale. Every afternoon they were split into groups and would take part in activities. In the evenings they cooked and ate together in the larger of the cabins.

One afternoon it happened that he was left behind. As the groups were being selected he was engrossed on his own, a little distance into the forest. The instructors, for whatever reason, didn't notice that he was not present as the other children climbed into the beaten minibuses to make their way to the activity points. It was only when µ heard the silence that he realised he was alone.

He remembered that silence even now as something pure and utterly different from the lack of sound you could hear elsewhere. In the city, silence was normally fleeting, a simple respite, a break in proceedings until the next noise, but there, alone, amongst the mountains, he felt something far deeper, far more terrifying, sat looking out on the trees and the lake below.

He had at first enjoyed it and taken the opportunity to jump between the cabins unhindered by the grownups, but after some time the sheer emptiness of the location washed over him. It was a bare, hard emotion only partially revealed. The volume of pure silence.

It was oppressive to stay near the cabins and so he wandered out, further away from the site. The loneliness and desolation he felt was not due to the absence of the other children or the instructors. It was something far more fundamental and indelible. A terrible solitude was transmitted directly through that silence.

It was something that frightened him and yet, at the same time, he could sense with a coldly rational, logic that this silence was the only true form of completeness. The silence was what had existed before the beginning of the world. The silence was what slept inside everybody. Was it possible that everybody felt that at some point? The roar of nothingness.

The instructors and other children were gone for several hours, completing their afternoon activities. When they returned they found him huddled in the front seat of one of the instructors' cars. He was listening to the static of the radio, trying to tune in to radio stations that were miles out of range. They presumed he was missing his parents.

He remembered that feeling years later when he saw a documentary about the Gnostics, an ancient pre-Christian religion who believed that 'the true form of nature was hidden by the illusion of our reality'. As far as he understood it, they believed that the physical world was, at best, a frivolous illusion, and at worst the creation of an evil deity.

The true god, the supreme divinity, was something remote, unimaginably distant from humans. This God, Bythos, or Profundity, was the single source that encompassed everything else. From this true source emanated further divine beings, known as Aeons, aspects of God that existed in hierarchies, progressively and gradually more distant from the true source.

The everyday reality that humans were stuck with was the creation of one of lowliest of these Gods, an altogether inferior being, a demiurge, a false God. The whole of creation was nothing more than an illusion and mankind needed to battle through this if it wanted to progress towards the ultimate source. The documentary had mentioned, sarcastically, that union with the ultimate deity was impossible according to the Gnostics, but that that didn't stop humanity having a go.

There had been a detailed section on the life of Simon Magus, the supposed founder of Gnosticism in the Western world. He had been a sorcerer and heretic and μ remembered the camera had zoomed in on an ornate mural of him and his accusers painted on the wall of a church in Milan.

The documentary had then veered off into the wild theories of some quantum physicist, called David Bohm, who believed that modern society had become fragmented due to the fact that mankind regarded itself as separate from nature.

He had derived some complicated-sounding equations that apparently proved the traditional quantum theories wrong. Rather than the strange particles and quantum cats of Schrödinger there were in fact many different 'hidden' orders of reality.

These implicate orders of reality were somehow different to the 'illusion' predicted by the Gnostics, but μ had struggled to follow most of the technical stuff. He didn't doubt there was something wrong with modern society, but still, what did it really mean to be connected?

It had been so long since he had felt a real connection with anyone that he struggled to imagine a deeper reality where everything was connected. Even when he had been more or less content with Alberta for a few short weeks, he had always been outside, separate from the true nature of things.

It had started to rain more heavily and μ's jacket stuck wetly against his skin. It was colder in this rain and, reluctantly, he stood up to leave the marshes. As he plodded back towards the underground he suddenly felt a wave of nausea as he remembered the events of the previous night. Why did it have to be him who had stumbled into that shop?

The walk back to the underground led past several cafés and bars. The heavy rain had driven most of the customers inside, but as he approached one bar he could see a bunch of rowdy people sitting outside under a giant awning, completely protected from the torrential rain. They must have been smoking heavily, for the air under the canopy was thick and grimy. As μ drew level with them a man with a severe flinty face and thick blonde hair gave him a stare that seemed to pierce him to the core. Some unknown instinct made μ pull his jacket closer around him and increase his speed as he went past.

He wasn't sure why, but he felt an overwhelming pressure to be on time for his meeting with Ddunsel. He had never met the man and had only spoken to him once, on the phone that morning, when he had sounded extremely drunk and not especially agreeable, so there was no particular reason for µ to even turn up, but somehow he was sure Ddunsel was at the centre of all of it. It was not something µ could put his finger on. More a feeling that he was entering a giant web, at the centre of which lay Ddunsel.

He remembered a type of charity collection box that had been popular outside supermarkets when he was a child, a sort of wishing well or coin funnel. They were always covered by a clear plastic dome and had a slot on the top where you could slide a single coin. Inside, under the dome, was a convex surface, typically painted with lurid green and white spirals, that sloped in towards a small hole in the centre.

You would drop a coin in the side and it would orbit slowly at first, ringing around the bowl, following the lines painted by the spirals. Gravity would pull it down and gradually it would pick up speed, moving in ever-decreasing circles towards the centre until it was a blur of motion, spinning around the dark hole in the middle. Faster and faster it would whirl until that indefinite point when suddenly it disappeared with a clink to the unseen depths of the box.

Whatever Ddunsel was, or represented, was both dark and mysterious in its pull. He was the hole at the centre. µ knew next to nothing about him but felt himself spinning faster and faster. His life had grown so empty recently that, whatever the consequences, this encounter was something he craved, an axe to the frozen sea inside.

In some way he was – had become – separated from something, something intangible, something that he had once apprehended more clearly, though never touched, as a child. It pained him to realise how lacking his existence had become.

It was as if a parallel µ existed side by side, travelling an adjacent path, but one which ran an altogether more perfect course. He imagined this perfect 'twin', his double. What would he make of µ' s tawdry life? He felt this twin must exist somewhere, even if only in the platonic realm of ideals.

This twin had succeeded in everything he had not. This creature, identical to μ, had achieved every potential that it could as a living organism while he had merely wasted his time.

Where he had careened from one place to the next, job to job, relationship to relationship, meal to meal. This other perfect μ had continued with steely resolve, deflecting any obstacles, never encountering doubt or dilemma. This perfect μ was not something to be jealous of, he simply represented the natural order of things. It was μ himself that was at odds – had slipped or dilly-dallied on his way.

As children, the two μs, himself and his perfect double, would presumably have been similar. In fact, μ could almost pick moments where the two were indistinguishable. That was not the case any longer, now that an enormous distance loomed between them, a distance so huge that μ could no longer make out the shape of his more perfect self. He could only imagine it as a memory.

It was unclear how, when or where the distance had been gained, but it was quite clear that μ had strayed. No longer was his life even comparable to his twin. He had stumbled – transgressed. He was somebody to be viewed with a mixture of sympathy and disgust.

He remembered Alberta, speaking to him through a drunken haze; he had drunk a whole bottle of rum.

'Have some dignity for yourself,' she had said in a hushed tone of contempt. 'You owe it to yourself to have a bit of respect.'

He had barely known who he was at that point, so drunk, spinning in a kaleidoscope of warm sensations, but something about Alberta's icy tone and those words 'DIGNITY, DIGNITY' rang through his fuzzy world.

And what was dignity? Where did one acquire dignity? At some level it was not where you were but where you were heading. Something that one carried with them. A duty, a commitment to being an honourable person – a good person, a dignified person. A duty not only to act in a certain way but something altogether deeper. It was a responsibility to be better, to improve oneself, lift oneself up from the mud and shit and detritus and find his long-lost perfect twin. It was an almost schizophrenic thought.

But if it was an obligation, to whom was it owed? Your country, your wife, your children, your workplace, to yourself even? What did it mean to owe a duty to yourself?

If the debtor and creditor were one and the same person then the debt itself was meaningless. 'If I both owe and am owed the same amount it adds to zero,' μ pondered, sensing the drugs were addling his powers of arithmetic.

'Unless there is some way to separate the two parties? A version that is owed, the perfect version, the perfect twin that receives the offering and another version that does the owing, the you that has a duty to improve, the you that wallowed in the mud and the shit.'

Anyone could appear dignified to others by diligently following the rules, but within oneself was it possible without admitting to a split personality? The greater the betterment, the greater the debt of duty one owed. The person that gave up their life in usury to the image of the perfect self must surely be the purest. The question was only what depths one was willing to go to, what debts you were willing to take on.

It was an absurd idea – the most dignified man must be the most abject, the most pitiable, for it was he and only he that could have the largest burden of duty to improve. It was only those with nothing at all that relied completely on hope, those that had nothing but debt to themselves that were the most dignified. The greatest distance to travel was from the gutter to the stars. Yet this made no sense, for surely the man living in filth and moral decay could hardly be called the most dignified?

μ trudged on, pulling his jacket off. The rash was by now furiously itchy again and he realised that he had left his pills on the bench. He was hot and angry under his clothes and he scratched feverishly. He felt trapped in his own head, drug-addled logic swallowing him voraciously, thoughts uselessly chasing after each other.

To The Expo

He was in a strange part of the city. Refurbished factory blocks now masqueraded as gated flats, the occasional Mercedes or Daimler whooshing in or out of a gate. Those factory blocks not designated suitable to accommodate the rich classes and their glitter and parties and bon homie were left in their original state, sad corpuscles on the face of the city.

The map at the tube station exit had extended far enough to show μ where he needed to go, but he had no idea what he would find when he got there. He presumed that it would be a lavish building, glass and metal, probably an apartment on the top floor, a penthouse, with all that that suggested.

He pictured alternative possibilities, arriving to find nothing but a scrubby wasteland, a brazier burning dirtily by a crumbling wall and a man in a grubby sack suit shaking his hand and saying:

'Ddunsel. We spoke on the phone.'

μ quickened his pace. He was anxious both to meet Ddunsel and to get the interview over and done with. Whatever was coming could only be dealt with once he had spoken to this man.

When he arrived at the address μ was a little disappointed to find that it was neither a lavish glass penthouse or a scrubby wasteland but merely a typical block of modern looking flat conversions. The same as all the others in the area. Ddunsel's apartment was on the fifth floor, number 4. μ stood outside and took a couple of large breaths before venturing to knock. The door was decorated with roman numerals:

IV

He tried to picture what lay on the other side of the door. In his mind Ddunsel was still drunk, partying, swearing at the heavens, surrounded by a coterie of artists and junkies; μ leant towards the door but couldn't hear anything. Had they gone home? Was it empty? Perhaps they had fallen asleep, overtaken by the drugs and alcohol, or maybe the door was simply too thick to hear anything through.

He raised his fist and rapped twice. The knock disappeared, velvety, into the door, dampening away almost instantly. μ checked his watch. It read

16:03

He raised his fist and knocked again. Three times this time. The only noise was a muffled cough that came from behind a door further down the corridor. μ was perplexed. He had been certain that some form of reception awaited him, even if it consisted only of the dregs of Ddunsel's debauched party.

He had been sure that the mysterious script, the dead boy, Hearst, even his rash would somehow be explained by this meeting with Ddunsel. He had been counting on it, in fact; counting on some thread to tie up all the confusion in his life.

Abruptly, he sat down, exactly where he was. His legs couldn't carry him anymore. The thick pile carpet underneath him was very soft and he sank into it gratefully. He was so tired. Disappointing as this turn of events was, something was still bound to happen here. It was his duty to wait until something was revealed. He settled down, ready to hold vigil for Ddunsel or his emissary. Nothing happened. Five minutes passed. μ felt exhausted.

A couple of people passed by, stepping over him with an audible tsk tsk. μ didn't respond but kept his gaze firmly locked on the door. The corridor returned to silence. He had been there over twenty minutes.

By now he no longer cared to get inside or to meet Ddunsel, he just could not face leaving the building empty handed. To return with nothing. His flat, his job, it all seemed entirely unsustainable now. He knew that he should leave, but his eyelids were heavy. He couldn't remember if he had had anything to drink at the café that morning. He must have done. At least, he should have drunk something before this meeting. But now why was he feeling so tired?

It didn't feel dignified to sleep here in the hall, but the carpet was exceptionally thick and inviting. He would be sure of meeting Ddunsel this way. He curled up, making sure that anyone walking down the hall had room to pass, and felt the tide of sleep pull at him.

He awoke to a rough, slapping force, then lagging somewhat behind came a frightening, distorted noise. μ concentrated, trying to decipher what the noise could mean at the same time as fending off the blows. He tried to move but could not feel his legs under him. Then, suddenly, the noise turned into a voice. It was someone shouting out at him – shouting at him and slapping him about the face as he lay on the ground.

With this rush of insight he was able collect himself sufficiently to fend off the attacker and sit up to get a good look at his assailant. In front of him was an old man wearing a guard's uniform, replete with shiny peaked cap who, sensing that μ was now compos mentis, had stopped his barrage.

'Right, come on, on your feet,' he spoke belligerently, but μ sensed that this man was unused to dealing with confrontational situations.

'I was sleeping,' μ replied.

'No, sorry no, you can't go sleeping here.'

'And who are you?'

'Me? I'm security.' The man leaned towards μ conspiratorially, showing him a plastic badge with some writing and an emblem on it. 'What do you think?'

'I'm waiting for someone,' μ spoke loudly. This security guard may think he had stumbled upon a drunk tramp but μ's intuition told him that a firm tone would give him the upper hand here.

'No, not here, get moving or we'll have to get the police round.'

'This is Ddunsel's flat? Well I'm waiting for him.' μ folded his arm with a defiant shake of his head. The security guard narrowed his eyes before laughing under his breath.

'Oh really, are you now?' A self-contented smugness had

descended on his face. 'Well I know for a fact that's a lie.'

'What are you talking about?' μ was exasperated. 'I spoke with him this morning and he told me to come here at four o'clock to meet him.'

The security guard glanced at his watch before speaking.

'For starters, it's four forty-five so I would say if you were meant to meet him at four then you've already missed him.'

Here he grinned as he gripped μ's shoulder. He clearly liked the idea that he outwitted μ so easily.

'Secondly, I just saw Mr. Ddunsel on his way out downstairs not five minutes ago.'

At this μ jumped up. Ddunsel had been here? Had he been in the apartment all the time? Had he stepped over him on his way out, failing to recognise the sleeping body curled up in front of his door as the visitor he was expecting?

'Where? Where did you see him?' questioned μ. 'Where was he going?'

The security guard stiffened, evidently keen to get on with his task of kicking μ out of the building.

'No, that's enough. Think I'm going to tell you where Mr Ddunsel has gone to just like that?' he smiled, his professional knowing smile again. 'No, no, no, you can't just break in here, set up home in the hall and start asking questions about our residents. Really you've got to get out or I will call the police.'

μ was taken aback – this man clearly still believed he was some kind of drunken hobo. He rummaged in his pocket. The security guard was on his feet now and with a surprisingly steely grip was hauling μ along the corridor.

'Look here. I'm sure you're just doing your job but Ddunsel told me to come here himself.' He produced the card he had received from Hearst. Although it was crumpled and didn't in fact contain the address, it had the desired effect. The guard stopped and examined it, his eyes narrowing again.

'Did he now? And how do you know Mr Ddunsel?'

'I don't... he asked me here for a... meeting.'

'And you thought it would be a good idea to fall asleep on his doorstep?'

'Obviously I didn't mean to fall asleep. I was tired. I thought he would be there soon.'

Reluctantly, the guard withdrew his hand from μ.

'Well you can't stay here,' he said. 'I'll let Mr Ddunsel know you came when he returns.'

'Ok.' μ started to feel a little more confident. 'But I really need to find him now. Do you have any idea where he was going?'

The guard looked surreptitiously behind him in the hall.

'I shouldn't really tell you anything but if you start leaving I suppose....'

μ nodded his ascent and made a move towards the exit with guard.

'It's not like he keeps it a secret I suppose,' the guard mumbled, seemingly for the benefit of his own conscience. 'He's at that big Art Expo I believe.'

μ stopped and looked at him blankly.

'Now get going, come on.' He ushered μ again towards the exit.

'Ok, ok I'm going. What's the address of this Expo place?' μ tried his best to leave at his own pace without directly resisting the guard's pushes.

'The address? How am I meant to know? It's somewhere on the left bank. I'm a security guard not an art critic, come on now, scoot.'

When they got out of the lift at the ground floor the security guard held onto μ's arm, evidently unsatisfied that he wasn't going to run off back into the building. μ walked with his head up, as slowly as possible, just to underline who was really in control. He felt the security guard's eyes on him the whole time, but he walked through the double doors with some sense of pride intact.

In the bright crisp sunlight outside μ felt the start of a headache coming on. The short sleep on Ddunsel's doorstep had left him groggy and bad tempered. As he had left the apartment block he had intended on going straight to the exposition, but by the time he reached the end of the block he was already beginning to change his mind. He squinted into the bright light as his face fixed into a frown.

What was he doing chasing after this figmentary Ddunsel? Did he not have enough problems of his own? He had no reason to believe that Ddunsel had anything to offer him and in any case what was it he wanted? It all seemed so ridiculous. He just needed to get healthy, relax.

But it was all a lie, wasn't it? He looked up at the neat, clean towers of apartments on either side. Contentment, balance, mental stability – it was all nothing more than a series of tiny white lies sewn together to make an overall contented truth. Once you started picking away at the little lies the big truths start to crumble.

'Of course everyone knows, even children, that we lie to ourselves to stay happy,' μ thought. 'Subconsciously everyone moves the goalposts, a little left or a little right so that we can take the winning shot, and when that doesn't work we change them again.

'The model life – family, savings, success, power, achievements, contentment, love – everyone need a few white lies to paper over the smaller cracks. The man with a fine family and wealth may achieve many things, but there will always be parts of his life where he has failed, areas where no matter what he says, what lies he tells, he is jealous of his neighbour's lot. He will try of course, goodness knows we can all be quite blatant in our dishonesty, letting the most outrageous nonsense fall out of our mouths.'

'He can be so cruel to me, but I know he has a good heart.'

'She cheats on me, but I know she loves me really.'

μ had always felt, instinctively, that it was better to see the cracks, put them right out in the open and travel on to your destination. Now it struck him how delicate the process truly was. Life required a constant, almost compulsive obsession with lies, with fictions. The perfect life was not just one lie but a complex web, hung together only by the act of spinning new stories. Like a tightrope walker constantly revising each movement, listening carefully to each slight shift in pressure, ready to lean this way or that, constantly adjusting to his surrounding, ready to tell himself anything rather than fall down to the depths below.

From a distance, certainly it may look like the tightrope walker is perfectly still, balanced, content, but he, the tightrope walker, knows differently of course. He realises that each step is in itself a struggle. The tightrope is never-ending.

When eventually he does reach the other side, there is nothing there but a blank wall, the illusion is shattered. The moment he steps off that rope he is nothing; he is simply the empty space waiting for its time to start again.

Now he could see that his own lies were no different from those that anyone told themselves. Where he thought he had escaped, he had simply moved to another city. When he thought he was over Alberta, he had simply suppressed his hurt. It was not that he had chosen a more truthful path, but simply that he had chosen to tell himself different lies.

While his friends had moved on, busying themselves with buying houses, selling property, raising families, μ had contented himself with the knowledge that he was not settling for second best – he was not going to sacrifice the important things in life for a second car, or even a first car. In reality of course there was no second best, only being alive and whatever story that happened to entail. Truth and fiction were two sides of one coin.

Bright sunlight blanched μ's pupils so that he winced and furrowed his brow. People passing by on the pavement cast sharp dark shadows, and μ glared at them indignantly. It was so much easier to enjoy things when you didn't have the sun in your eyes.

After ten minutes' walk he reached an older part of town, narrow and shaded. The wood clad buildings rose to four storeys and shielded the pavements below. μ instantly felt more comfortable and, seeing a half empty bar, decided to stop and sort his head out.

It had been a long time since he had stopped to have a drink in a bar on his own, but things had been getting so out of hand that he needed it. He ordered a Schnapps, a drink he never usually had, and drank it greedily, the sweet fruit-like flavour dissolving his misgivings as it dripped down his throat. He stayed for another and ordered a beer to chase it down, expecting the bar to fill up as the afternoon wore on, but instead the few customers that were in the place left, leaving the small room even emptier. Even the barman disappeared, ducking through a small hatch into the back and telling him to shout if he needed anything.

Inertia held him to the stool. Half-heartedly he watched the flickering television in the corner. Snippets of sound reached him, but they all flowed together meaninglessly. He tried to remember how long exactly he had been in the city but gave up. The programme changed from politics to football.

The door made no noise as Hearst walked in. His craggy face held a wearier expression than the first time he had seen him, but it was undoubtedly the same man that had given him Ddunsel's card.

'You didn't make it today,' he spoke slowly, deliberately.

'I tried,' said μ. He didn't feel surprised that this man was here, but annoyed that he should have caught him alone this time. 'He wasn't in.'

'He waited for you. He is a very busy man. He had to leave.' Hearst whispered.

'Well I was there.'

'You were there,' the man repeated the phrase with a weary contempt. 'You were there.'

'I fell asleep on his doorstep. The security guard...' μ trailed off. This all seemed irrelevant. Whatever reason the man had for coming here, it was evidently not to commiserate with μ about his tribulations.

'Despite your failure, Ddunsel is still anxious to meet you,' the man spoke, as if offering some much needed advice to μ.

'He will be at the exposition until 9pm. You can find him here.'

The man pushed a small cardboard leaflet towards μ. On the top face was a brightly coloured floor plan of a building – presumably the exhibition centre. The man had circled one of the stands in blue biro.

There was not really any need to respond to this and so μ sipped his drink.

'What is this? What is happening here?' μ scratched at his arm as he spoke.

The man carefully considered μ's blotchy red arm before speaking.

'Look, I shouldn't be giving you advice.' μ wasn't sure if Hearst's brittle tone was angry or sympathetic. 'This is your affair after all. But let me suggest, if you really want to find out what is going on, you are going to have to make a rather more decisive break with reality.'

'Who exactly is Ddunsel – is he behind all of this?'

'He is a powerful man,' was all Hearst said, and with the slightest of nods indicated their meeting was over. With that he abruptly straightened and left the bar. μ watched him go before turning his attention to the card in his hand.

49th Exposition of Art Memorabilia – 19th-22nd

Underneath there was a meaningless list of words. μ couldn't make out whether they were names of companies that would be presenting at the Expo or individuals who were speaking. It was quite possible the list related to something else entirely – exhibitors, gallery names, funders, maybe even office stationery or agricultural machinery manufacturers for all he knew. On reflex he crumpled the paper and then, realising that he might need it later, he smoothed it flat on the bar. On the reverse were printed four bullet points in clear script:

- All language is an attempt to describe the world
- Human relationships are defined by this description
- The existence of intelligence in the world is a necessary hypothesis
- We should seek to understand the ultimate intelligence

μ considered this for a moment. It was definitely out of context for a flyer advertising an Expo, but then he had no doubt that this flyer had been printed for him alone. He slipped it into his pocket without another thought.

A sudden dark panic engulfed him then and he felt the need to leave the bar as soon as possible. The barman had long gone and as he peered towards the back nothing moved. A terrifying claustrophobia swelled to fill the room and, clutching his jacket, μ dashed for the door, running out without paying.

The way to the Expo was no more than ten blocks but μ wasn't sure he could make it. Some mania was descending on him. His breathing was tight again and he wished he had more of the pills he had been prescribed. Instead, the buildings around took on monstrous forms. Shadows leered and wheeled out at him as he stumbled through ever more decrepit housing estates.

It was easy to get lost in these labyrinths – everything was covered in concrete. Walkways and stairwells snaked around ugly modernist blocks in such a way that you forgot where ground level was. Hooded figures appeared at the periphery of his vision. Hearst had tricked him? Had sent him this way to his death?

He was sick in his stomach. What had Hearst meant with 'a decisive break from reality'? Had he meant to imply that μ was losing his mind? He scurried through the dilapidated concrete blocks, keeping his face out of sight, only too aware of the hot burning of his rash. The people he passed were all too aware of it as well. He saw their disgusted gawking. A rag-haired woman pulled her child away from μ as he staggered past. The stairwell stank of urine.

It was as he crossed a scrubby, shrub garden that he spotted the figure. Hooded like the others, this one kept his distance. μ tasted bile. There was nothing specific in the stance, but μ recognised his presence instantly – could tell he was following him.

At first he almost made the mistake of waving to him or attracting his attention before he sensed the danger he was in. Running at full pelt now he smashed through the garden and down a flight of stairs on the far side. He had to reach the Expo.

The figure was gaining on him. A quick glance and he saw

the flash of a weapon. Some sort of hammer. μ doubled his pace, the tightness in his chest wrenching. The hammer was no doubt intended for him.

The way ahead was dark and μ was forced down a small alleyway. He stumbled, frantic, like an animal, the figure closing in. Why had he chosen this way? Why had he not stayed where he was safe? Surely it was only a few steps before he was caught.

Then, out of nowhere a giant space, a building, a gigantic advertising hoarding. It was the Expo – he had made it. Crowds of people milled around near the entrance. They talked on phones or else stood in small groups speaking earnestly; professionals with serious business to conduct. It couldn't be more than fifty metres away. He pushed himself harder. The figure surely couldn't attack him in plain view?

Thirty metres away and a horrible realisation struck. A towering mesh fence cut him off from the crowds. How had he not seen it? It was evidently there to keep non-delegates out of the conference. He was so close. He let out a terrified yell but no one heard him above the hubbub. There had to be a way around it.

Frantically he dashed along the perimeter, looking for some gate or entrance, but there was nothing. The crowds, only metres away, ignored him as they hurried in and out of the entrance to the Expo. Sobbing, he rushed towards the nexus where the fence met the wall of the building, hoping to find some chink in the structure.

The first swing knocked him to his knees, the searing pain in his shoulder causing stars to jump. As he fell he caught sight of his assailant, the hooded figure, pulling back to smash the hammer down again. A black liquid started to seep into the edge of his vision and he was filled with terror, as he used his final strength to crawl towards the exposition.

THE WAVE

INT. EARLS COURT 1 - LONDON BOOK FAIR - DAY

Large crowds of people mill around near the entrance to the Earl's Court exhibition centre. Some people talk on their phones while others cluster in small groups talking earnestly. Awkwardly clasping an iPad, UP walks purposefully towards the escalator that leads to the upper level. In the distance a white haired man waves enthusiastically to her and rushes over.

DOWN's hair is now pure white but his lined face has been replaced with a beaming smile. He hugs UP enthusiastically.

                    DOWN:
    You're here.

UP looks astonished at the sight of him. A look of hurtful mistrust flashes across her face before she fixes a smile in place.

                    UP:
    I didn't expect to see you today.

                    DOWN:
    Like a bad penny.

                    UP:
    You look different, Tob. Better.

                    DOWN:
    Why thank you. I feel great

                    UP:
    ...the last time I saw you...

                    DOWN:
    Another world.

139

DOWN puts his arm around UP's shoulder.

                    DOWN: (CONT'D)
     Let's get a coffee. I have some news.

INT. WRITER'S CAFÉ - LONDON BOOK FAIR - DAY

UP and DOWN squeeze through the crowded seating area clutching their coffees. They reach a small table wedged in one corner and sit down.

                    UP:
     I was worried you know?

                    DOWN:
     What can I say, I am an arse, I behaved
     terribly.

                    UP:
     This is serious, Tob. It really hurt to
     see you like that and then... nothing?

                    DOWN:
     I know, I'm sorry. I was a mess.

                    UP:
     I was really angry with you. I couldn't
     believe   after   everything   we've   been
     through... You can be so selfish.

                    DOWN:
     I didn't know how to deal with anything
     for a while.

                    UP:
     It's not like it's the first time you've managed
     to hurt me. I thought we had a professional
     relationship. I convinced myself.

THE WAVE

DOWN:
We did. We do. It was a... momentary lapse
of reason.

UP lets out the tiniest of smiles

UP:
God. You are impossible. You didn't need
to shut me out.

DOWN:
I don't know how to explain it. I behaved
abominably. Let me make it up to you.

UP:
And then to say those terrible things.

DOWN:
Please can you forgive me?

UP considers DOWN quizzically for a moment.

UP:
Of course I can. You knew I would as well.
That's what really infuriates me.

DOWN:
If it helps it wasn't just you that I
pushed away. There was a long time I
didn't want to speak to anyone.

UP:
I tried to forget about it, when you
stopped answering my messages. I was in
Australia promoting 'White Lilies'.

DOWN:
Yes, congratulations on that by the way.

                    UP:
I only found out about the hospital when
I came back.

                   DOWN:
Yes. Margo.

                    UP:
Honestly I don't know whether to be happy
or not. You look better, but Christ, Tobs.

                   DOWN:
You take things too seriously you know.

A look of fury sweeps across UP's face and she
jumps to her feet speaking loudly.

                    UP:
Christ you have a nerve. To tell me that.

                   DOWN:
Calm down. I'm sorry. Sit down. Please.

DOWN smiles apologetically and holds UP's
forearm. UP hesitantly relents.

                DOWN: (CONT'D)
Please.

                    UP:
I take things too seriously? When we sold
the flat, when I moved out, I swore I would
move on. I wouldn't give a shit about you
anymore, but really, after all this?

                   DOWN:
I'm sorry, I forget. I feel different now,
that's all.

THE WAVE

UP:
They've given you something.

DOWN:
Yes, yes, they can fix anyone these days.
Even someone like me.

UP:
I didn't realise. Not till after. The
hospital, I emailed but... they told me
you were already discharged.

DOWN:
Yes.

UP:
They told me they didn't know your new
address.

DOWN:
I told them to say that. Like I say, I
couldn't face speaking to anyone for a
long time.

UP:
God, I should have visited.

DOWN:
Forget it really, it's behind me.

UP:
I do feel terrible.

DOWN:
You feel terrible. I should be the one to
thank you.

UP:
Oh nonsense. You wouldn't let me do anything.

143

                    DOWN:
Well I suppose it was that shitty gun
that really saved me. It was antique
apparently. My brother sold it for a
healthy price. Told me it wasn't safe to
have it lying around, but he always had an
eye for making money.

DOWN lets out a booming laugh.

                    UP:
You never understood my feelings, Tob.

                    DOWN:
You, you're as tough as boots.

                    UP:
Well thanks a lot.

                    DOWN:
It's good to see you.

                    UP:
So you've left the business?

                    DOWN:
Left it? What, that bunch of snakes? Ha,
no, I am retired now. I haven't been back
to the office since you walked me out of
there.

                    UP:
And you've recovered?

                    DOWN:
God yes.

                    UP:
I can only imagine... in the hospital.

144

The Wave

DOWN:
Yes, I was in some state back then. Really. It feels like I was a different person.

UP laughs nervously.

UP:
You've not found God have you?

DOWN grins.

DOWN:
God? No. Well, perhaps you could say something like that. I never properly thanked you.

UP:
I told you there's no need, really I didn't do anything.

DOWN:
No, but you brought me the manuscript.

UP:
The manuscript?

DOWN:
μ

UP:
You didn't tell me you had read it.

DOWN:
Read it? It changed my life.

UP smiles nervously.

UP:
It changed your life?

DOWN:
Yes, I was wreck in that hospital.

UP:
But I don't understand. When did you have
the chance to read it?

DOWN:
After you left me with Margo I stayed
there a few days. I thought it had just
been a moment of weakness. Everything was
fine. I thought everything was fine... and
then I made another attempt.

UP:
You still had the gun?

DOWN:
That, no. It didn't work in any case. No,
I should have followed the advice in those
books, but I thought I would take the easy
way.

UP:
The easy way?

DOWN:
I didn't realise, but most modern cars
are fitted with catalytic converters that
make carbon monoxide poisoning almost
impossible.

UP:
Margo found you?

DOWN:
Physically I was fine, but I couldn't stay
with her any more, not after that. They
checked me into St Edwards.

THE WAVE

UP:

So I don't understand, how did the manuscript save you?

DOWN:

I was there for weeks at St. Edwards and horribly bored. Rosie sent me my files from the desk and of course you left that µ manuscript lying there. I was in a very raw state of mind.

UP:

And you read it?

DOWN:

It started me thinking about a lot of things.

UP:

I've never known any good to come from you thinking about things.

DOWN:

To everything there is a season, and a time to every purpose under heaven.

UP:

Well, God, I hope that certain seasons won't come back.

DOWN:

Oh I think that season has gone.

UP:

And the cancer... it's still...?

DOWN's smile fades for a fraction of a second.

147

DOWN:
The cancer?

UP:
Yes, the doctors, have they been able to...?

DOWN:
Oh yes. No, they were finally able to operate.

UP:
They got it out?

DOWN:
Yes, for now.

UP leans forward and clamps DOWN's forearm.

UP:
But that's amazing.

DOWN:
I'm not that changed that I would say I'm optimistic about it, but yes, for now it's gone.

UP:
That's marvellous. How long have you known?

DOWN:
Oh it's all quite recent. They say that it's in remission. But let's not talk about that.

UP:
But really that's fantastic. It calls for a celebration.

THE WAVE

                    DOWN:
Yes.

                     UP:
No come on, let's get out of here. The air
in here is all recycled.

                    DOWN:
But you must have meetings to go to.

                     UP:
Oh sod meetings. Let's get a drink.

                    DOWN:
A drink.

                     UP:
Don't tell me you're not drinking?

                    DOWN:
Dear lord no. I may have changed my ideas
but I'm not that radical.

DOWN leads the way out of the conference centre.

INT. BLACKBIRD PUB, EARL'S COURT - DAY

UP and DOWN sit at a table around the corner from
the main bar. On the table sit two flat looking
Gin and Tonics.

DOWN   speaks   enthusiastically,   his   shoulder
hunched over the table.

                     UP:
Why did you not return my calls?

                    DOWN:
I don't know. I can't explain. I wanted to
be nothing, to know no one, to disappear.

                    UP:
Well it certainly seemed like you had. If
I hadn't been there that day, what then?

                    DOWN:
I honestly don't know.

                    UP:
You're just such a frustration sometimes
Tob. Why turn everyone away?

                    DOWN:
I think I had to hit bottom. I wanted to
hit rock bottom and hit it as hard as I
could.

                    UP:
Well you made a bloody good job of that.

                    DOWN:
I started to realise that there was a
connection between things. I spent a lot
of time reading like I hadn't done in
years. Devouring information. Looking for
meaning.

DOWN's eyes glow with an infectious energy.

                 DOWN: (CONT'D)
I had been naïve, I had presumed the world
was nothing more than an empty shell, but
I started to see there was an order, an
implicate order.

The Wave

UP:
An implicate order? What does that even mean?

DOWN:
Every molecule, every atom is connected.
There is no spooky action at a distance,
only a deep connection between everything
in the universe.

UP smiles sceptically

UP:
So you did find God?

DOWN:
No. I was wrong. That's all that mattered
then. I was wrong and something could have
meaning.

UP:
Great. I guess.

DOWN:
You're not taking me seriously.

UP:
Should I?

DOWN:
I've started to write.

UP:
Really? You're a writer now?

DOWN:
It's a little project. Let's put it that
way.

UP:
Well pitch me then.

DOWN smiles knowingly.

DOWN:
I'm keeping it under wraps for now. The section in your manuscript, about David Bohm, it's piqued my interest.

UP:
It's not my manuscript any more. At least, that is, I'm no longer representing it.

DOWN:
What? Why?

UP:
God knows? Depression? Perfectionism? The author... requested I return all copies. I thought your copy had been pulped.

DOWN:
Well I'm glad you got it to me. Sitting there in Whitstable everything clicked. I could see that my dark feelings, the problems around me, they were all part of something deeper.

UP:
And what is that?

DOWN:
The Wave.

UP:
What were you doing in Whitstable? Did they give you smokeable medication?

THE WAVE

DOWN:
After they discharged me I went to Whitstable. My brother has a cottage. The sea is beautiful there.

UP:
So is this what you're writing about? The beauty of the sea? Self-help from the waves?

DOWN:
Don't joke. If you must know I'm writing a biography.

UP:
A biography? Of who?

DOWN:
David Bohm.

UP:
What, is it quantum physics meets new-age Buddhism?

DOWN:
No, its not spiritual mumbo-jumbo at all. His ideas on wholeness... how we become separated by the fragmented nature of the modern world... our inability to connect with the deeper reality. Fascinating concept.

UP:
Well, from what I remember the manuscript didn't touch on any of that...

DOWN:
Yes. The manuscript you sent was nearly all fantasy. But I started reading... The McCarthy era.. His work with

Einstein... Holonomics.

                    UP:
So you're setting down the facts.
                    DOWN:
I'm writing about reality. It's about
religion, philosophy, quantum mechanics,
lots of things. It's a big novel.

                    UP:
A 'novel of ideas'?

                    DOWN:
Don't be sarcastic.

                    UP:
Well it's marvellous to see you have
something, a project.

                    DOWN:
It just feels like it's the right time.
To pull together all these strands in my
life.

                    UP:
You certainly have a few strands to pull
on.

                    DOWN:
It suddenly feels... it's a very exciting
time. It feels like I am part of something
big.

                    UP:
Well that's great. I wish you all the best
with it.

DOWN considers UP thoughtfully, and slowly
reaches to caress her face. They are silent

for a long time.

                    DOWN:
    I've been a shit. I'm sorry. We could
    have spent so much more time together. All
    these years.

For a moment the pinprick of a tear enters UP's
eyes but she blinks it away. As she looks at him
a lump forms in her throat.

                    UP:
    Look what you've made me do.

                    DOWN:
              No, I'm sorry.

UP smiles tearily and clasps DOWN's hand. She
stares pensively at his bare ring finger.

THE WAVE

We are enfolded in the universe.
David Bohm

Brazil

It was suffocating, like living at the bottom of a giant sweating sea, a grey iron mass that pushed down on your head inexorably. The clouds, the sky, the faintest current were all aspects of this giant ocean that encased the earth. Not even a whisper of fresh air existed down there. Any breath of wind coming from the Atlantic was transformed, turned into a stifling wet wave of humidity.

The sun too was different – strangled, fierce. It was the engine that continued to drive the infernal hydrosphere. Sweaty drops of moisture dripped out of the air but rarely did it rain. Most of the time the moisture simply hung there, like a leaden curtain, dampening everyone's movement and thought.

Bohm had been there only three weeks but already he was slipping away from his old life in the States. It was a disgrace. He had no desire to remember the details that led to him having to leave. A bad taste still lingered in his mouth from those last weeks before he got on the flight.

Those first few days after he crossed the equator he had hoped there would be a new beginning, new leads in his work, some new approach to help him understand the role of the μ variable. Colleagues that were open frank, stimulating – something different from all those destructive relationships in Princeton, a chance to act on all the things that really made a difference. Now here he was and all he wished for was a cool drink.

The House Committee on Un-American Activities had expelled him for 'Acts in contravention of the interests of the state' which, according to his legal counsel, meant that he was on a par with some of the worst terrorists and war criminals. He hadn't attended a communist event in years. It was hysteria, the whole world was going mad.

The prosecutor had said that in light of his academic achievements and the character testimonials they had received there was a willingness to look favourably on his political affiliations but that, ultimately, there was little that could be done. He might have been able to stay in some other role if the university authorities at Princeton had not buckled to pressure and turned their backs on him.

Well, he didn't need them anyway. His research had been leading further and further away from the applied sciences in any case. The thought of discovering anything important, anything truthful, inside of some particle collider or by rubbing atoms together seemed ludicrous now. No, for his research he needed only a piece of paper and a pen and the chance to concentrate.

If only he could concentrate. Could it be that hard to have a proper rest, to find somewhere where this horrible, clammy heat didn't invade? The food too was making him sick, he was sure. Before he left, a colleague, Jim Briant, had told him at great length how great the food was in Brazil.

'You're going to love the Salgadinhos, man,' he had said. 'Yeah, great fuckin' food, and the steaks?' Here he had stretched his hands out wide before patting his belly, 'Boy, superb steaks, man.'

Jim Briant was an idiot. He had known that at the time, but somehow he had thought he could trust his opinion on food because of the size of the imbecile's stomach. Well, he had been suckered on that point as well.

He was sure some of the food might taste fine if it were possible to think about putting it in your mouth, but the hygiene in this country was virtually non-existent. The mere look of most dishes was enough to get a dose of embrillis bacterium. He had tried to brave things, but he had only been there three days when he caught a particularly nasty virus.

After that he had tried eating only in the more expensive restaurants, thinking that their kitchens must surely operate at a higher level of cleanliness, but the food there was no better. Eventually he had resorted to living on 'Quesitos', a brand of cheese crackers that were somewhere between flavourless and disgusting. At least they were shrink wrapped.

Needless to say, his work had not moved forward at all. The university had provided him with an office as agreed when he took the contract, and had left him free to pursue his own research direction. However, the stimulating conversations, the academic fervour, the fresh talent and insight – all the things he had hoped to find when he left UCAT – none of these things seemed to exist here.

The local professors seemed more interested in their cortados and in lolling around on the second floor veranda puffing on cigars than in discussing any of the tantalising concepts at the core of their subject. The Portuguese they spoke was a vulgar dilution of the language, lacking in any poetry, and their accent when they attempted, brokenly, to speak English was for the main part impenetrable. On some days it felt as if he had moved from a world class centre of knowledge to a third rate parochial secondary school.

It was not that the physics department in the University did not have an international dimension – indeed, if anything, there was undue influence from abroad – and this was yet another reason to be unhappy with his new tenure.

Long before Bohm's arrival, a faction of German professors had pitched up at the university. By the time he arrived, they were so well ensconced in the Faculty of Physics that some of the teaching assistants even spoke a few words of German. While Bohm had, at best, a patchy relationship with the native professors, the Germans he openly detested. The feeling was well reciprocated – his Jewish heritage was not something they approved of, to say the least.

On the first day he had made the mistake of sitting with them at lunch. They were all impeccably dressed in shirt, tie and waistcoat despite the intolerable heat, while Bohm wore shorts and sandals. Their stares remained fixed on him as he approached. Professor Heinz, a once feted academic with thick black eyebrows, gave him a particularly withering stare as he sat next to him. The group spoke rapidly in German. He heard his name mentioned. They were evidently discussing something to do with him.

'Dr Bohm,' he began, 'we have heard much about your work.'

Bohm smiled stiffly. He was dismayed to discover the Professor spoke perfect English.

'You are enjoying this country?'

'It's a lot to take in,' Bohm replied primly.

'The country is not up to your standards perhaps?' At this, Heinz smirked towards his colleagues. 'I hear you have had some bother with meeting certain standards yourself. We are also, how do you say, "in the same boat".'

Bohm was acutely uncomfortable but found no words to reply.

'Of course we are practical men, quite uninvolved with politics, but it does seem that we have at least that in common.' Here he turned theatrically to his companions. 'After all we are also fugitives from our fatherland thanks to, how shall we say, the international "problem".'

Both the university and the Germans made every effort to ensure that their background and career history were kept vague, but it was quite clear to everyone that, far from avoiding politics, they had been very much involved in it before arriving in Brazil. It added insult to injury that Bohm was the only one that seemed to care.

They had arrived, it would seem, with a considerable amount of ready money – several trunks worth of the stuff – in a mix of European currencies. The cash-strapped university had been only too eager to welcome them in and commission a new 'Propulsion Engineering' building on the site of the old 'Department of Theoretical Natural Sciences'.

This meant that Bohm's office was now housed in a flimsy pre-fabricated block on the side of the campus. It was not the atrocious facilities or the lack of air-conditioning that got to him the most, but that those vile criminals should now be lording it up here in São Paulo, a few years after everything that transpired over in Europe.

Not only had they got away with their crimes scot-free but they were the toast of the town. While they were lauded by everyone from the freshman students to the city's mayor, he was classed as a 'political agitator' and forced to work in miserable conditions. When he thought of the people he had mingled with at Berkeley, world leaders in thought, it seemed almost a cruel joke.

His first few months at Berkley had had the flavour of one of those grand tours of the Continent undertaken by Englishmen in the nineteenth century. A boy from narrow and repressed Wilkes-Barre, Pennsylvania, was suddenly introduced to the cultural world outside physics. He had been encouraged to explore philosophical, social and political issues and to consider the wider implications of physical theories.

Above all, he had been captivated by Oppenheimer. He remembered his first impressions of his old teacher – an immensely exciting personality with such an intense interest in scientific and philosophical ideas that students could not help but be swept away. Bohm's feelings for Oppenheimer extended far beyond admiration – he had based his early career on him – but he had his bad side just like anyone else.

What Oppenheimer termed his 'beastliness' occasionally surfaced in his dealings with his students. Years later when Bohm had finished his book, Oppenheimer had cruelly commented:

'The best thing Bohm could do would be to dig a hole and bury it.'

Now where was he?

Stuck in a miserable backwater with war criminals.

As well as personal disgust there was also healthy professional derision between Bohm and the Germans. He viewed their work as little more than boys playing with toys. Their work was nothing more than applied engineering. While he was grappling with the concepts that governed the universe, trying to discover deep truths about the nature of our perceptions – the nature of existence, even – they were arrogantly wasting time firing rockets.

The Germans, for their part, acted as if he was something of a con-artist, spending his time as he did writing pointless equations that never produced any tangible results. To their eyes science was something that should be firmly tied to the yoke of human progress. The pages of scribbles he wrote did no good for anyone and certainly did not warrant him drawing a salary, meagre as it was, from the university. For them his work was mere sophistry; yet another sign of the malignant disease of Jewry.

One of the Germans had even gone so far as to approach the university authorities about having Bohm removed from his post, although on what grounds it wasn't clear. Luckily, they had decided not to act on this request.

So it was that he sat in his apartment, feeling sick and miserable. He had hit something of a brick wall in his research and had decided to stay away from the university for a few days to avoid the negative energy there. In any case there was little advantage to working in that place.

Books he ordered from the library never turned up, or if they did were always the wrong volume. His personal secretary spent all his time chasing girls and would only condescend to carry out any assignment if the trip coincided with some place he was already planning on going for a liaison.

Bohm turned over his papers. A letter had arrived from Princeton, from Albert no less. He knew he should feel happy that his erstwhile collaborator, such a titan of the physics community, continued to correspond with him, even in exile, but he couldn't help feeling frustration that the man had done so little to protect him. Was he not also Jewish? Had he not been hounded out of Germany? Had they not been friends? A word from him could have made all the difference in his defence with the university.

He slid his finger under the damp joint of the envelope. There were no more than a couple of lines enquiring after his health before Einstein got onto the crux of the letter. As Bohm read, he slowly felt himself relaxing. He had a sharp intellect, there was no denying it. It was a pleasure to read Einstein's opinions, follow the cool, concise logic of that funny little fellow's arguments.

He talked of his much-loved EPR gedanken experiment – his thought experiment, aimed at highlighting the paradox behind the concept he referred to as 'spooky action at a distance'. As ever, he was concerned by the notion of non-local interactions and the potential of entangled states.

A noise outside disturbed Bohm and he rushed to close the

window. When he returned to his seat he found his concentration was gone. He could tell there was something important buried in there, but his brain refused to make any sense of it. He read it through three times, but the damnable heat meant he just couldn't concentrate.

The concept of order, an implicate order in nature, folded into the very fabric of existence, was something he had been pursuing ever since he was a child, but on days like this his brain refused to see things as any more than fragmentary – jigsaw pieces that would never join together.

He looked at the paper again, '...thus non-local interactions may be capable of transmitting along non-timewise vectors...' and put it back down on the desk. He could feel some invisible barrier as he groped mentally into a new space.

Every action was the cause of some outcome, causes led to effects, and effects were the cause of new actions. Everything in the universe was linked in an unending chain: cause –> effect –> cause and so on, ad infinitum. The universe was a perfect machine, but the new quantum theories, the ambiguity, meant it was impossible to predict events with any certainty. This was the established orthodoxy and everyone from the brutish Germans on campus to the brightest minds back in So-Cal believed in this.

That there was another truth, a deeper order of existence he did not doubt, but to understand it he had to find some way to describe it – an explanation that would be convincing, undeniable – an equation that would show the paradoxes that he could feel were inherent in all the theories of Bohr and Schroedinger and their ilk.

It didn't seem like he was going to achieve anything with the day. If only the heat would let up, he was sure he could concentrate so much better. Standing up, he let out a disgruntled breath and walked over to the window. He would try opening it again. He was never sure if it was better to keep the window closed and prevent hotter air getting in, or to open it in the hope that there would miraculously be some cooling breeze.

As he undid the latch, a thick waft of asphalt-laden air burst into the room. He peered out through the thin brown curtains. Across the street a building was in the process of being demolished. One half of it had already been partially torn down. Diesel excavators clanked, making a dull racket, chewing through the concrete. The other half was evidently still occupied, as he caught the occasional glimpse of movement and washing hung out to dry. How did they carry on living in there?

He had expected something far different before he arrived. The few photos he had seen all painted the place as some sort of grand fiesta – brightly coloured carnivals, catholic excess, celebration, colour, life. Not that these things didn't exist here. In fact, all those aspects were, in a sense, more present than he had supposed.

The problem, the thing you couldn't see in the photos, was the sheer grey dreariness of this country. The brighter the colours of the carnival floats, the more they seemed to emphasise the mud on which they stood. The more outrageous the celebrations, the more one was aware of the awful poverty and closed-mindedness that drove them. His dreams of a dynamic, intellectual bustle into which he would easily assimilate seemed so stupid now. It was clear his nature was as much a mystery to Brazil as its nature was to him.

He thought again of a recent conversation he had overheard about the new Jewish state of Israel. Gloomily, he considered how unlikely he was to fit in there either; religious faith was something he had given up well before he ever started school.

He was trapped here now. What a fool he had been to leave so quietly. He should have thrown everything at his case. It was as good as admitting guilt to run away. At least if he had stayed to fight he might have got somewhere – some other position – but now he was as good as on the run. A fugitive without any trial.

As soon as the authorities realised he had left the States, the case had been thrown out, of course. There was no point wasting taxpayers' money after all, but his passport had been confiscated by the US embassy shortly after he arrived in Brazil. They had issued a temporary travel document while they conducted 'administrative checks', but he knew this was only a pretence in order to deny him return entry to the US.

The last thing he wanted to do was fight the authorities. After all, he had barely been involved in the communist party, but there was clearly some vendetta coming from up on high. He had imagined that a few months' sabbatical in South America would be enough to let them lose interest, only now his having fled the country was probably as good an admission of guilt as they needed. Slowly, he was starting to realise that he might never be allowed to return back home. It annoyed him how such petty concerns could ultimately stand in the way of his work.

He had been in the taxi for nearly 45 minutes and was already feeling slightly better. The cool steady stream of air coming in the window helped for starters and they were nearly clear of the last favelas that surrounded the city. He didn't know why he hadn't thought of this before. It cost next to nothing to hire a taxi, and the back of the old Chevrolet was quite comfortable now they were out of traffic and on the motorway.

He was sure that the driver had understood very little of what he had said, but that didn't matter. He had no desire to go anywhere in particular, only to keep moving, feel a breeze on his face. Motion after all was the basis of matter. Everything came from motion; physics was governed by the ebb and the flow. The quantum world provided definite proof that the old classical theories were simply wrong in placing emphasis on a static Cartesian model.

For most physicists, quantum mechanics had changed nothing, it merely added a froth of uncertainty on the surface. Like the froth on a cappuccino, it was easily forgotten once it was mixed into the hard mathematics that underlay the subject. It was not entirely his colleagues' fault. Underneath it all, science was quite unconcerned about the actual nature of reality. Scientists shied away from tackling the truly fundamental questions as much as the next man.

But there was something deeper to be discovered – something meaningful that was usually brushed under the carpet with all the talk of probabilities and uncertainties.

That everything was connected seemed self-evident to Bohm, but such ideas were unfashionable. The new creed stated that there was only probability, ambiguity – nothing beneath it all. For every apparent link in the theories there was always some counter-argument, a quantum uncertainty that frustrated attempts to understand.

There were plenty of left-leaning intellectuals in Caltech. After all, he was not the only one who had attended a communist event, but they were sheltered. They towed the accepted line when it came to their work and while they might talk about politics they clearly were happy to renounce their feelings in the face of McCarthy's band of inquisitors. They viewed any issues outside the realm of their immediate mathematical conundrum as entirely unimportant. To their masters they were dependable, focussed only on the goal at hand. It was Bohm's earnest talk about the overlap between physics and real life that got him branded a maverick.

The idea of himself as a maverick rebel, banished from the fold, struck Bohm as ironic. He who had been as timid as a mouse at school. He rested his head back on the headrest. They were out of town now and heading into the mountains.

He stared up at the sky. The omnipresent mass of clouds was broken in places here and there. Moments of bright blue sky pierced through the thick layer of vaporised water above his head. It was almost as if the further they went into the mountains the more could be peeled away. Perhaps on the top of the highest mountain, the entire cumulus layer would peel back to reveal only perfect blue in every direction. He smiled at the thought.

But what was that blue but another layer of wrapping around the planet? Clouds or no clouds, didn't the sky just mask another colour behind it?

He remembered lying on the beach in the Californian sunshine. While everyone else was splashing in the waves, soaking up the heat, or enviously eyeing one another's barely clad bodies, he had been puzzling over a differential equation in his head, huddled on his towel, feeling decidedly miserable. The woman nearest to him aroused no feelings in him other than a sense of the general absurdity of the human race.

It was shortly after that he made his break through regarding spin variables and, for some inexplicable reason, although he should have been feeling elated, it was as if a crushing weight was pressing on his skull. He had rapidly plunged from 'the world of light' into 'the world of shadows'. He was used to migraines of reasonably high intensity, but that was the first time they had been accompanied by such dark, interminable thoughts.

Nowadays he could feel it coming – the moment when his mind was slipping into such a state. He realised of course that it was entirely unproductive to dwell on 'depressive pathways', as his therapist had called them, but at the same time there was something undeniable in their logic. Whereas in his day-to-day life he might stumble from problem to problem, grumbling about his health or thinking about minor practicalities, when he slipped into this way of thinking he 'knew' he could see things as they really were.

It was as if his thoughts untangled for a moment, giving him a chance to let go. He intended to breathe out but the breath never came. His lungs pumped gallons of nothing in and out. The sky sheltered us from the vast set of stars behind and these in turn masked a thousand questions. Questions about nothing.

There was nothing beyond this because everything was contained right here. If you peeled back that blue sky and the stars and the questions you always found the dark black of nothingness behind it. That was the only true colour, because it was no colour at all.

The layers of meaning in the world, produced by cultures over the centuries – the reference books, the stock exchanges, the flowering of languages, feelings between lovers, sexual tensions, slave trades, sex traffic, music, criticism, pride, humiliation, tenderness, violence, obsession and birth – all of these were simply layers, blue summer skies, that masked the eternal night time behind.

He realised this in a very measured, clinical sense. He had never been afraid of the night as a child. It did him no harm to realise that this earthly facade was only a temporary sheet covering the face of something deeper.

This insight was, in a sense, awe-inspiring and yet, inexplicably, it was always accompanied by a deep feeling of melancholy. Not sadness over the loss of something, a regret at a missed opportunity, a sexual encounter that never happened, a love that turned out bad, but a sadness that came from outside him. He observed this sadness, but it also permeated him. In a way, it was unconnected with the world around him and in another it was precisely because of it.

His therapist would probably have told him he was having feelings of dissociation. He was sad for the loss of childhood or was reacting to stress, but this feeling had no core. It went deeper than he was able to travel. It encompassed everything. It was how all humans perceived nothingness. It was the real world.

The taxi driver pulled to a stop in the windswept square of a small mountain village. He evidently believed they had reached their destination, as he turned with a sour smile and motioned for Bohm to pay him. They had been driving for hours. At a guess, Bohm thought, they were somewhere in the Serra da Mantiqueira. Reaching in his pocket he pulled out a 10 real note and handed the crumpled bill to the driver. The taxista made a great show of counting the change, laboriously opening several flaps and loudly counting out each coin individually. Bohm waved his hand to indicate that the man could keep the change and opened the car door.

Outside, the air was icy. After so long in the sweltering heat of the city he had forgotten what it felt like to shiver. He walked towards the edge of the plaza as the taxi sped off back towards the motorway.

He had no idea where he was. It was something of an adventure to travel out here on no more than a whim. The country surrounding the city was as much a mystery to him as the deepest reaches of the Amazon. His colleagues at the university rarely discussed anything outside of city life. When they did, it was usually to deride the peasant mentality of the rest of the country.

As a result he had developed an image of the land somehow

frozen in time, peopled by half-savage natives or else by Gallegos who had initially come to conquer but had eventually been sucked into the primitive way of life. He had imagined that the people lived an almost symbiotic existence with the earth, accepting the ravages of disease and death as placidly as the earth accepted their transgressions.

He remembered discussing the subject with a visiting French professor, Pierre Menard. The Professor had argued that the prevailing view of the conquistadors as victors bringing civilisation to the continent was entirely fallacious. While those first native tribes they encountered were decimated – subject to disease, rape, plunder, and ritual humiliation – it was ultimately the Spanish that suffered the defeat. Although they put up the most remarkable struggle to preserve their church, those that remained were broken by the land and in the space of a few short generations had turned into the very unbelievers they had come to vanquish.

Bohm had pointed out that the Catholic faith was probably stronger in Latin America than anywhere else in the world, but the professor had simply turned his lips up in a thin smile.

'I am an atheist,' he had said. 'What do I know about these things?'

The town where Bohm now stood, however, was far from the savage Brazilian interior. The little square was tidy and sober looking. A simple church dominated one side and short well-tended trees ran away from it in three neat rows. Green benches had been laid out around the edges of the square for passers-by to enjoy the mountain air and, beyond these, brightly coloured houses spread outwards in a grid pattern. The village sat in the saddle of two sheer mountains. To the north and south, terracotta coloured rock formations shot up towards the sky in alien-looking towers that reminded him of picture postcards of The Grand Canyon back home. To the east and west, steep valleys fell away to the Atlantic below.

The instant the taxi disappeared from view, Bohm was quite at ease. There was not a person in sight and, feeling almost light-headed, he strolled towards the church. He had brought nothing with him, but the moment he had arrived the thought hit him that he would stay the night here – drink in this refreshing air and recuperate before returning to the city. He would need to find a hotel.

He wandered down several streets but saw no sign of any lodgings. The village was in fact much smaller than he had first thought. The houses extended no more than two or three streets away from the main square. Beyond these dwellings there were only a handful of scattered, barn-like structures, presumably used to house whatever animals the villagers managed to rear on this hard ground.

He returned to the main square without seeing a single person. It was like a ghost town. He had no idea where the villagers could be. Most of the houses were simple single-storey affairs and, looking through the windows that were open, Bohm could see that there was no one inside. He was just starting to imagine the possible causes for the disappearance of an entire village when the church bell broke the air and the heavy wooden doors were flung open, sending a tumult of people out into the square.

In an instant, Bohm found himself surrounded by a sea of sobbing, wailing villagers. Despite being, on average, only half his height, the crowd swept him along, away from the church doors. A seemingly endless flood of people poured forth onto the square, evidently overcome with grief. No one appeared to notice him, even though he stood out quite plainly amongst the hordes of bodies.

Eventually, when it seemed the square could not possibly hold any more people, the bell rang again and two pallbearers, dressed in black, appeared out of the gloom inside the church carrying an ornate coffin. They were taller and paler than the rest, long bony limbs, thick wiry hair on top of their heads.

The crowd stifled their sobs and straightened their shoulders as the pallbearers started a slow, laborious march down the centre of the square. Bohm was quite unsure what to do. Clearly whoever had died had been highly valued by the villagers. Should he join them in paying respects? Should he leave them to their grief?

They didn't even seem to notice his presence, never mind object to it, and it was quite transfixing, this sudden outpouring, both of people and grief. Perhaps it would be rude to try and slope off from this sort of ceremony?

As the pallbearers crossed the far side of the square, the people fell in behind them quite naturally forming two rows and Bohm found himself stepping in line. They reached the far side of the village and a small graveyard. By this point, the wails of the villagers had resumed and built into a sort of crescendo. It was as if the entire village were wailing in tandem and as the pallbearers lifted the heavy coffin to the edge of the open grave the noise was all but deafening. Several swarthy men came forward and, half-blind from tears, helped the pallbearers to lower the casket into the grave.

No sooner had they done this, however, than the wailing stopped dead. For an instant, not a sound could be heard from anyone. Slowly, bit by bit, whispered conversations started up, here a group of men patting each other on the shoulder, there a couple chatting amiably, but nothing to suggest that the whole site had been full of fervent mourning only seconds before.

It was only now, too, that people started to take notice of Bohm. He heard shouts.

'Olha! Um estranho.'

'Onde ele veio?'

'Leite Azedo.'

There was suddenly a hubbub of interest surrounding him, but his limited grasp of the language meant it was hard to know exactly what they were saying. One of the men approached him and spoke Portuguese with a strong dialect. He had a surprisingly deep voice for his relatively small stature. With an effort, Bohm managed to grasp most of what he said.

'Come…visitor… this day… corn gathering… stairwells.'

It was hard to tell if he was translating each word correctly, but the man's demeanour at least seemed friendly.

'I come… after… the city,' Bohm replied, brokenly stumbling over each word and extending a hand towards the man.

He was not confident the man would acknowledge him with

a handshake but to his surprise he grabbed hold of his hand and shook it vigorously.

'You... now... eating,' was all Bohm managed to catch before being whisked away by the crowd.

Without quite realising how he got there, he found himself sitting at a table in one of the small houses that lined the streets of the village. The place was very small and Bohm's head nearly scraped the roof. The entire ground floor formed a single room with a kitchen and hearth in one corner and a living area with two chairs and a few ragged looking books on a shelf in the other. A thick layer of soot seemed to cover everything and Bohm instinctively looked to the fireplace, but it seemed it had been unused for a long time as a variety of boxes and crockery filled it. In the centre of the space sat a dining table, behind which the man ushered Bohm, before crowding in next to him along with several other villagers.

The man chattered jovially as food was served. Bohm was worried that they would try to make him eat some of the food laid out in front of him – gritty, earthy looking fare that he was certain had not been prepared in a hygienic environment – but after a cursory prod in his direction they didn't force any of the plates on him.

They were less flexible about the tea, however. A tray with herbs and boiling water was produced and with deep ceremony the man brewed the tea in mugs made from the husks of some fruit. Having prepared the drinks, the man thrust one at Bohm, indicating he should drink it.

He took a big gulp and they nodded eagerly, so he drained the rest of the small mug. They guided him to one of the armchairs. He was drained, slightly nauseous. What had they given him? His eyes grew heavy and the villagers slowly receded from him. The man started talking again. Bohm did not understand everything, but could make out enough to determine that he was relating a parable of sorts:

THE WAVE

The Indian's parable

At first, we only vague aware of things. This fact know every man. Every fire start and end with coldness. As children we know only half-ideas, half-beliefs. At first, flames are weak and surrounded on all sides by darkness. They fight. Nothing is clear, only kindle at base of fire is burning. Slowly, with help, next branches they catch flame, logs and coal begin pick up, the flames grow strong. The fire multiplies and chases shadows away.

As more heat it give to the burning, more light. People start gather at fire looking for each other. Talking loud. Standing around the fire they see that it good and huddle closer. Light shines brightly and they can see. Not everything, but the light is bright, it is good they see shapes, they see forms.

They glug, glug happy as the bottle it pass round. They are not blind. Up close they can see their neighbours wink or smile. With light is easy enough, see hands and feet. Friends that are most close, you see perfect. They understand every line of friend face. When they look sad or looking at the ground that they know why. They able share feelings.

Sounds coming, cheering. Shadows are still there, dance to the fire rhythm, jumping here and there and playing surprised, happy face. All this goes on and on, big fire.

We share this fire, share warmth, light. You, me everyone. We talk, see others, speak and how to hear him speak. But always real darkness is close. This for sure. No man see so far. Wise man see beyond. Very wise man, good eyes, good vision can see the rabbit or hare out but only little further. Visionary man.

But what is outside fire? What is beyond it too difficult say? Is this good question? Is not it better get it out of mind? Why worry about what surround us outside when fire is warm here? Light here strong.

He remembered the flames and the spire. He had been charged with building a cathedral. It was to be the largest in the land and he had been chosen from amongst many to lead this project in praise of the almighty. He had detailed plans that had been submitted by the architects, models submitted by the stone masons, teams of workmen ready to go, cooks, slaters, carpenters, glassblowers, even specially blessed beams shipped from Rome itself. It was his job to ensure that all these separate parts fitted together seamlessly, that God's vision was accomplished.

It was something that weighed on his mind constantly and as a result he found it difficult to sleep at night for the worry. He would often walk around half the day in a daze, struggling to deal with the clamour of people seeking his attention, desperately wishing he could rest, and then once he was lying in his bed at night would toss and turn, worrying that he had wasted yet another day where something more could have been achieved.

It was because of this that the project fell hopelessly behind schedule. Mistakes were made. An entire section of wall had to be torn down and rebuilt because of a problem with the measurements and this delayed progress. Several tonnes of the wrong material were ordered and, while the stained glass was finished far ahead of schedule, every pane was only three quarters of the required size.

At first he thought that he would be sacked.

'As soon as they realise the mess we are in it will be my head,' he thought.

But miraculously that day never came. In fact, quite the opposite – the more mistakes he made, the less sleep he had, and the more bleary eyed he became, the more the authorities appeared to value his work. They allocated him more resources with each mistake and heaped praise on him at every opportunity. The number of workers on the project doubled in number.

All the while his sleep deteriorated. By now he barely closed his eyes at all each night. He was sure that he had lost his faith in God entirely, but that in a way seemed almost irrelevant.

'What did God matter in this equation anyway?' he thought to himself.

For some unknown reason, it crossed his mind that this could actually be written down in some mathematical form. Perhaps he could actually write it down – solve the equation using differential calculus or some similar method and prove God's lack of involvement in the cathedral or anything else besides.

All that mattered, it seemed, was to finish the building, to complete the edifice, but that was the one thing that was not possible. Every delay engendered further delays. Every increase in his resources delivered further bureaucracy. What had initially seemed a finite, glorious task now became an interminable burden. Eventually he sought out the high priest in despair, determined to hand in his resignation.

Reaching the priest's chamber, he prostrated himself on the ground and confessed all his weaknesses.

'I have sinned, Father. I cannot go on with this work. I have discovered that I no longer have faith. I am a sinner and it is because of this that the project is failing. This cathedral will never be built as long as you leave me in charge of it. You must remove me from my duties.'

The priest looked at him long and hard and started to speak.

'My son,' he began, 'I cannot release you from your duties, as it was not I who gave them to you but God. As for the cathedral, you may have lost faith, but everyone has faith in you. We are sure it is progressing well. True, there is little to show for it on the ground, but God's strength is in the spirit.'

'But I cannot sleep, Father,' he begged. 'Every night I try to rest, but doubts torment me.'

'You are right to doubt, my son,' the priest said in a low voice. 'That is the way to God. You do not need to rest only because God has decided you do not need sleep. Dreams are our sign on earth of the almighty, of the doubts he has sown himself.

'When we dream, the land we enter is of fantasy, uncertainty. Nothing there is real; we see castles in clouds, friends long dead, all manner of beautiful, puzzling sights that shimmer. Yet when we awake they are as nothing. If we remember them at all it is only as a vague memory and even then a memory of something fabricated.

'And yet there is something, something in every dream that is solid, more solid than all the cathedrals of this world. When we awake we know that above the floating castles, behind the smiles of long dead friends, there is something real.

'In those first moments of waking we look at the world around us with the eyes of a sceptic because we feel we have been tricked by our dreams. If all the things that felt so real in our dreams are false, then what is true? What does it mean to live a fiction? Might not everything we see around us be just as false as the objects of our dreams? It is an old question, but one from which we cannot hide. That is the basis of all doubt, the very essence of the uncertainty that plagues you now. That is the essence of God himself.'

The priest collapsed in a fit of coughing on the floor. Bohm tried slapping him on the back, but to no avail, and in the end he was forced to drag him outside in the hope of getting some help. As he stumbled out into the bruised dawn light, he saw smoke coming from the direction of his cathedral. There on the skyline he saw angry flames eating their way around the scaffolding, the barely completed stump of stonework wrapped in a thick black shroud of smoke.

A bitter tear formed in his throat. He heard the shouts of his workers desperately trying to save the building from destruction and the crackle of the blaze. He wanted to shout to them, to tell them there was no point trying to save it – the structure would never survive those flames.

They would have to start again from scratch. He had been a fool to think it could be completed so easily, that this work could ever be finished. Wearily, he started to make his way in the direction of the inferno. There was no need to rush; the construction was going to take a long, long time.

Bohm was exhausted. He remembered nothing. All he felt was a deep warm ache. His entire body was depleted. He was at the bottom of a deep hole. Then from somewhere high up above, people appeared. Up there, near the lip of the well, faces peered over at him. Strange looking faces. They were built wrong. One of them had two eyes, another only had a single mouth. They were terrifying. His brain struggled with recollection. The eyes, yes, that was correct, two eyes – the correct amount.

He struggled to take a breath and focus on the faces again, but now they were swimming closer. He heard sound now too – babbling, running, breaking – it came from all sides, all around the faces. It strained him, this noise. Agitated, insistent, but wait – were they not speaking to him?

With a click, everything fell together. He was on a bed, the villagers leaning over him. He must have fallen ill. And where was this village? In the mountains, that was right. He had come here by taxi. They had fed him and then?

'Dr Bohm? Dr Bohm?' A gaunt looking man leaned in close to him. He was quite clearly not one of the villagers.

'Yes,' Bohm managed hoarsely.

'You're awake? I'm afraid you had a reaction. It happens. Nothing to worry about. A mild fever.'

Bohm managed a faint grimace which the man took as a sign to continue.

'I'm Doctor Olle Ruddsn. Lucky I was here in a way. The Apamai thought you'd been possessed by a devil, poor souls. Goodness knows what they would have done after all that's happened here.'

Bohm found he was rapidly returning to himself and gratefully drank the cup of water proffered by the doctor. Seeing that his patient was recovering the doctor then turned to the villagers and started to converse with them. Now that he could focus in the poor light of the house, Bohm saw there was something highly irritating about the doctor's face. Perhaps it was the angle at which he leaned over him or the imperious way that he spoke to the villagers as if they were children. It conjured up the picture of an irate schoolteacher and Bohm had the desire to squirm from underneath all the grinning faces and escape into the street.

'Dr Bohm. Dr Bohm.'

The doctor was speaking to him again. Even the way he spoke irritated him. He had a strange accent and mispronounced his name

– Boom. Should he correct him?

He propped himself up on his elbows with a grunt. As he lifted his head from the floor he could tell that his body was far more drained than he had at first imagined. His reaction, whatever it was, had inflicted a physical beating on him. Surprisingly, he felt mentally wide awake; there was a tremulant, almost expectant air to his thoughts as he assessed his position. Despite the numerous villagers crowded into the shabby dwelling, there was a stillness in everything. He was mentally poised, waiting for the coming storm.

He struggled up until he was sitting fully upright, pushing the doctor's hand from his shoulder where it rested, deterring him from moving any further.

'I don't believe we've met?'

Ruddsn smiled and waved his hand in view, clutching Bohm's travel document. How did he get that?

Bohm was suddenly quite furious at this man and struggled up to try and snatch the paper away from him. Seeing this change in his patient, Ruddsn jumped back a little. Bohm seized his chance and scrambled to his feet. The doctor was a good few inches taller than Bohm.

'That's mine,' Bohm snapped, somewhat superfluously, as Ruddsn was already proffering the wallet to him.

'I understand you are agitated. It's a common side effect, but I would suggest you try to calm yourself.'

Bohm snorted loudly at this.

'They seem to think it's an acceptable way of welcoming someone, but I've already given them a piece of my mind, I can tell you.' At this, Ruddsn cracked a twisted grin quite unsuited to his face. 'No sort of welcome for an eminent scientist such as Dr David Bohm.'

At this, Ruddsn broke into a deep booming laugh that filled the entire room. Was he being sarcastic?

'They published a short article about you in A Gazeta when you first arrived.' He paused. 'A local rag. There were several pictures and I must confess it caught my eye. A Commie, eh?' At this he gave a short, brittle laugh in what Bohm guessed was meant to be a friendly way, though he failed to see what was humorous about socialism.

'You must be tired?' Ruddsn spoke sharply to the villagers surrounding Bohm and instantly they stepped in, supporting him with firm arms. Bohm's first reaction was to shrug them off, but he realised he needed their help if he wasn't going to end up back on the floor.

'You can rest at my villa,' Ruddsn continued. 'It's up at El Tropes. You'll need to go that way if you want to catch a lift back into the city anyway.'

With that he clapped his hands and the villagers followed him out of the building, half dragging, half carrying Bohm who gave no resistance, eager to find his way somewhere he could rest. He felt the first stirrings of curiosity about Doctor Ruddsn.

The villa was some distance further into the mountains and so they took Ruddsn's car. It was an ageing Mercedes that had evidently been up and down these ragged mountain roads on several occasions, for it was covered in dents and a thin layer of dust. It was parked in the shade of a scrawny ipê tree. The villagers took Bohm round to the rear door and helped him into the back seat. The old leather was hot but inviting. Ruddsn, meanwhile, got in the driver's seat, warding off the villagers who crowded around the vehicle.

With a roar Ruddsn gunned the engine and the car shot off in the dust. The force of acceleration pushed Bohm's neck deep into the headrest. As they careened downhill, away from the village, fatigue gripped him. He was tired, tired of everything. He tried to think of his work. What was he doing here, moving even further away, out into this unknown space, when his work was so far from completion?

It was curious, he thought, the way that routine wheedles its way into life. He had always appreciated order but now, as he careened into the unknown, he wondered quite how he had become so cloistered.

As a child he had wanted only to play, to experience new things, to learn this or that as the fancy took him, never to sit down and persevere. If something became boring the only wish was to move onto something else more interesting. The world was full of wondrous, inexplicable things as a child, each strand of thought or experience sparking a chain of new questions and interests. At what age had he started to train himself to sit down and learn, revise, persist with an idea of self-discipline?

'It's unnatural,' Bohm thought, 'to continue with an idea once it loses its freshness. A thought that has lost its interest is in a way dead, should be left to decay.'

What did his obsession – his compulsion – with re-treading dry theories and ideas gain him? A way to prepare the dead, like an embalmer preparing bodies? Was he some freak, working over and over the dead flesh of ideas?

Why not just move onto the next experience? What would he achieve in his little office anyway? But he had no choice. He had not chosen his obsession. What at first was tedious, repetitious, after time had become invaluable. How could he explain it? It was something personal, discipline, a dedication that nobody could share. Prostrating oneself before something, a personal devotion.

What made it a true devotion of course was the doubt, the uncertainty, the deep urge to kick all of it over. The simultaneous appreciation of the pointlessness of his work and the pig-headed desire to carry on anyway. What good was dedication if it was mundane, unthinking?

Was uncertainty after all at the crux of everything? Did discipline spring up not as a counterbalance to doubt, as some people seemed to think, not as some protection against the uncertainty of this world, a rock to depend on when everything else was changing, but as a shrine, a submission, a surrender, to the true nature of reality?

It was uncertainty that had plagued him more than anything these last few years, uncertainty both of the familiar existential kind and of the more formalised mathematical variety. The possibility of the hidden variable, the μ variable.

His academic work had progressed well by the standards of his peers – papers had been published, conclusions stated, promotions awarded – but he had answered nothing that he set out to. The quantum equations all suggested the universe was inherently random, but what he wanted to know was if there was something beyond this, some deeper law.

His preliminary research on hidden variables had generated some interesting equations that pointed to a guiding wave, a 'hand of god' acting at some deep, fundamental level.

He had developed the mathematical basis for this guiding wave from the delsun-D wave, a wave that permeated all space. Like the Luminiferous aether, beloved by the nineteenth century electromagneticists, his wave was an invisible constant, a blanket that connected the seeming randomness of the quantum world.

A way to understand these things – a philosophy, if you will – that was coherent, something that allowed one to understand the quantum world without resort to solipsistic get-out clauses. That at least was the holy grail. Perhaps there was no final answer, but the idea that beneath the surface of reality there was only chaos was not something Bohm would countenance.

If he could understand the role the hidden variable played then he felt sure he would have the clue that let him understand how these 'spooky' quantum states arose, how particles separated by great distances were correlated with each other, how seemingly contradictory states could exist at the same time.

In the traditional physical world it was easy enough to simply correlate events, work out the locations and count the number of centimetres, inches, metres or miles. In the quantum world, however, things became confused, complicated. Quantum particles did not always have a definite location. But how did you determine the distance between objects when you didn't know where they were? And if there was no fixed location then could one even say they had a fixed reality?

But once he started on this course of thought he found it extended beyond sub-atomic particles. What did it mean to say that he was 5,000 miles away from home? What was the significance of the fact that London was 3,465 miles from New York? In a sense, was it not all an elaborate fiction?

In Hemingway's the Old man and the Sea, how far exactly did the fisherman, Santiago, sail out into the ocean? Everyone would agree he must have travelled some distance. Three days dragged by a giant Marlin in his tiny craft – he was certainly not near the shore when he finally delivered the fatal blow with his harpoon – and yet could it mean anything to say he was a certain distance from the shore? Could you measure the distance between two characters in a book? What was the distance as the crow flies from Homer's Odysseus to Ivan Ivanovich in the Brothers Karamazov?

The question was nonsense but the paradoxes it implied… If only he could formulate an expression for the guiding wave. The μ variable offered hope of a deeper understanding, but he had been hampered these last months with so many external worries. Perhaps a rest here in the mountains would do him good.

Looking up from his seat he took notice of the surrounding landscape for the first time. They had moved from the dry, mountain ground on which the Apamai's village had been built. Here the valley had broadened out. Lush trees stretched up from the road on both sides, reminding him of a trip he had made some years before to the Poitevin Marshes in France.

The heavy creeper-laden vegetation, the sleepy slow moving water and the light that broke only slowly through the canopies all brought back memories of that place. There had been a dreamlike quality to that trip, or so it seemed as Bohm recalled it. As in this valley, strange animals had populated the forest; donkeys hidden under layers of coiffured hair, river snakes that shambled with difficulty onto the banks as they had rowed past. He shook his head to dismiss the connotations that flooded back from that trip.

How far are we? He leaned toward the driver seat, suddenly eager to speak to Ruddsn.

'Not long,' Ruddsn spoke without moving his head from the road, as he executed a tight corner at speed, sending dust and grit into the air, 'ten minutes no more.'

'Thank you,' Bohm said. 'For offering to put me up for the night.'

It was as if they were travelling along a road they had travelled many times before.

'Oh, don't worry, there's plenty of space there. I'm a scientist as well, you know.' At this Ruddsn let out a laugh. 'A botanist, at least. I studied molecular biology in Cambridge but I was, how would you say, 'disenfranchised' with the academic system in England. These days my research is more psychotropic.'

They continued on in silence for a while. Was that really true? It seemed rather unlikely that Bohm should run into a Cambridge academic conducting research out here in the wilds. But then why would he make it up? To impress him?

'I am writing a history.' Ruddsn glanced round briefly from the road to check his passenger was listening. 'That's what I'm doing up here. The peace and quiet gives you a chance to think. I'm not sure if my work is any better for that, but it progresses much faster and that's the main thing isn't it?'

'Yes, it might be a good idea to spend some time away from the city.' Bohm leant forward so that he could hear Ruddsn over the roar of the engine. 'Do you know, is there a hotel in this town we are heading to?'

'A hotel, no, just the house. The nearest town is 10 miles further down the valley but I wouldn't wish a stay there on anyone. No, I insist you stay at the house as long as you wish. There is far too much space for me on my own and in any case I could use a hand in keeping the servants in line.'

At this Ruddsn let out a shrill laugh and turned his attention back to the road. Bohm wasn't sure how to react to this invitation. While he was keen to stay away from the city for a spell, he didn't want to feel obligated to stay with this Dr Ruddsn should he decide to go elsewhere and so without replying he sat back in his seat and waited.

As they pulled up to the villa it was obvious that Ruddsn had been telling the truth when he said there was plenty of space. Hidden from the main road by a mass of sprawling trees and vegetation the villa sat in remarkably well-tended gardens. The building itself was in the Spanish mission style with numerous outbuildings and roofs extending off from the main block.

It was certainly not modern – the newest addition must have been over a hundred years old – and yet it was not only its age that made the building seem out of place. It just did not belong there. The undergrowth, teeming around the perimeters of the well-kept gardens, jostled to reclaim the land. The building was an interloper, a trespasser on this land. It was perhaps for this reason that Bohm felt that he could stay here quite comfortably after all.

The two men quickly settled into a working routine. For Bohm the mountain air and change of scene was revitalising, and he would wake early at around 6 a.m. A maid, one of the many half-invisible workers on the property, would have his breakfast prepared the moment he stepped into the sunny breakfast room.

It puzzled him that she was able to second guess his wishes so well, laying out exactly what he was wanting without a single question. In fact, in the time he was there he rarely had to ask for a single thing, always finding it laid out in front of him already.

The villa was well staffed. Far above what was necessary, as far as Bohm could tell, but he rarely had much chance to speak to any of them as they seemed to live a strange parallel existence, as if inhabiting a shadow universe ever so slightly separated from his.

His existence there reminded him of the muon, the tiny sub atomic particle that travelled at the speed of light, passing through the matter of the universe quite unhindered. He remembered his late discussions at Oppenheimer's house, purported tutorials. He had sat beside Seth Neddermeyer. A peculiar, twitchy yet confident man. They had talked about the muon; Seth's discovery, his baby. A child he shared with Carl Anderson at Caltech.

The muon was a sub-atomic particle that Neddermeyer represented by the Greek letter μ. A meson of the lepton family, it shared many properties of the electron and yet interacted only weakly with matter. Half as a joke, Bohm had started to use the same symbol to represent his hidden variable as he grappled with his concept of the guiding wave.

He remembered how Neddermeyer and Anderson had been so excited when they first discovered the muon, discovering the existence of these elusive particles through a series of accelerator experiments in the university labs. They had thought they had produced something new, but in fact muons had always existed. Tens of thousands of muons hurtled towards every square meter of the earth undetected each minute. Save for the occasional detector, laid out by a curious scientist, the human race was oblivious to the existence of muons.

Similarly, Bohm felt that he passed by the the villa's staff unobserved. They approached living with an almost unpleasant fervour – affairs were conducted, sexual encounters took place in empty rooms, gossips were spread, jealousies and amours flowered and amounts of money changed hands. All the aspects of a grand healthy force that Bohm was somehow cut off from.

The house was full of life and Bohm passed through its midst, wraithlike. Increasingly he found he had to stare hard at his hand or dig the nail of his thumb into his thigh just to convince himself that he was not fading away.

The greater his sense of dislocation, the greater the servants bustled. Even the smallest activity seemed to require the involvement of twenty different people. If Bohm did occasionally ask for something – a sandwich, for instance – the kitchen would instantly fill with people supposedly concentrating on the task. Rarely did any of them do anything productive, however, and the end result could barely warrant all the attention.

Bohm found it hard to distinguish amongst this horde of bodies that filled the house every day. He had a sneaking suspicion that they must be arriving in numbers from some nearby town. Had word got out of a cushy life here at the villa? Two foreigners without any idea how to control a house. A walkover.

When he had arrived he had estimated there were no more than a dozen servants, already more than enough to look after the needs of Ruddsn and himself. Now he realised their number was far larger. As soon as one of them appeared in a room they were shortly followed by a horde of others. Children, grandparents, enemies, lovers, the garrulous and the taciturn were all drawn together as if by some invisible force. A force which ignored Bohm.

This was not something that bothered him – he had little interest in dissecting their chaotic behaviour – but Ruddsn, on the other hand, appeared to take delight in the pointless foibles of the servants. While they undoubtedly classed them both as outsiders, Ruddsn nonetheless persevered in speaking their language and maintained relations of a sort.

Bohm was sure, for instance, that Ruddsn was sleeping with at least one of the girls. He had seen them together on several occasions and the bashful look the girl gave whenever she found Ruddsn and Bohm in the same room was more than enough to confirm it.

Bohm tended to stay in his own quarters in any case, concentrating on his work most hours or else wandered the grounds 'cogesting', a word he was pleased to have invented to describe the process of simultaneously cogitating and digesting.

One evening, Ruddsn arrived in Bohm's rooms full of energy and intent on conversing. It was rather late and Bohm had been preparing to go to sleep, but Ruddsn was insistent. In one hand he held a half empty bottle of wine and in the other a large canvas backpack.

'They are a bunch of damnable idiots, I tell you,' he had declared. 'I have no interest in how people are made up. I'll tell you that straight, they're only good for spouting nonsense. Everyone out there, with their therapy, psychology, and other pseudo investigations – they all want to understand themselves or, what's worse, to "realise their inner potential"'. He spat this phrase out with venom.

It was not altogether unusual for him to appear like this, when the mood took him, and Bohm had diagnosed him with at least some of the symptoms of a manic depressive disorder.

'Have a seat, Olle.' Bohm wasn't sure if drinking was good for

Ruddsn when he was in that state, but he poured out two large glasses of wine in any case. 'I'm sure we are well away from any psychoanalysts out here.'

'No, that hogwash doesn't wash with me. What is the point of unravelling a perfectly good psyche, a perfectly screwed up, normal character, and turning everything into ambitions…? I need to be recognised in my work, I need to be loved… Good god it's enough to make you sick. That's all great if you want to get rid of the mystery in your life, if you want to get the big promotion and cut out all the tricky questions, but who wants that?'

As he spoke, Ruddsn was frenetically scouring the room, packing items into the rucksack.

'You're planning a trip somewhere, Olle?' It was obvious Ruddsn had set his mind on some adventure. His jaw clenched and unclenched as he spoke.

'Of course, we know, the physical world… this shit hole… the so called "real" world is nothing but a surface. Your whirring atoms and little electron, all this shit that everyone assumes will carry on long after they die… it's just a covering, a slip of material, a bag to hold the parts that make up the actual world.'

Ruddsn waggled his unlit cigarette at Bohm.

'Everyone lives their life… their real life… here.' At this he jabbed vigorously at his own forehead.

'The physical world is simply a nasty itch we are rubbed against with enough regularity to make it seem unavoidable.'

Bohm examined his companion sceptically. Was this some sort of trial? In moments of depression he was prone to exactly these sorts of solipsistic thoughts. Was Ruddsn trying to bait him? Was this in some way related to his work?

'God doesn't play dice.' Bohm did his best to look outraged as he plagiarised Albert's words, but he was sure Ruddsn was too far gone to take much notice of anything he said.

'Dice… God… obviously not… you think I'm not saying that. Of course everything is controlled. You scientific types… you bloody minded people… you assume that the supernatural must be some other world, some other existence, but it's all the same old shit.'

He seized the backpack, which was by now nearly full, and lifted it up to Bohm's face.

'This rucksack, the physical world… it's a giant sack… that's where we… our essence, do you hear…? It is necessary of course, quite necessary. Without this rucksack where would we carry our lives, or existence? I don't deny it is possible to live… but the mysteries cannot be diminished so simply. Life has a way of making its point felt.'

Their conversation had quickly passed the point of constructiveness. He had heard many similar arguments as an undergraduate; alcohol never uncovered some important truth about reality. Ruddsn may have been seeking something – something intangible, something true – but it seemed unlikely that he would find it that evening.

Bohm's thoughts slipped away from Ruddsn and his pointless philosophising. What was he doing here in this godforsaken country? What was he running away from? Emptiness? Hopelessness? But then why did he long to get back? And his work? Was that only to provide a justification for his existence when the judgement came? Was that not the common prayer: 'It's not my fault. I didn't know any better. I've been busy working'?

He wanted to crumple his face in his hands but Ruddsn continued talking.

Finally, with an exclamation Ruddsn sprang up, the rucksack was full.

'So… you beer stain… you crumbler… are you with me or not? We must go at once.'

'It's dark,' Bohm mumbled. 'Leave now?'

'Darkness is the perfect cover.'

Ruddsn leaped to the window and pulled the huge pane wide.

'We need to leave at once.'

Bohm remained obstinately in his seat, clutching his half-finished glass of wine.

'Well fine, stay here if you want. I'm off!'

With that, Ruddsn took two small, pirouetting steps and swept out of the window into the black ink of the outside. Bohm remained in his seat, drunkenly staring at the trajectory of his now vanished partner.

The following morning the activity in the house was at an even more fevered pitch than normal. He heard screams and loud lamentations drifting into his sleep as he woke to find himself slumped in the same armchair as the previous night. Ruddsn's young girl rushed in to his room in floods of tears.

'Mr Bohm, please, Mr Ruddsn he go.'

'Yes, I know he go,' Bohm spoke angrily, before correcting himself. 'He's gone.'

'But Mr Ruddsn he go, he go.'

'I was with him,' Bohm heard himself saying. 'I was in this room last night when the drunken fool jumped out that window and ran off into the darkness on some idiotic mission.'

He was on the point of repeating this to the girl when something about her demeanour, something about the conversation the previous night, made him stop. Was there another meaning to her garbled speech? Where exactly had Ruddsn gone?

Bohm racked his brain but found no memory of exactly what the plan had been that they had discussed in such detail only a handful of hours previously.

'Where has he gone?'

Bohm took the girl in his hands as if to shake an answer out of her, but it was all evidently too much for her and she collapsed sobbing. She managed only one word.

'Dead.'

There was chaos for the next few days and Bohm understood very little of what was happening. More and more villagers descended on the house until it was quite impossible for Bohm to do any work. From morning to night there was a heavy presence of mourning in the house. The women would wail and cry at all hours and, from time to time, gather as if attending a funeral.

As far as Bohm could ascertain, no body had been recovered and he could see absolutely no reason to get concerned. Ruddsn had left fairly drunk, but he knew the land and would no doubt be back in a week or two. Even if he never returned it proved nothing, as he owed nothing to this place. He may simply have grown bored with the isolated life and flown back to England or wherever he was actually from.

No, Bohm wasn't concerned. Nonetheless without the knowledge of Ruddsn's presence a heavy mood descended on him. Whereas before he might easily go a whole day without speaking to the man, at least he knew that Ruddsn was there should he desire some conversation. Now, however, he was truly isolated.

He started to wonder exactly how long he had been out there. The days melted into each other so rapidly that he had soon lost track of what month it was. Hot sweaty nights made it difficult to sleep and then the mid-day sun would drive him to take a siesta, so that he no longer woke up to a new day, but merely slipped in and out of dreams.

He had thought that with Ruddsn's disappearance the servants might become closer to him, but if anything they were even further away. It was their house now. They stopped bringing him food and so he started to make his own meals. They didn't seem to mind him eating in the kitchen.

The girl that had slept with Ruddsn came to him one evening. They made love awkwardly.

'Are you happy?' she asked him.

'Happy?' Bohm was irritable that she should ask him this directly. 'I am busy, that is the main thing.'

'I am happy,' she spoke slowly, thoughtfully, 'but is it strange sometimes I wonder what it's like to die?'

Bohm studied her face carefully. She wore a fierce determined expression. It was time to leave this place, he thought.

The next day he made his way to Ruddsn's quarters. The servants had closed it off as if it were a tomb the moment his disappearance had been reported. Outside they had draped linen over the doors and the few girls who milled around in this part of the house walked reverentially, as if they were approaching some religious site. As he came near, Bohm had to convince them he had the right to enter at all.

Inside he found the place in chaos. He wasn't sure exactly why he had come: To find some clue as to where Ruddsn was? To satisfy his curiosity? To look for something to help him in his own escape from this place?

The room depressed him and he was about to leave when he noticed a thick binder lying half covered on Ruddsn's writing desk. The cover was a waxy, heavy material and inside it appeared to contain some form of script – clips of dialogue and descriptions of scenes. He scanned a few of the pages half-heartedly, but the content was pretentious and dull. He wondered if it was the history that Ruddsn had claimed to be writing. It didn't seem to amount to much.

'I have to get out of here,' he thought.

The villa and its grounds had started to become all he knew. With Ruddsn gone it was growing a negative energy, intent on expelling him, like a cancer. The entire place was degenerating, he could feel it. He no longer had a foothold and the jungle was circling the house, preparing to take it back into its fold. The walking palms, the kapok trees, even the servants that pretended to tend to the house; they were all part of the machinery of the jungle, slowly swallowing the house back into its guts.

Returning to his room, Bohm readied to pack his bag, putting the few possessions he had onto the bed. There was not much of value now he looked at it. The pads in which he had written notes these last months were voluminous, but he knew in his heart there was no more than ten pages of original work between them. He piled everything into the two battered suitcases from on top of the wardrobe.

The thought that the jungle was closing in around the house –

was in a sense trying to erase all trace of him and Ruddsn – gave him a peculiar impetus. Perhaps he shouldn't pack anything? What was the point of trailing these pointless belongings with him through the jungle? He had no clear idea where he was going in any case.

On impulse he took all his belongings back out of the suitcases and positioned them more or less where they had been originally. Satisfied with his work, he selected his stoutest pair of shoes and left.

Once he had put some distance between himself and the house a curious feeling engulfed him. On the one hand there was a sense of relief – elation, even – at having escaped, at being free, being his own man again and yet, on the other hand, he felt enormous trepidation, as if he had made some fateful error, leaving safety behind to venture out where the risks were high. It was something akin to the feeling he had when he had first left home at the age of 17 – left his home state to go and study in California.

And how had that turned out?

His first thought was, of course, that it had been a success. After all, his teachers back in Philadelphia would have been amazed at the people he mingled with there. Important, powerful people: Oppenheimer, Pauli, Feynman, Einstein. It amazed even him that he had sat and discussed physics, philosophy with such luminaries, how quickly he rose to the rank of professor, and yet that was all so far away. Here he was relegated to Brazil, excluded for political reasons that, when he looked at them rationally, made not one bit of sense.

After several hours, he reached a junction with a busier thoroughfare. Although nothing more than a dirt track, it was still a wider dirt track than the one he had been on. Mud red trucks roared up and down, carrying loads held together by tarpaulin and string. At the side of the road an ancient woman stood beside a stall selling juice and snacks made of dried banana. He approached and tried to start a conversation in his broken Portuguese. She shook her head.

'Soy Colombiana... Colombiana.'

He took a bag of juice and clumsily attempted to drink it with the straw she provided. Most of it ended going down his front.

That night he was several hundred miles away. A truck gave him a lift. They had passed out of the dense overgrowth and down, down towards sea level. On the drive he had started to realise how rash he had been to leave. The food at Ruddsn's retreat had miraculously settled his stomach and his nerves. In fact, he hadn't worried about eating for all the time he had been there. The climate too had been perfect – balmy without being overpowering.

Now that he was descending into the tropical haze, his body started to remember the torture that had been São Paulo. The heat, the food, the sweating masses.

At the first decent-sized town, Bohm got out and booked himself into the best hotel he could find. The city was a nondescript criss-cross of wide thoroughfares; it was newly industrialised. For some reason, Bohm imagined the inhabitants had also only recently arrived, the population swelling in the space of a few weeks, no doubt with glamorous dreams that were never going to materialise. Once in his room he turned the air conditioning on full.

He was restless. His mind was frenetic once again, another side effect of his discomfort. He felt, reluctantly, that he had returned to his real self. The calm he had in the jungle, the reflective contemplation he had shared with Ruddsn, it had been nothing more than a brief oasis.

Using a sheet of the hotel paper he noted down a few random state vector diagrams. The embryo of a thought was growing in his mind. With rapid, scratchy strokes he hurriedly wrote down a series of calculations. Each line flowed after the other, spurred on by a tightly wound logic; he was suddenly close to something. To catch it quickly, that was the trick, to employ a certain delicateness. To catch it while his concentration was intact, that was all he had to do.

His pen flew across the paper, but then, no, he had forgotten something, the μ variable was represented twice in his calculation. When he adjusted for that it cancelled everything out leaving him with an empty statement. Frustrated, he pushed the paper away from him and half stood then, crouching again, wrote hurriedly in the margin:

- State
- Collapse
- μ
- Action at a distance
- The Guiding Wave
- Uncertainty?

He looked at the list, satisfied, then licked his lips and added another '?' after the word 'uncertainty'.

It was getting late. He stretched out on the thin mattress. Outside, the torrential sound of cumbia and samba, shouting and traffic, drilled into his head. Already he was frail again.

If he was to understand cause and effect, the guiding wave was key. The Copenhagen interpretation was insufficient; the complete collapse of the wave function was meaningless without some external frame of reference. There must be a framework, a formulation.

Implicit in the equations was a structure, wrapped up in the syntax. An implicate order, a parallel wave that predicted the outcome of each measurement. An invisible hand behind the seemingly random. Eternal, outside of time, outside of this realm, even, but silently giving direction to the physical. It reminded him of the religious texts of his boyhood. The same ideas that had equally infuriated, sending him chasing his tail through alleyways of thought and guilt.

Taking the paper from the table, he added the following in the margin:

Can we measure 'spooky' action at a distance?
Can we talk about others as an objective reality?

The second of these he circled three times.

* * *

The next morning he was drained. It was curious how quickly he had returned to his old self – pre-occupied, anxious, sickly, so concerned with the reality of his knowledge and so little concerned with the real world around him. He had worked well into the small hours and now, groggily, he bundled up the frenzied papers he had scribbled the night before.

He had made a breakthrough, he was sure. He was about to start re-reading his notes when some superstition stopped him. Better not to change anything now, send it back intact. He would post it and read it over when he returned.

At reception they provided an envelope and pointed the way to the nearest post office. He had to queue for what seemed an age, the dread heat starting to seep into the morning air. Finally, he reached the gridded window, and the bored teller snatched his envelope and affixed a multitude of brightly coloured stamps that between them must have featured every Brazilian head of state since the founding of Olinda.

He walked through the poorly maintained streets, looking for a pharmacy to buy some painkillers. Of course, nothing was open. How did these people live like this? Was there no sense of pride in their city, no sense of shame to be living in squalor? Evidently not. Around him there were only seas of smiling faces. Even those drivers hitting their horns did so with a beatific happiness. Was this natural? Why did he feel such a need to unravel it all, to understand the fundamental structure of the world? What good did it do him to pursue these skittering trains of thought?

To look at these people, the idea that there was anything more that needed understanding was somehow ludicrous, but why then did he feel so wretched? For a moment, panic engulfed him. Why had he sent his papers by post? His work, his breakthrough, who knew where that envelope could end up? What if it was lost?

His headache was returning. He finally found a shop to buy painkillers. He could make neither head nor tail of the packaging. The dosage appeared to be 500mg. He took three. What was it that made him this way? What cloud had lifted, momentarily, while he was in the mountains, hidden from view in Ruddsn's den?

He wondered what had happened to that man. A part of him was jealous of his spirit: unafraid, adventurous. No doubt Ruddsn was already embroiled in some other escapade, his manner made it easy for him. He would flit from one adventure to another effortlessly. When he greeted strangers they instantly felt they were his friends and when he met people he had known for years they would still get the frisson of the excitement of a new acquaintance. He was a man at ease in the world, and for that Bohm felt jealous.

In his imagination it was clear what sort of man Ruddsn was. He was hearty and well built. Intrepid and fearless. Bohm was jealous of his luck. If he did not suffer from such acute health problems he too could afford to take risks. He would be fearless if he did not have to worry about his digestion, the stomach pains and falling ill. Without his diabetes or his epilepsy he would be capable of adventure and daring. As for Ruddsn's easy way with people, well, was it Bohm's fault that they never treated him with the eager interest they greeted Ruddsn?

Bohm realised he was getting carried away. He did not know in reality how Ruddsn behaved in society, having only seen him in the confines of the remote jungle. What difference did it make how Ruddsn carried himself? Bohm's problems were his own. Suddenly he felt an overpowering urge to take some risk, to gamble, to throw his hands up at the senseless, grinding probability, to kick out at the statistical stew that drove everything. What did it matter if he was not in such fine health, did that not in fact show his courage all the clearer?

For a healthy man to take chance by the jaw was one thing, but for an invalid to venture outside the bounds of safety required much greater courage, much higher disregard. A euphoria lifted him. What better challenge than to throw himself head first into adversity, fully aware that he was ill-equipped for it. The idea seized him. What could be greater than to realise fully how deficient one was but to continue nonetheless?

THE WAVE

What could he do to make a decisive break from it all?

The idea occurred to him to take a job – was that crazy? Was it ridiculous that honest, tough work could cure him? What philosopher was it that had renounced an immense inheritance and moved to Norway to chop wood and solve the problem of semantic meaning?

The thought occurred to him that he must find a job where it was difficult for the manager to simply sack him. Then, and only then, would he be forced to deal with the situation without the option of leaving.

'A boat, once it sets sail, is an island. There is no way out. If I board at the last minute they will be stuck with me.'

In fact, his legs, perhaps unconsciously, had been carrying him towards the river. Already through the gaps in the cheap boxy houses he could see the ships' towers belching thick smoke. He was surging on the crest of wave. Was it the painkillers? An image grabbed him of the romantic life, travelling the length and breadth of the country, vast miles of uncharted river ways, vessels passing each other so slowly, bound for unheard of locations with even more obscure cargos. The knowing glance between decks as crews passed, eyeing their mirror images across the water, judging the length of each other's journey by the masses of tangled beard on the opposite crewmen's faces.

Yes, a romantic life indeed, to take on the life of the river: rapids, icy churning water and all hands on deck, tossed about, no time for wasted words, only commands barked with a desperation that comes from facing capsize, the loss of a cargo that none of the men would ever have profited from, but for which they risked their lives nonetheless because they were kept afloat by the same beams of iron.

And then, the next moment, the river sludgy and brown, moving at a snail's pace, baking in the tropical sun, inching past the tree-lined shores, all the crew splayed out with nothing to do, the captain even submitting to the dolorous boredom, no space for dreams, other than perhaps a cool shower, and even that not a rest but a constant test of one's mettle.

The ships, when he reached the dock, were far larger than he had imagined. Rather than stained, beaten tug boats there were shiny transporters, each several decks high. The crews too looked thoroughly professional in white, creased uniforms. He approached a group smoking near a container, but when he attempted to ask them a question they were none too interested. Bored, one of them pointed over to a shack with 'Oficina de Empleo' painted above the door.

The grizzled man inside looked him up and down and shook his head. Here out of the light Bohm felt his head spinning.

'Trabajo, busco trabajo,' he stumbled. The wave he was on threatened to collapse for a moment, but no, the euphoric feeling swashed around him once more. He smiled helpfully at the old man who sucked in his breath.

'Oro?'

At least that's what it sounded like to Bohm. He nodded. What harm could come of this. Now he thought of it he truly felt good, for once, having made this decision. He was ready to show them, whatever the numerous obstacles. He would show what he could do when he put his mind to it.

The old man whistled and a young boy appeared at the door. Tugging Bohm's sleeve, he led him to a boat. It looked much the same as all the others, a little smaller, perhaps, but still, to Bohm's untrained eye, most seaworthy. Standing there at the quay Bohm got his first true glimpse of the river. The water was terracotta red, like a thin paint or gazpacho.

A man appeared, evidently some form of officer by his uniform.

'English?' he said.

'No.'

He tilted his head slightly to one side and eyed Bohm up and down. Eventually he took a step to the side, allowing space for Bohm to walk up the gangway. Hesitantly, Bohm passed him to enter the ship. It looked like he had got a job.

THE WAVE

*   *   *

The crew was small and about half of them had worked together before. They told him to wait below deck. Bohm managed only a dazed smile, his head still spinning from the drugs. This first leg of the journey there would be little work for him. Nobody seemed to take the idea seriously that he might be needed as a member of the crew, but they were unsure what to make of him. As a Yankee he surely did not need the money?

The day passed away like a wisp of cloud. The afternoon sun blazed, a perfect oven. The hectic flurry that had accompanied their departure fell away. Bohm followed most of his crewmates in taking a siesta. Below deck he was instantly coated in a thick oil-like sweat. Dark reverberations tolled through the body of the ship. Heavy sleep. Thick Sleep.

And so the day was finished. The room was dark, windowless, still hot and stifling. Struggling to the deck he was greeted by a star-laden sky. Deep blue. Such a dark blue. The open heavens startled him as he first poked his head above board. There, raw above his head, the universe, uncountable points of light shimmering purposefully.

Nothing moved. Even the slow progress of the ship along the river seemed only designed to keep everything still. It cut effortlessly through the thick jungle, embankments of vegetation falling into the water. On deck three crewmates played a hand of jass. Bohm climbed up onto the higher deck and stared upward.

A gelatinous thread of light shot across the blue. A shooting star? A particle? Cosmic rays, travelling from the depths of space and time were constantly bombarding the upper reaches of the earth's atmosphere. These packets of energy made their journey across galaxies, taking a frozen eternity to reach the earth and splinter – crashing, cascading towards the ground.

The muon had a lifetime of 2.2 microseconds – a blip, nothing more. It barely interacted with this world. Arriving from the heavens, it died moments later deep in the ground, passing sheer through solid rock, passing through the earth itself as if it were invisible.

Their lifetime was the briefest of flashes in the sky. A blazing death. A transitory becoming and unbecoming. They travelled unimaginable distances through nothingness, formless and perfect, only to burst into this world, to be thrust here with a shuddering volt of reality.

And what about man himself? Did he not arrive here from somewhere else, thrust into this atmosphere for the shortest time, only dimly aware of the world around him, aware of his mortality, but intent on ploughing forward anyway?

Bohm looked up. The blue above him had drained away to reveal a black, star-flecked sky.

And before – what was before? What happened in the space before he was born? Was there anything? Did it make sense to ask that question? And, if so, what sort of answer could there be?

There were stories, passed down from those that were older, who lived through long gone times. We take their word for it, and why would they lie, that they lived and saw those things in that time before we were born.

They tell their stories with the utmost conviction about countless events that took place before we were born. A wedding, a car crash, an assassination, a great war, a ceremony, a gathering, all real to them, no doubt, but forever out of our reach, before our time, before we were born, existing, but not existing for us.

Before that, even, before the time remembered by any living person there was something, stories, always stories. Of great deeds, of the most mundane deeds, Kings and Queens that shaped the nations. The whole of history was only a patchwork of stories designed to explain the great lead up to birth, to provide some reason that birth should be not only natural but entirely normal.

Yet what did they mean, this collective mass of stories, this collective history carried by mankind? What weight could any of it carry when none of it could be experienced directly? It may neatly explain countless centuries of progress that provide us with the way of life we see around us, but can it ever be any more than a feasible description, a possible explanation?

The Germans, Professor Heinz, Professor Mendel, they hated the Jews, but why? Had they personally had reason to despise a whole race? It was doubtful, even if they had had extremely bad relations with several Jews, they would simply not have had time to gather sufficient information to extrapolate that dislike to an entire race. There must be some underlying narrative, a thread that they followed, or which followed them, a thread that made sense of their hatred as a continuation of past inequities.

What was it then? The history of their families, the defeat of the First World War, the Crucifixion of Christ centuries earlier, a need for national pride, the insularity of the Jewish people, the political machinations that had left Germany ruined? Which of these threads had truly resonated with Professor Heinz and made him subscribe to the Nationalist Socialist propaganda?

Which of these narratives had been lived by the people of Germany and which were passed down from the time before they were born? Which of these had fuelled the story of the Aryan myth? What was it in those stories that could motivate tens of thousands to march?

Were they searching for a return to an empire that most of them had never known? An image of something they had been told about as children? Kaiser Wilhelm, the Radetzky March, Viennese coffee houses, the rigour of a military life.

Could there ever be anything truly original or new if people were always contaminated by such tales of the wonderful long-long-ago? Was there any hope for causality if you could not ever reach the first cause?

Yes, the first cause, what was there before all this? He was no closer and, looking up at the black curtain above him, knew that he could never get nearer.

'Before we are born,' Bohm thought, as he looked at the night sky. 'Whatever exists before we are born is made of the same formless stuff as the star that lies just beyond our view, the bird just over the horizon, the tree falling just out of earshot. As soon as we find it, it becomes quite ordinary and, in the process of becoming ordinary, it is insufficient. Always we need something beyond our ken, a grand history to bolster our view of ourselves, a furthest star to reach for.'

Leaning forward, he reached out his hand, as if for a moment he believed he might be able to touch the firmament above him.

'Why can we never be satisfied with ourselves?' he thought.

The ship was travelling upriver. They made a few short stops along the way and Bohm slowly got used to the pace. Bit by bit the crewmates got used to him. Each time the ship docked, some of the crew changed. Slowly, Bohm became one of the older members of the crew. They tolerated him, called him cerebro – brain – somewhat affectionately.

As they neared the upper reaches of the river, the going got harder. There were less crew willing to travel this far upriver. On deck there was always talk. There was danger from headshrinkers in these remote areas, so the rumours went. Bohm was indifferent. He had long since stopped suffering from his previous ill-health. In truth, he had become almost ascetic. He barely ate anymore and seemed to pass through the ship like a ghost. He barely interacted with the world.

The last crewmembers to see the ship disembarked at the remote jungle town of Sao Mungo. They all reported that the remaining crew were in good health when they left, but that the ship was under-manned.

Later, when questioned by police about the disappearance of the Hesperus, each of them separately made comment about cerebro. They spoke in a respectful tone about the Yankee. 'Kept himself to himself,' they said, 'a bit of a thinker'. He had been travelling with the ship upriver as far as it would go, they said – 'in search of gold'.

THE WAVE

INT. HOLIDAY RESORT ROOM, LANZAROTE - DAY

A holiday apartment room furnished in white with a double bed, breakfast bar and kitchen and ensuite bathroom. A wall-length window opens onto a balcony, looking out onto the Mediterranean.

DOWN stands by the bed, naked apart from a bright yellow T-shirt that he struggles to pull over his head. UP lies next to him, her left leg wrapped in the white sheets but otherwise naked, save for a sheen of sweat.

                    UP:
   Why do we need to go anywhere today? Come
   back to bed.

                   DOWN:
   We may as well have stayed at home if we
   are just going to lie in bed all day.

                    UP:
   You know what I mean. Come on there's no
   rush.

DOWN succeeds in pulling the t-shirt over his head and turns to face the bed. On the t-shirt is the word 'Loco'.

                   DOWN:
   I'm not in a rush. It's just... what are
   we doing here?

                    UP:
   We're on holiday.

                   DOWN:
   I know we're on holiday, but from what?

UP pulls the sheets around herself protectively.

UP:
Why are you talking like this?

DOWN:
I'm not talking like anything.

UP:
Yes you are.

DOWN:
I'm just asking.

UP:
Do you not want to be here? Is that it?

DOWN:
No, you know that. I'm the one who wants to go outside. Of course I want to be here.

UP:
Well there's no rush. Its too hot yet.

DOWN:
So what, are we going to just sit here all day?

UP:
Is it so terrible to share a room with me?

DOWN:
I'm just saying, why don't we see some more of the island?

UP:
Do you ask her the same questions?

THE WAVE

> DOWN:
> No, why would you say that?

> UP:
> I know you don't like talking about this,
> but you've got to understand this is hard
> for me. How long have we been doing this
> and nothing has changed?

> DOWN:
> Ok then, look, let's stay here.

DOWN wanders to the breakfast bar and pours
himself a glass of orange juice. He takes a sip
and raises the glass towards UP.

> DOWN: (CONT'D)
> It's so nice, this orange juice.

> UP:
> When was the last time you went on holiday
> with her?

> DOWN:
> I don't think we should talk about this.

> UP:
> You know I thought this would be a chance
> to fortify our relationship, but this
> holiday was a mistake.

> DOWN:
> Don't be crazy. I've been dreaming about
> this for weeks.

> UP:
> Did she go with you to New York?

                    DOWN:
                (defensively)
        No. You know that was a work trip.

UP sits up in the bed.

                     UP:
            She did, didn't she?

                    DOWN:
            No, she was at her mother's.

                     UP:
            We can't do this anymore.

                    DOWN:
        I thought you wanted to come on holiday.

                     UP:
            I did.

                    DOWN:
            Well let's go outside.

UP turns away and DOWN drops his arms by his
sides, exasperated.

                DOWN: (CONT'D)
            I used to believe in fate.

                     UP:
        What are you talking about? Why can we
        never have a serious conversation?

                    DOWN:
        This is a serious conversation. What is
        more serious than fate?

THE WAVE

UP:
You always turn everything into some abstract debate rather than just talking about your feelings.

DOWN:
How can we be in love if there is no fate?

UP:
Why can you never just talk about the situation? This has nothing to do with fate. It's about you making a choice... if you are with her then how can we be together?

DOWN:
But that is fate.

UP:
You make everything so abstract, but it's really simple.

DOWN:
Well why don't you do something?

UP:
What can I do? I can't make a decision, it's up to you. You are the one that has to decide.

DOWN:
Why me?

UP leans forward, looking around on the floor for her clothes. Finding her bra she starts to put it on.

UP:
Christ. I thought we could have a nice

time away from London - forget everything
- but I was stupid. How am I going to
forget any of it?

> DOWN:
> Look, I don't know what to say.

> UP:
> You never know what to say. There is
> nothing to say.

> DOWN:
> Look, if you don't want to go out, why
> don't we just stay in?

> UP:
> No, I don't care, lets go outside. See the
> island. You're right. We're not going to
> see each other when we're back.

> DOWN:
> You're overreacting.

> UP:
> No, no, I'm not. You're underreacting.
> I can't do this anymore. You won't do
> anything, is that fate?

> DOWN:
> We can only do what we do.

> UP:
> What sort of excuse is that? How
> conveniently fatalist.

> DOWN:
> Look, I'm in this situation for whatever
> reason, but it takes time to change.
> I'm leaving Margo. Believe me, I want

to be with you.

                    UP:
I try to believe you but... it's always the
same. Are we ever going to be together?

                    DOWN:
We are together.

                    UP:
You know what I mean - properly together.

                    DOWN:
We are properly together.

                    UP:
I need someone that cares just about me.

                    DOWN:
I don't know what to say.

UP wrestles her clothes on, snatching each item
off the floor. DOWN paces back and forth still
wearing nothing more than his T-shirt.

                DOWN: (CONT'D)
What if I left as soon as we're back?

                    UP:
Really?

                    DOWN:
Yes, as soon as we land.

                    UP:
You're not going to do that. You enjoy
having two women too much.

                    DOWN:
I need to. We're not right for each other.
We could move in together?

                    UP:
You won't do it.

                    DOWN:
Why not?

                    UP:
It's been like this for so long. You're
not going to leave Margo.

                    DOWN:
You don't know that. We're not so old.
We've still got time to start a different
life. We could get a flat together.

                    UP:
You can't just turn your back on Margo.
You've told me that so many times.

                    DOWN:
No, but she won't want to be with me after
I tell her.

                    UP:
I can never tell when you're serious.

DOWN crosses over to the bed and takes UP's hand.

                    UP: (CONT'D)
Really? You are serious?

DOWN nods imperceptibly.

THE WAVE

<pre>
                    DOWN:
    Let's not go out. I don't feel like it
    anymore.

UP pulls DOWN on to the bed.

                     UP:
    Well take that T-shirt off then - you look
    ridiculous.
</pre>

213

LOCHLAN BLOOM

THE WAVE

"You must dream up beauty and goodness and justice. Tell me do you know how to dream?"

Johann von Gunten

The House in Girt-Thrum Valley

Why was he so weak? He struggled with the thick duvet. It was so dark here. He didn't even have the strength to lift himself out of the bed. Shit. He slipped back into the soft cushion of pillows. Fuck.

A panic rose up in him. How had he got here? His memory was obstinately blank. Work. The room was filled with an antique gloom. Where was he? He could see the dim outlines of furniture. A large French dresser filled the far wall, rosewood drawers and shelves housing porcelain jugs and ceramics, an embroidered chair, cushions, swirling thick pile carpets… Slowly, his eyes adjusted to the darkness, playing tricks on him, gummy, thick. He must have been asleep for an eternity. Had he always been asleep?

Currents of dreams swirled beneath the surface of his thoughts. A river… An immense river, he had been trying to reach somewhere, somebody, attain something. Had he made it? Had he even been there, aboard a ship? It had been so hot, like a giant sweating sea of moisture. The image evaporated. It was nothing – a fiction, a dream – but then where had he been?

On the opposite wall heavy patterned drapes reached from floor to ceiling. Behind these, he presumed, lay windows, but they could equally have hidden a door leading to an adjacent room. The thick material blocked out even the smallest chink of light. It was impossible to tell if it was day or night.

The bed sheets were wet against his skin. How long had he been there, poaching in this bed? He threw back the covers and his body was brushed by the breeze. It came from the direction of the drapes and carried a delicious fragrance. It was not so much a smell as a clarity in the air. A stark pure wildness, an untamed wilderness extending from the outside. He yearned to catch some glimpse of it. To get out of this stifling bed.

And now, a city, he remembered a city. He had lived there? Was he still there? He was sure this place, wherever it was, was somewhere far, far away.

With a chill he recalled the image of a hooded figure. The hammer swing. The searing pain. He had been only feet away from the crowds; so close to the entrance of the Expo. Instinctively he reached to touch his head. Apart from a vague ache there was no wound. What had happened after he passed out? Had someone found his body? Or had his attacker been sent to kidnap him? It did not appear that he was being held captive, but then again there was no way to be sure the door was not locked.

Now, more hazy memories arrived: a stern looking man who had fed him pills, others coming in and out of the room observing him, a nurse who had brought him food, another who had bathed him. He had been ill. Very ill. A fever? Hallucinations? He remembered a girl sitting by his bed. She had been crying. She had thought he was going to die. She was so familiar. Tendrils of fever clung to him.

How long he had been there? Snatches of real memory mingled with those brought on by fever, but none of them made any sense. He remembered a black presence framed in the window. He wanted to cry out, to make some noise, to summon help, but the building was filled with an almost overbearing silence that he could not shatter.

'How are you feeling today?'

The girl had spoken quietly, her eyes twinkling with a leathery tranquillity. She had been there beside him on the bed. Had she been there all the time? Her eyes had been red, red and wrinkled.

No, it was not a girl, now he remembered it had been an old woman. Someone he knew? Her face had looked lived in. What was her name? He had held her face in his hand. He remembered his own arm, covered in grey hairs, wrinkled skin.

'Old age is never a pretty sight,' he remembered thinking. 'We have grown so decrepit, so decayed, both of us. We have aged together like two old wrinkled prunes. Is this what we all become? Old wrinkled prunes? We expend the greatest energies, overcome huge obstacles and after all that, age is our only prize? The same grey emptiness for everyone from the highest to the lowest. We survive years of hardship, we follow all the rules, just to become indistinguishable lumps of wrinkled flesh.'

What was her name? She was so familiar, her face like a worn pebble that had been with him for years. He knew this woman intimately, every line, every half-formed gesture or sign that she thought he didn't notice. It was all there inside him. Was that not what growing old was? Getting accustomed to it all?

His memory was dreamlike, hyper-real. Why were his thoughts so muddled? He had to think rationally. He was recovering from some attack? Or was it an illness, a rash? He remembered itching his blotchy red skin. He looked down at his body, but the skin was young, unbroken. He wasn't so old after all. Had it all simply been the fever, did old age really exist?

Despite the lack of light he knew he was better. Whatever treatment they had given him, he knew that it had worked. The rash belonged to wherever he had been before. Had that been in a different life? He had a rash and had been looking for someone…

Ddunsel. That dreaded name, it washed into his brain like

a tsunami. Ripping at the cobwebs of his memories it crashed deathlessly on, wiping out any glimmer of light. His body was wracked with a hideous tension, followed promptly by the onset of a coughing fit. He leant forward, grasping for something to steady him, his brain reeling.

The name Ddunsel rang out in his mind.

This was Ddunsel's house. The thought came to him forcibly, suddenly. He couldn't remember why he was here, how he had come to be transported to this place, but something unmistakeably marked it out.

He tried to focus, but his head felt as if it were about to split.

He called out frantically; it was as if the room was melting in front of his eyes,

The room a cage, he chased frantically after the dissolving fragments of his dream state, willing himself to slip back under the blanket of sleep, but he was awake now, he was here in this place in Ddunsel's domain.

This was real and he was many miles from home.

The panic rose up inside him again. He had nothing to cling onto, he didn't even know his own name. What was there in him that he could rely on to be true?

He grappled with his memory. The woman, the face of the old woman returned. What was she called? He knew her, but why could he not remember her name? Something about her had been so familiar, he felt that she was the one that would lead him…but to what?

He closed his eyes with an effort.

He had been looking for Ddunsel. He had been in a city and he had been looking for that man. He was obsessed with Ddunsel but he had had no idea who he was. He had a room – yes, that was right – and a job. He commuted on the underground. How long ago had that been? It seemed impossibly distant.

And before that? He struggled. Sygeton. Another place, smaller, more like a town, he had been there with someone, a girl, Alberta. Had that really been her by his bed or was it a fever? It was impossible. She had been so old, so decrepit.

He remembered his name.

Outside, the sound of motors rang up from the courtyard below and with an effort μ pulled himself over to the drapes. Behind the drapes lay two thick oak shutters attached by wrought iron clasps. Fumbling in the murkiness he managed to remove the fastenings and fold the shutters back, revealing two leaded window panes constructed in a lattice pattern.

Luxurious cars lined an expansive gravelled driveway that led up to the front doors of the house. It was semi-dark by now and the headlights shone golden in the dusk. Even from such a great height, μ could tell that the patrons descending from the cars were wealthy beyond all measure. Their pose, their elegant costumes, the glitter of diamonds. Everything suggested that the great and the good were all gathering here for some kind of party.

Servants and valets scurried around, the worker ants providing for the queen bees, a gathering of the hives. μ wondered how the honey tasted to those down on the ground as a bitter taste travelled up his throat.

He was aware of his body. He was weak – he must have been in that bed for weeks, months even. Had he been unconscious so long? What had they done to him? He looked down at his pale body, the skin hanging, his shrivelled cock. He had to get dressed and leave, find his way down to the exit.

The dusk light provided little extra illumination, but with the shutters open μ was at least able to see something. He needed to find some clothes. The wardrobe perhaps? Taking unsteady steps he crossed the room and pulled the wardrobe door.

It was a sturdy mahogany wardrobe and inside hung a solitary clothes hanger supporting a dark grey suit. He pulled it out suspiciously. Who had left it there? A starched pink shirt was tucked inside the suit jacket and from the bottom poked the legs of the trousers. Holding it against his body it looked to be his size. In fact, it looked exactly his size. But these were not his clothes, he was sure. There at the bottom of the wardrobe lay a small pile of other appurtenances: a belt, underwear, a pair of soft leather shoes.

He set the suit out on the bed and bent to pick up the other items. It seemed to be too deliberate. A single set of clothes, left pressed and folded for him. Was he expected to attend whatever event was unfolding down below? How could they have known he would awake at that precise moment and not sleep for further weeks? Unless, had he been drugged? Held in some kind of coma?

It was evident he had been brought there for some reason, but he had no trust for Ddunsel's motives. Despite this he felt compelled to stay, at least until he had some idea of what was planned for him. He dressed. He was pleased to find not only that the clothes fitted him perfectly but that they were made of the finest materials, slipping softly over his frame, surrounding him in an armour ready to take on whatever discomforts were outside.

He checked the pockets – they were all empty except for the inner left breast which contained a worn rectangle of card. He pulled it out but had to go to the window to read it. It was an old business card. He remembered it now – he had received it from Hearst. It was now annotated in blue ballpoint pen:

- All language is an *(failed)* attempt to describe the world
- Human relationships are ~~defined by this description~~ *(illusory)*
- The existence of intelligence in the world is *(unproven)* ~~a necessary hypothesis~~
- *(We can never hope)* ~~We should seek~~ to understand the ultimate intelligence

It made no more sense to him now than it had when he first saw it. Who had annotated it? And why? Looking closely, the scratches of blue ink appeared similar to his own handwriting, but he couldn't be sure. Had he written those scribbled notes? He certainly had no recollection of having done so.

The card was old and crumpled. It had evidently been well worn, but what had happened to it? Had he had it with him all this time?

How much time was that? How much time was he missing? His previous life, the city, Sygeton, Alberta, it seemed almost like a fiction to him now.

The door to the bedroom opened effortlessly, despite his fear that it might be locked. He placed one foot in the hall and stepped into the darkened corridor.

Outside, the hallway was dimly lit and stretched off to his left into blackness. μ felt the need to make distance between himself and the room in case anyone should come looking for him and so he strode off into the depths of the building. The decor in the hall was just as rich and faded as that in his bedroom; rich navy carpets patterned with elegant swirls muffled each step.

There was no sign of anybody in this part of the building and it suddenly occurred to μ that he may not be allowed to be out in the corridor – perhaps he was meant to stay in his room until called for? But did he need permission? Was he not a free agent?

And, after all, they had not asked his permission, whoever had transported his sleeping body to this house in the first place. He didn't exactly feel like a captive, but without doubt he had not reached this house under his own volition. Ddunsel had not asked permission before he had carried him to this house.

Then again, who had the right to say where their body should or should not fall? Certainly μ was not asked before he was born if he was happy with his designated point of entry to the world. Nobody asked his permission to enter the world over here rather than over there; if he would rather arrive on earth in a sunny clime or surrounded by snow; be born to rich parents of poor parents. Nobody asked if he was ready to appear on life's rich stage or if he would, perhaps, rather wait twenty more minutes before dropping, kicking and screaming through a crack into the world?

There was no pre-birth questionnaire to choose the qualities that would ultimately hold ties over him for the rest of his or her life. No survey to check he was happy with the body or personality he was set to start life with. No, the course of all life was set without so much as a pretence of permission. It carried on blithely without such idle concerns as liberty or equality.

It was only some deluded individuals that presumed to believe in freedom, the idea that it was the highest goal of humanity to in some way be free. That freedom is something to earnestly strive for or, at the very least, think about working towards. But this freedom was an invented concept. One could only ever hope to be free within narrow confines.

If everything was permitted, then what action could be better or worse than any other to the free man? And who wants to end up in a state where no judgements can be made? Where is the point in life if we cannot judge it? For μ, it was sufficient merely to tread carefully and avoid alerting any of the staff.

The only natural light came from a double height window at the far end of the corridor next to the door where his bedroom had been. It was an ornate pane of brittle, ancient glass framed with thick lead and inset in a mahogany sill. Although it covered a large area of the wall, very little light penetrated down the corridor and μ had to turn after only a few steps to reassure himself that some strange force was not sucking away the light.

Another few steps and he found his eyes were adjusting to the gloom of the place. He could see several doors on the left-hand side ahead of him and beyond those a wider corridor opened out. There was an opening of sorts and several tables and chairs had been put out for the guests to wait. A couple of bored men lounged around on armchairs. None of them spoke to each other and they had the air of husbands waiting for the wives to get ready. Perhaps they were going to whatever event was meant to be taking place downstairs? They sat, picking at their teeth, their wives' handbags and coats on the seats beside them, waiting for the last minute adjustments of make-up to be complete.

μ walked past, keeping his eyes fixed ahead of him. He hoped to find some stairway that might guide him to the ground floor, but the further he walked the more labyrinthine the corridors became. What was this place?

Most of the doors he passed were closed and he guessed they were bedrooms similar to the one in which he had recently awoken. He was able to glimpse through the occasional open doorway a maid changing a bed or dusting a fireplace.

At one doorway he paused, hearing a raucous noise from inside. Peering through the gap in the doorframe he caught sight of a group of young men toasting flutes of champagne. They looked like the sons of bankers or lawyers. Sons of privilege and excess, expensively reared and educated.

One of their number had a bottle and was going around the rest topping up their glasses the moment they had downed the contents. Catching sight of μ he yelled in the direction of the open door.

'Wilsen, Wilsen! What the hell are you doing out there?'

The others all turned to look at μ, letting out a braying roar.

'Wilsen get in here!' 'Where's your glass?' 'Fill him up, Charlie.'

μ said nothing but was reluctantly sucked into the throng of well-groomed young men. He was thoroughly out of place and had no idea why they should have mistaken him for Wilsen, but it was somehow easier to go along with it all and raise the glass that was suddenly thrust into his hand.

There was a celebration planned, that was for sure, but for what or for whom was unclear and perhaps unimportant. The boys were all quite drunk. Arrogant. Friendly. They were certainly capable of being quite forceful in their frivolity, rolling backwards and forwards, pressing μ in amongst them, clasping his head or planting a kiss on his cheeks. Twice they started singing a song evidently composed for this Wilsen that μ had been mistaken for. μ could not tell if it was meant to praise the prowess of Wilsen or denigrate him, but in any case the crowd knew only three lines of the song before collapsing into rounds of laughter.

'Have you come to see Ddunsel?'

'How do you know the host?'

'Did you come from far?'

μ's attempts to garner information about the location of the gathering or the owner of the building were met with blank looks.

'You always were a funny one, Wilsen,' said one of the boys, before slapping µ's thigh in a way that µ couldn't help feeling was inappropriate.

µ was starting to feel a little funny, if truth was told. He had no idea how long he had been lying unconscious, or what illness it had been which sapped his strength, but he had already had three rather large flutes of champagne and a wave of euphoria now lifted at the tails of his coat.

Fighting off the affectionate hugs and pummels, µ struggled out of the room. He had to keep his wits about him. Ddunsel was here somewhere and he had to find out something about this place before meeting him. He was very close now, he could feel it.

In semi-euphoria µ tripped down several corridors. He even stopped to speak excitedly to some of the guests he came across. None of them really seemed to understand his questions and in response only gave him directions back the way he had come. He was lost now. Lost and drunk.

This building was dizzyingly huge. He had been walking some time already and had come across nothing but corridors leading off corridors and endless flat-faced guests. Instead of leading him closer to the main body of guests, every turn took µ further into the depths of the house, the grand, thick pile carpets becoming more threadbare. In place of elegantly clothed guests, staff members appeared, scurrying around carrying heavy platters and magnums of champagne.

'It must be an enormous event,' µ surmised. 'The number of bottles going backwards and forwards is enough to fill an army.'

The staff were even less helpful than the guests and refused to respond to µ in the least. There was something disgustingly servile in the way they carried themselves but this did not translate into any form of civility. Whenever he approached them, they avoided eye contact and made off as fast as possible, hurrying about whatever errand they were sent on. It was somehow entirely in keeping with their servility that they should ignore him so completely.

'I wonder what passes through their heads,' µ paused for a

moment, leaning against the wall. 'That champagne was quite powerful after all!'

He had to keep moving, try and work out what was going on here. Find out what had happened at the Expo and what Ddunsel's plans for him were. Wandering the vast house it felt that Ddunsel must be some kind of demi-god, if he was a person at all. Could Ddunsel be more than one person? Why did μ feel the compulsion to seek him? Did he expect salvation?

A short distance away, a trolley was placed in the hall for staff to leave dirty plates and collect new orders. It was a passing point for the various waiters and they took the opportunity to pause there and exchange brief remarks. Although they passed μ in unfailing silence, he was able to overhear snippets of conversation from the far side of the hall when they thought he was out of earshot.

'I'm telling you, it's no laugh.'

'I've got a good mind to...'

'He has got a doctorate, you know.'

'Of course, but the poor girl, what can she do now, who is going to take her side?'

'Give me a cigarette.'

'Ha, get out of here, how do you suggest you do that?'

'My god, but is he not so repulsive.'

μ was preparing to leave when he spotted a pale, timid girl approach, struggling with several plates. Where the other waiters were so deft at transporting a seemingly impossible number of plates, this poor girl laboured to carry just two. Although the plates she carried were the same size as all the rest they looked unfeasibly huge next to this girl and her twig-like arms appeared about to snap.

μ followed her awkward movement as she deposited the half-eaten plates and tried to pick up three new orders. A young waiter, who was standing close, helped her and she thanked him with a flustered smile. μ was preparing to leave too, when he overheard a whisper of a name floating from her lips.

He wasn't sure if he had heard her correctly. Had she said 'Ddunsel'? What did she know about him? By the time he turned she was off, already some distance down the corridor. µ chased after her, trying to catch up. It wasn't too surprising, he supposed. If this were Ddunsel's house, then all those working under its roof must technically be his employees. Of course they would know about him, even if it not on a personal level.

In any case he was drawn to this girl, compelled to follow her, reassure this pale shadowy figure. She might lead him closer. Closer to wherever he needed to get to.

The girl walked surprisingly quickly, quite in contrast to the awkward way she had approached the trolley moments before, and µ struggled to keep up. He didn't dare to raise his voice and shout after her. Although the drunken young men had been making a huge racket µ could not let out a shout here.

µ picked up pace and had almost caught the girl when she stopped abruptly, sending him crashing into her. With a quick twist of his body he avoided knocking her to the floor, but the surprise upset the girl, causing her to drop one of the plates. It smashed on the wooden floorboards with a cracking of ceramic. The girl instantly reverted to the fearful creature he had watched a moment before.

'Why did you do that?'

'I was following you,' µ coughed uncomfortably, instantly regretting having said this.

'Karl's going to kill me,' the girl sobbed. 'Thanks to you.'

'Here, let me help you clear this up.' µ bent to pick up the fragments of plate. 'Who is Karl, the boss?'

The girl examined µ more closely as he straightened up.

'What are you doing wearing those clothes?' She moved closer to him as if sniffing him out.

Although she had in fact made comment on his outfit, µ suddenly felt naked, as if she could see right into him.

'I'm a guest,' he blustered. 'I'm a personal guest of Ddunsel.'

At his mention of Ddunsel the girl looked at him strangely, confused for a moment. She stared searchingly at µ as if for some sign of irony.

'But you're not a guest,' she finally managed.

µ felt anger rising in him. Who was this gloomy little child that she should seem so sure about what he was or was not? How could she know he was not a guest? What right did she have to say that? However he had arrived there, it was no doubt at the behest of Ddunsel.

'Look, take me to this Karl. If he is your manager, he will sort this out.' µ was suddenly convinced that he had to speak to someone in charge if he ever wanted to find Ddunsel and make his way out of this rabbit warren of a house.

'Take you to Karl? But he won't be pleased to see you dressing up like that.' The girl bowed her head and set off down the corridor, apparently leading µ to Karl.

µ followed, unsure what to make of this latest turn of events. The sickly girl was convinced that he was not one of the guests, but did what he said anyway. Was that because she had simply become so used to following orders? Was he not in some way a guest? After all, he was certainly not an employee of this place.

What was it that she had seen in him that marked him as an imposter in these clothes? Were his clothes not identical to those worn by the boys drinking champagne he had just left? Was it something in his face – something that marked him as too crude, unrefined or vulgar?

They passed quickly along the corridors, the girl apparently familiar with every turn and twist. Several times she opened doors that to µ had appeared invisible, hidden by pillars or cunningly placed to blend in with the walls so that guests might not notice the staff coming and going.

Away from the lavish passageways designed for the guests µ was amazed how much of the building was crumbling or badly repaired. This place, this house, was huge – quite unending.

Eventually they arrived at a corridor that bustled with staff, evidently some sort of offices. The girl led µ to a door then pulled up short, blocking µ from seeing through the open doorway. Intensely she turned to µ and brought her index finger up towards his nose.

'Are you sure you want to disturb him?'

'Disturb who?' μ suddenly began to doubt this was such a good idea.

'Karl, of course.' The girl's pale face looked exhausted in this light. She really was a strange creature. The dark, shadowy bags hanging under both her eyes were just a little too sallow to be attractive, and yet there was something so timid and breakable in her that he wanted to reach out and stroke her face.

Should he disturb him? The decision was made for μ as an elderly man with a tall, skeletal frame suddenly appeared in the doorway.

'What are you doing standing out here,' he roared, then, catching sight of μ, 'wearing those clothes?'

μ jumped up, instinctively straightening his posture in the gaze of authority. Karl was clearly the boss.

Despite the fact that the man bellowed his words, there was nonetheless something comical in his demeanour, as if he himself didn't take his role particularly seriously but merely acted out the part of the hard-hitting boss to goad a reaction from his underlings.

'These are the clothes they provided me with,' μ piped up, suddenly feeling the need to niggle this man in return.

Karl squinted at him and then at the girl.

'Well, Alice where did you find him?'

'He was hanging around the drop-off tables.'

Karl considered this for a long time.

'And you claim to be a guest here, do you?' The old man stood perfectly still. No tremor or frailty seemed to pass through his aged frame.

'I don't see why I need to claim to be anything,' μ carried on with his impudence, 'I am a free citizen and they left these clothes in my room for me. I can do as I please.'

'A free citizen indeed!' At this the old man let out a low, wheezing laugh. 'But of course you are. What a delightful idea – so you are neither a guest nor a member of staff.' He laughed even harder at his joke, though μ could not see what was so funny.

'Well, it is certainly clear that you are not a guest, but then the mystery remains of what exactly you are doing carrying on around the halls dressed like that instead of working.'

Karl bent his frame down to µ's level, for he was a good head and a half taller than him.

'Come into my office, perhaps you can expedite yourself.'

Inside, the office was not ornate but tastefully decorated with antique looking furniture. It was obvious that the old man spent most of every day in this room and invested much effort to create a virtuous working environment. Positioning himself in the seat behind the huge oak desk, he motioned that µ should sit opposite him.

'You probably think I am out of touch with what's going on out there, that you can just get away with whatever you want? Well let me tell you, it's not by chance that I am in this position. I have to hang on by my teeth, let me tell you.' He spoke now in an almost conspiratorial tone.

'If others had had their way... well, let me just say I don't let them knock me down. Main amongst them being my own brother Karol, of course.' At this the old man twitched his lips bitterly. 'Brother of mine.'

µ could see the memory of this brother cast a dark shadow across the old man but couldn't help interjecting.

'What funny names for two brothers – Karol and Karl!'

'You think it's funny we have such similar appellations?' he roared. 'Practically the same name? Why, they are nothing alike. He is my greatest curse. I am nothing like him. Karol.' He stressed the second vowel, drawing out the word. 'Does the name alone not suggest to you a truly feckless individual?'

Talking about his brother had clearly made the old man angry, and he had jumped out of his seat animatedly as he repeated the name.

'Do you think anybody called Karol could become deputy butler at the age of 19? That he could go on to manage a team as large as mine? That he would be trustworthy? Or reliable? That anyone with that name could make sure all these countless souls turn up each morning and find work enough for each of them to do?

'God, I have worked away all my life in this place.' Here he ran his hand lovingly along the seam of the table. 'I have achieved something. Do you not believe this is something, some accomplishment?'

He glowered at μ and it took a second before μ realised the old man was expecting some response. He cleared his throat to answer in the affirmative, but by then it was already too late. The old man flopped, deflated in his seat, a look of childlike pain crossing his face.

In that split second μ understood far more about the man than if he had talked for three hours.

'Maybe we can never achieve anything after all. The idea of serving anybody has been deeply unfashionable for a long time, I admit, but I clung onto it in any case. It's only recently that I've started to wonder, old age no doubt, whether it is not simply about the weak and the strong, as the philistines have always said.

'Isn't old age the ultimate weakness? it goes beyond any other form of weakness or disability because it is amplified by the knowledge that an end is to come. What is the point of doing anything when the end is close? What is the point of changing anything? Of fixing anything?'

μ fidgeted nervously.

'But what would you know? You are so young.'

The image of the aged Alberta sitting on his bed flashed through μ's head. He struggled to remember how old he really was.

'And you came here to work, I presume? Despite the costume you are wearing.' Karl suddenly leant forward on the table quite seriously, instantly banishing any cobwebs of his previous ruminations. μ felt as if he had been put under the spotlight.

'You are an earnest young man, that much I can see. You must of course ignore my meanderings. There are rules here, obviously, but that is not to say that it is not possible on occasion to bend them. I run a tight ship, but my position certainly gives me the opportunity to nurture those that offer promise – not break the rules you understand, I must uphold them, but to make certain exceptions.

'You, for example: Clearly, I could not give you a very significant role. What would the others say? No, certainly not straight away.

'Straight away, there is merely the chance to work, and work is after all the main objective – gainful employment. Who knows what can happen in time. Yes, anything significant would be quite unsuitable, but perhaps something in the kitchens.

'The girl, Alice, that brought you here, she is a good worker. A little simple, it is true. She works in the kitchens with Emile. Simple tasks – cleaning dishes, running errands, nothing too taxing. It is true that Emile is a bit of a handful, and quite work-shy, more interested in molesting the younger girls than anything else... but I can see you screwing up your face. Perhaps you feel you have more aptitude than to be working with those two? No doubt, believe me I am making no statement about your skills or potential... as I say, there are rules.

'How would it look if I were to just give you a job higher up, just because you were able to do it better? No, this is the absolute best I can offer you, and don't worry that because the job title may be lowly you will not be able to shine; there is always work to do, always. You will find there is quite enough to keep you fully occupied even if you are technically subordinate. No, most certainly you should not scoff at this role, far from it. It is a monstrous stroke of luck for you that you managed to get this audience with me today, believe me, you could be a lot worse off.'

μ couldn't tell if Karl was being serious. The last thing he wanted was a job as some sort of menial kitchen helper to a pair of mentally challenged teenagers like Emile and Alice. He didn't know quite how to respond to the old man's rambling delivery. Certainly he could not make any acknowledgment of this offer of work.

'I'm looking for Ddunsel.'

At the mention of this name, Karl again flew into a rage. He threw himself across the room with an energy far exceeding that expected of a man of his age. In a single bound he had leaped up on top of the writing desk, and with his spindly legs pounded his feet against the oak, inches from μ's face.

'What is that you say? Where in the hell do you think you come from?'

μ told him where he was from, but even as he spoke the words seemed thin and unconvincing.

'Oh, you have a real delusion I see,' Karl roared, 'but I don't, for one fucking moment, think that you can really believe that.

'You execrable fucking cunt, where the bloody shit do you think you are? You go about saying you're some kind of... foreigner,' he spat this last word, 'telling me you're looking for Ddunsel.'

μ was taken aback by the old man's expletive laden invective. He couldn't quite believe that such profanity had come out of the old man's mouth. Only a moment before he had seemed so respectable and well-mannered. Had μ really done something to provoke this?

No, he had only mentioned Ddunsel's name, hardly a crime. It was not like he didn't have a good reason to be looking for Ddunsel, who was presumably responsible for his being there in the first place. Who was this old man after all to scream at him like this? Was he just going to give up now and work for this crazy old fool just because he yelled at him? Intimidating as this verbal onslaught was, it strengthened the desire in μ to needle the comical old man.

'I am sorry that I appear to have upset you,' μ stood solemnly, intent on maintaining a show of dignity despite the fact that Karl still stood on the desk in front of him, red in the face. 'I will leave and continue my search for him elsewhere.'

This infuriated Karl to breaking point and he angrily kicked at the screen on his desk, sending it splintering into the wall.

'Go on your own, will you? Do you know how many people are clamouring for a job here you little runt? How many would give their right hand to work for Karl? And I was about to give you a chance, to think! Oh no, well I'd like to see your chances.'

μ beat a hasty retreat, staggering into the hall confused by what had just taken place. As he closed the heavy door behind him he was aware how sterile and silent the hall was. The few staff that had lingered outside Karl's office when he entered were now nowhere to be seen.

He had to find someone who knew the order of this place and could take him to Ddunsel, or he was never going to get out of there. He was keenly aware that he was a visitor there. He didn't belong there, not in the same way as the others did. The staff were compelled, for whatever reasons, to work in this place, while the guests were so carried by their god given arrogance that μ could not imagine any of them had any feelings but utter entitlement.

He imagined a future in which the favoured progeny of these guests were served canapés by the children of the current staff, a future where new generations drank copiously from the champagne glasses delivered to them by the hands of a new unborn servant class.

Perhaps there would be some interbreeding, between guests and staff. Who knew the rules on these sort of things, but that would not change the fundamental operation of the machine.

For it was a machine, when you viewed it from a certain distance: the participants, the cogs, each played a part in driving forward production. All action was simply a reaction. The staff and guests together – this society – were actors in a production line, each action triggered by the previous line in the script, all intent on creating some as yet unidentified end product, a product that would not be realised for generations to come.

What that product might be, or even what form it might take, was at best a hazy approximation, but it seemed to μ, standing there in the silence of the hallway, that it must in some way be tied to Ddunsel.

At every step μ had sensed some intelligence controlling things, an intelligence he had attributed to Ddunsel. Was it possible now that Ddunsel could be a mere man? Was he not something larger, some guiding hand? If μ could only make contact with him he was sure he would be able to glean some inkling as to the ultimate purpose, whatever that may be. Ddunsel seemed inextricably linked to this unseen order, and some part of μ yearned to be subsumed into that plot.

There was a shuffling noise at the end of the hallway and μ squinted to make out who was there. It dawned on him that he might do well to leave this section of the house if he wanted anything done. Suddenly he was an intruder in the staff quarters. Here, he was liable to find himself sent on an errand or lost forever in the bowels of the kitchens.

The noise in the corridor repeated. There was somebody there lurking in the shadows. He caught a flash of a white face but it disappeared a moment later. Trying to master an authoritative tone, μ took a step forward and projected his voice.

'Hey there.'

There was a crash and a scrape as whoever it was shrank further away into the shadows. μ took a couple of steps towards the lurker. The figure retreated, despite having been spotted, and μ strode forward, intent on catching whoever it was. A web of limbs propelled itself away from μ, clattering down the hallway.

There were two people. One of them turned around as they passed a lamp and he got a glimpse of a face, turned backwards in hurried flight. A shock of recognition went through him. Two sets of long bony limbs topped by wiry black hair awkwardly tried to stay out of sight while at the same time running at full pelt away from him. The pair from the bookshop. How long ago that was.

'Hey, you there,' there was a desperate edge to μ's voice as if seeking their approval.

The pale bodies of the assistants paused briefly to share a look before continuing away from μ.

'...From the bookshop,' μ finished weakly.

They were aware of him. Afraid of him. Timid now. It was imperative that he catch them, they were his only link to the outside and what's more he was sure they worked for Ddunsel and knew how to reach him. Doubling his pace, μ chased frantically down the corridor.

The two assistants were able to move surprisingly fast, despite being badly co-ordinated, their long gangly limbs giving them an advantage when it came to running. It was sheer luck they happened to round a corner as a guest was coming the other way, drink in hand.

The combined momentum of the twins sent all three of them flying in a ball of arms and legs and sent the glass shattering to the wall. μ rounded the corner just in time to find the twins awkwardly attempting to help the guest to his feet. He was furious.

'What the hell were you doing?!' he gesticulated wildly at the stain on his expensive suit where his drink had been spilled.

The twins simply stood mute, shaking their heads dumbly, which visibly enraged the guest.

'You think you can fucking spill a drink all over me. I'll have your fucking job. Where's your manager?' The guest had grabbed one of the twins by the lapels and had pulled his face down to his level, spitting bile at his chin. The twin didn't flinch but instead grinned stupidly at this abuse.

'I'm terribly sorry, sir,' μ stepped forward, 'I will see to it they are both disciplined.'

The guest relaxed his grip on the lapel and turned his attention to μ.

'And who the fuck are you?'

'Assistant Services Manager,' μ eyed the twins disapprovingly. 'I was of a mind to give them a good beating myself anyway, but now I see what they have done, on top of everything else today,' here μ lowered his voice to a conspiratorial whisper, 'you can be sure that they are for it.'

The guest seemed pleased by μ's speech.

'Well it's not on. Staff running around the halls like that.'

Grimly, μ nodded his agreement.

'Believe me, they will be severely reprimanded.'

Grabbing the closest of the twins, he pulled his lapel as the guest had done a moment before so that he was at eye level.

'Severely reprimanded indeed.'

'Let me take your jacket.' μ motioned to the other twin with his free hand and he helped the guest take his jacket off. 'We'll have this cleaned straight away and have a replacement sent to you immediately.'

The guest's anger had by now completely dissipated.

'The jacket, will it be ready for the event?'

μ slapped his head as if remembering something.

'Yes, of course, your room number?'

'217.'

'And where you are dining this evening…?'

'The Venetian Aquarium.'

'I'll have a bottle of our finest from the cellar sent to your table.'

'There's no need.'

'No, really, we'll make it a case.'

The guest smiled broadly and even went as far as to shake μ's hand. μ apologised again for the incident and, while doing so, managed to shoot off a glare at the twins to indicate they should be left alone in order for the reprimand to begin. The guest drunkenly staggered back the way he had come.

As soon as the guest had disappeared from view, μ rounded on the twins.

'So it is you two, what are you doing here? Ddunsel sent you to spy on me again?'

The twins looked abashed, shrinking away from μ. In their eyes there was the definite glint of impudence but it quickly faded, replaced by a glazed panic.

'I saw you in the bookshop, you were watching me.'

'No,' one of them burst. For some reason, μ took him to be the younger of the two. 'No, that wasn't us.'

μ could tell he would get nowhere questioning them directly; they had a certain defiance despite their fear. What's more, he could see they would withstand any abuse, take any beating or put up with any indignity, not through some inner strength but simply because of some dumb obedience. They shrank and twisted in front of μ, unsure whether to be afraid of him or the unseen authority that had sent them there.

'You can relax,' μ decided to try a different tack, 'we're on the same side, but you must help me.'

The twins looked at each other confused – they had clearly been expecting further beration. They stared glumly at their feet.

'I need to get into the event this evening. You have to help me.' μ paused, hoping to see some reaction from the twins, adding for emphasis, 'It's of the utmost importance to Ddunsel that I attend.'

'The dinner?' The older twin shook his head in disbelief. 'You need a ticket to get in there?'

μ let a sly grin slide onto his face. 'Come on, there must be ways to get in?'

The twins stood still.

'We need to get back.'

μ was unsure if they were always this ill-at-ease or if it was just in his presence that they acted so nervously. Were they as dumb as they appeared? They really were overgrown children.

'And where do you need to get back to?'

The twins looked worriedly at each other, afraid they had said too much.

'No... nowhere.'

Infuriated, μ grabbed at the jacket of the elder twin, shaking him aggressively

'We… you're not allowed back there.'

'Back where?' But they had clammed up. μ shook the hapless idiot. A red mist rose inside him.

'You tell me where this dinner is being held.'

The twins considered this.

'But Ddunsel…'

μ took a decisive step down the corridor, dragging the twins with him.

'We don't have time to dilly-dally.'

The corridors twisted and arced in the most confusing pattern. μ had the impression that, overall, their trajectory was taking them downwards, but he could make little sense of the route they followed. The twins steered him this way and that, up a few steps, across a landing, down a flight of stairs, through a crowded dining room. They passed through bustling hallways and tight passageways and, despite the twists and turns, they never seemed to hesitate. Whether they were leading him closer or further away from the centre of things μ could not tell.

As they progressed, μ got the sense that the building was in fact two separate structures, carefully inter-twined. Grand concourses, evidently designed for guests, were mirrored by threadbare passages, often separated by the thinnest of walls. Much of the convoluted layout of the building resulted from the fact that nearly all the architectural features were doubled to allow parallel operation.

Each intersection was designed in such a way as to make this coexistence almost invisible, at least to the guests. There was something terrifyingly organic in the way these two structures twisted around each other, like giant serpents fighting. As if the building was in some strange sense alive. Who could have designed all of this from the ground up? It appeared that the two halves of the building had grown around each other in a symbiotic arrangement. One feeding off the other, each with a grip around the throat, exerting just enough pressure to avoid suffocating its lover, just enough to keep it gasping for life.

The twins by now were flying along the carpet oblivious of μ, pulling him along in their slipstream. He could not tell what, if anything, was going through their minds. What, after all, did pass through somebody else's mind? Were other people not always an alien continent?

Unbidden, a conversation with Wijklawski sprung into his mind, reclaimed from some hidden corner of his memory. He had only just got to know the professor – it had been a sodden winter morning. The memory appeared fully formed, all the intervening time collapsing away like a fiction.

μ had been in Wijklawski's office and the professor had been talking about the nature of knowledge.

'…We can say, for example, that all knowledge is nothing more than a physical conditioning. A Pavlovian response, if you will, based on our physiological memory.'

'But not all knowledge,' μ had said. 'Surely we have reason, an intellect.'

'The intellect,' Wijklawski scoffed, 'there is no such thing. We are machines, nothing more. We gain knowledge in exactly the same way as Pavlov's dogs – from repetition, from the world around us. Pavlov rang the bell and his dogs salivated, their behaviour was a perfectly normal response. We are no different. We are organisms trained to react to our surroundings just as those dogs were. Our reactions are more complex, that is all. We might talk about high-minded ideas, about logic, or reason, or love, but all of it stems from our physical makeup.

'There is no a Priori knowledge. Everything is learned. As children we are conditioned to understand the rules of logic that hold true within our world. We apply these rules to ourselves and we think we have discovered "knowledge". We are nothing more than a series of conditioned responses. The result of complex feedback loops, we condition ourselves, we create a snake pit of feedback that we place on a pedestal and call our personality – our humanity.'

The professor paused on this last word, letting it float for a moment.

'We take it for granted that the universe is governed by logic, but in reality it only exists in the theories of lunatics. We do not "discover" laws, we simply learn appropriate responses to our circumstances.

'Life is a story we tell ourselves; we invent characters and swing them around on arcs, we make them follow predefined curves, we invent action to take place within a tiny range of possibilities and we imagine the most ridiculous events in order that we can say there is some logic.

'But logic is merely one form of story. The brain is remarkable only in its ability to store a thin trace of life, to record memories – a smear of existence that can be coughed up again at some later date. We are nothing but the story we keep telling ourselves.' The professor had let out a breath, the air clouding up the steamy window.

At the time, μ had thought the professor's words were utter nonsense and he remembered they had argued earnestly for almost forty minutes. Why that conversation should spring into his mind as he ran down the corridor he had no idea. Was it meant to mean something? He was aware of a dark, glimmering world that had been briefly illuminated. It seemed to point to some deeper future, a path forwards, but what? He heard an echo in the impenetrable fog.

'We are nothing but the story we keep telling ourselves.'

But it was gone. Already μ could feel the memory subsiding – the construct was threatened as other memories of Wijklawski flooded onto the scene, colouring the picture with prejudices and regrets. He could not separate this image from his other recollections of the professor, tainted as they were by his association with Alberta.

No sooner had the memory dissipated than a crushing sense of defeat enveloped μ. What, after all, had he achieved with his time? All those years that had passed – for what? The unexpected closeness that this memory had foisted upon him only highlighted the losses he had suffered... and loss, what did that word even mean?

The most purely individual process – a private, clandestine surrender – and all the more painful for it. After all, anything which could be shared was never really lost, was it? No, human beings had little hope to truly understand what loss meant for another.

'The main thing is that I don't lose these two idiots,' μ thought, quickening his pace to keep the pale twins within sight as they sped down the thick piled corridors.

They passed into an area reserved for some of the more well-to-do guests and the twins slowed to a more respectful pace. Now that μ paid attention, the mood around him was electric with anticipation. Snatches of conversation buffeted him as he passed, flapping through the air with drunken exuberance. Wherever they had arrived, it was certainly full of party spirit.

In this part of the house the wide corridors acted as crossing points between lavish galleries, each apparently decorated with a different theme from around the world. Rather than doorways as in the rest of the house, here giant entranceways announced the delights to be found in each great hall: Paradise Cove, Magiterium Rome, Wolfgang's Vienna... even from the short glimpses snatched as they passed, the level of detail was quite staggering.

In one, Marquesas Bay, a tropical beach was recreated with silver sand surrounding an 'ocean' of azure blue water which stretched far off into the horizon. Through whatever ingenuity, the designers had created the illusion that the water spread miles ahead, perhaps by using polished mirrors where the water met the wall.

Palm trees created shady hollows where guests reclined. They looked entirely at home, each guest wearing fancy dress impeccably matched to the style of the place. They drank bright cocktails supplied by beautiful Gaugin-esque beauties. Even the air carried a tropical, vegetable heat. A blast of warm island musk hit μ as they passed the entrance and a sharp salt tang stayed in his nose.

The twins were heedless of the decadent splendour, but μ's attention was diverted, trying to catch as much detail of each installation as possible, so it was a surprise for all of them when they were pulled up short by a burly stranger.

'Where do you think you're going?'

μ was almost about to respond, to excuse himself, when he realised the man was talking to the twins. They had both turned even more ashen faced than normal, gulping at an unnatural pace.

'We...'

They were visibly quaking. The man let out a terrifying snort.

'Well, there is no time to listen to your excuses in any case.'

μ tried his best to distance himself from the twins, without moving and attracting the man's attention, which proved to be an impossible task. The man looked him up and down disparagingly.

'Who is this? Are you drunk?'

'No, I'm simply looking for...'

'You two imbeciles!' Frustrated anger seemed to be the default mode of operation for this man. 'What are you doing dragging this drunk down here? What are you doing away from your duties? My god, this whole event is so finely tuned, you think there haven't been hundreds, thousands of hours of sweat put into creating this…?' He waved his arm around the magnificent entranceways. 'You think this whole thing isn't hanging so delicately, on the thinnest of threads, that you can come in here, come blundering in here, and it won't make any difference? That we can afford to have mistakes happening and still expect to have everything function? Are you trying to prevent this being a success?'

He spoke in a burning hiss, a roar that enveloped only the twins and μ. He was evidently an expert at creating a scene without disrupting the bonhomie of any of the guests. The twins stood dumbly as ever and, having let out his anger, the man deftly grabbed them both propelling them back the way they had come.

'You,' he spoke over his shoulder to μ as walked, 'wait here and I'll send someone for you.'

And they were gone.

It didn't take long for μ to realise he must move. Whoever was sent to collect him was unlikely to take him in the right direction.

He walked briskly in the direction they had been travelling, but now, without the twins to keep the pace and lead the way, he found the draw of the voluptuous installations too great. Giant statues carved from ice glistened in an arctic themed room: 'North Pole Attempt' was carved in the giant archway outside. A futuristic world hummed and throbbed behind a scrolling banner of electronic lights which read 'Utopia 3666.'

What made μ stop in front of 'Arabesque Dream' he couldn't say. The design was equal but not more impressive than the other rooms. Giant sandstone sphinxes and pyramids provided the backdrop for rich Bedouin tents. Veiled bellydancers wove in and out under hazy shisha smoke. Opium tones harmonised with the throaty sounds of rhaitas and bendirs.

A dusty desert wind blew across one flank of the tents and black, sharp shadows were cast by the 'sun' far overhead. The designers had excelled themselves. μ had barely gone ten steps into the space before he felt the heat beating on the back of his neck. What was this place? He had travelled a thousand miles away. It was with some relief that he staggered into the shade of the closest tent.

He was under a large canvas awning that protected the entrance to the tent proper. Sand whipped into this area from the desert outside but already the shade made it feel much cooler. Small groups huddled in this makeshift entrance, most of them within short distance of a makeshift bar. A barman poured them liquor in filthy glasses.

As in the other areas, the guests here wore fancy dress matched to the style of their surroundings – in this case mainly light khakis and sandals. There was something unsettling in their costumes, too scanty despite the heat, overly sexualised. Most of the figures paid little heed to μ and he ignored them too, pushing one of the heavy canvas flaps aside to enter the main tent.

Here in the comparative darkness it took a moment for μ's eyes to readjust. The thick canvas appeared to do an admirable job of isolating the desert heat. Inside it was cool and dark. Not a chink of light got in. The place was furnished with sumptuous rugs and cushions in the style of an Arabic Sewan but there was no wedding planned here. The guests were busy, greedily seeking other gratification than that afforded by well-made furniture.

Long cotton robes rustled revealing flesh, tied, harnessed for pleasure. Fucking, rutting shapes. Even with the dim lighting μ could sense the lust, the sex that hung in the air. It was curious there was no noise, no groans of pleasure, or of pain.

His eyes penetrated further into the gloom. He watched a young girl, perfect, trembling almost in her perfection, her tits rock-hard, her face angelic, twisted in a torture of sexual hunger. She was bound by a strap that splayed her rabbit anus twitching in the air. She was constrained completely, bound, gagged, unable to do anything but be pleasured, to pleasure.

Behind her a swarthy man in a suit handled her labia. He held her with contempt, swiping viciously at her cunt with a birch, each stroke eliciting a silent erotic scream from the girl, bringing the most delicate glow of desire to her face, a faint blossom of colour, a frosted breath of sex, she moaned, moving in her constraints. A plaything for her forbidding master, he a plaything for her pleasure, they neither had will nor control, only desire, mechanics, self-indulgence, their bodies yearning for absolution through the most wicked oppression.

μ moved through the tent. Everywhere he looked, fingers, tongues, toes, penises, cunts, were writhing in a sea of fucking, slapping, prying, pleasuring, torment. He was curiously untouched by the debauchery around him, this sexual ocean neither repelling him nor stimulating him. It was unclear who were guests and who were servants now. Those that inflicted the greatest suffering gleaned the least reward; those that allowed the greatest domination led the dance furthest. Cages hung from the roof filled with depraved girls, the boys no better.

'Who are these people? Begging for more, to be beaten, whipped into a stupor, their bodies' dolls, performing these acts on each other. Tied up, beaten, lowing like animals,' μ thought to himself, 'and how come I'm not in the least aroused by them? Some of these girls are fabulous, look at her over there with her ankles trussed up so delicately, like a pheasant ready to be devoured, or her there with her mouth screaming to be pleasured. There is no doubt these are some of the finest girls they could find and yet somehow they leave me cold. Is there something wrong with me?'

Despite these thoughts it was impossible for μ to leave the room, transfixed as he was, in a spell, one might say – but not a spell of desire, something quite different. One of the girls broke free and rushed towards him. He recoiled, her grip sweaty, moist with desire.

'And where did they all come from? Were they not someone's daughters – no doubt – after all, isn't everybody the son or daughter of someone? What difference did that make? Of course they were, even daughters must please themselves.'

He had passed to the far corner of the tent, by this point, where a flap of curtain covered the doorway into an inner room. Here the scene was much the same as in the previous room. In fact, what he had assumed was a single structure, a large marquee, appeared to be more a collection of tents, each joined to the next, separated by sashes, spreading in all directions.

It appeared each section catered to a particular perversion. Here, contraptions with steel struts and leather fastenings yoked bodies into astonishing contortions. μ stood dumbly by the entrance.

But there... who was that? Was it Alberta, there in the far corner? μ's heart juddered excitedly as his legs propelled him across the room. He couldn't be sure. Was she aware of his presence, playing with him? She moved quickly, ducking out of view just as he approached.

What could she be doing here? Was this another hallucination? She looked so young. His foot fell lightly on the plush Persian rugs. She was gone, ducking behind another flap of cloth. He must catch her, of course. He felt his desire suddenly aflame, like lightning on dry kindling he was ablaze with sexual hunger. He picked up his speed. There was no doubt about it, it was her. He doubled his effort.

'Alberta,' he caught her, with a gasp.

Instantly she stopped. Frozen. For the smallest fraction of a second she looked at him uncomprehendingly, then she smiled:

'You're here.'

'Yes, but how... you are so young... is this a dream?'

But no, this was no more a dream than the rest of life.

'I've been waiting for you,' she continued.

'How did you know I would come?'

'Of course you would come,' Alberta spoke in a prim, coquettish tone calculated to tease him, like a caricature of some cheap hooker. Had she always spoken to him like that? Like ripples on a pond, he recalled a hundred nuances of their life, long since forgotten.

He couldn't tell if she was pleased to see him or not.

'But what are you doing here?' He hadn't meant to say this so desperately.

Alberta let out a sharp laugh and gave a greedy glance around her at the bodies fucking.

Of course, now he looked at her she was dressed just as all the other girls in this place. A thin strap of material was all that covered her crotch. Her face too was made up with the same hideously lurid paint, no doubt designed to mark her role as sexual object. How had he not noticed this at first? Was this her work? To pleasure, to submit to this façade of an orgy.

'But you as well?'

'It's easy,' she let out another free laugh.

Her hand was in his. A jolt of recognition pulsed through him. This was not the time for recrimination. He was hard.

'You want to go with me?' Her playful touch was like a noose. He felt ready to explode.

She led the way through further curtained chambers until finally they were alone.

When μ drifted into consciousness it was on the sweetest, most merciful wave. Where had he been? Somewhere delightful, terrifyingly raw and beautiful. His body was released from some hated shackles. He could have been floating in a cloud for the weightlessness he felt, but he wasn't floating in a cloud, he was here in the tent. Alberta lay beside him, staring at him glossy eyed in the dim light, silent, animal-like.

'Where have you been?'

'Nowhere.'

'I thought you were gone.'

'I had to go. You knew that.'

He tried to remember if he had known that. What was Alberta here, now? She was real, solid beside him. It was hard to imagine anything more real, but at the same time his mind awoke to a thin sliver of doubt. What did he really know about her after all this time? It felt as if nothing had changed.

'How did you get here?'

'How did you get here?' She breathed the words back at him with a moist, warmth that doused his question. His eyes could see only love.

It was his brain that told him to be wary. She had left him. All those unhappy years. Had she not mutilated him in a way? Suffocated that childlike part that he had taken for granted. And yet did any of that matter? There in the dark everything was still and perfect. What was it he had been looking for in any case?

Her skin was so soft, unspoilt, it had never seemed so pure, an image flashed of the debauched scenes they had passed outside. He saw Alberta bound, her trembling mouth gagged, a flash of cruelty and fire, her face spitting sex, already he felt his desire awakening again. He pulled her roughly and from the resistance of a dream she moaned. It was strange there was no sound now from the rooms outside.

But why was she here? μ was suddenly furious. Here they were lying together, apparently two lovers, for the all the world the happiest two people in existence, shaded in the dark, unneeding of anything beyond their little shell, but in truth they were thoroughly lost.

What were they to each other? They had spent the briefest of time together so long ago. They had not even been happy then. Everything since had just been phantasms. And what about the old, wrinkled Alberta on his bed, what was she? Was he becoming delusional? Had he always been delusional?

'You work here?'

Alberta let out a deep laugh.

'You're paid to do this?'

'Oh no, why would they pay me?'

The question was pointless the moment he uttered it – nobody here got paid, that much was clear.

'What do they make you do?'

'Oh, everything... anything they want,' she giggled. 'They take me in turns, this way and that.'

'And what about now? Now we're together again?' μ struggled to finish his sentence, a murky helplessness ceasing him.

In truth his dick was harder than ever before.

Alberta's eyes twinkled. μ gripped her hair.

'You can do what you want with me too.'

μ was trapped, bound more tightly than if there were a hundred ropes. Half of him wanted to use sadistic force. To be utterly cruel, to turn her violently, to violate her, to penetrate her painfully like her eyes begged. The other half wished only to be cold, indifferent, to let this pass him by untouched, an otherworldly peace. He lay still, the only motion in the aching rock of his penis.

'Ddunsel brought me here,' Alberta spoke, as if sensing μ's dilemma.

'Ddunsel.' μ felt his desire draining.

'You know, he is a master, he is the only one that knows how to really work me,' she spoke so sweetly, her mouth prim. 'I let the others use me because that is what he wants.'

'He told you that?'

Alberta laughed again. 'He doesn't need to tell you things. I can feel that is his desire. He wants my body for the others to play with. That is why I was given this body – so that the others could take out their desires on me. Look, they marked me.'

Alberta turned her rump to him and he saw a red gouge in her white flesh. A few centimetres above her buttocks, directly in line with where her narrow opening lay invitingly buried, there was a metal ring gouged into the base of her spine. On the ring an insignia was carved – two interlocking capital Ds.

The last of μ's desire gurgled away.

'And what does he do?'

'He gives me power...' Alberta paused, as if weighing up whether the topic was a good idea to pursue. 'Who wants to be free any more?'

'So that's it? Some sex game, some power trip?'

She snorted.

'Does he love you?'

Alberta looked away, turning her body.

'I don't ask him to.'

'He is raping you, can't you see that? You've grown accustomed to it, that's all. No, more than that, you are learning to like it, to think it's normal, to enjoy it even. You are perverting your own nature and you don't even realise it,' μ all but shouted.

'There are only icebergs, that we cling to, transporting us from one lover to the next, from one continent to the next before they melt and we are forced to jump,' Alberta replied coolly.

There was stalemate. The old stalemate. Older than either of them. The oldest stalemate perhaps? That between man and woman.

He was hit by a stiff comprehension. He was nothing more than an ant, a minute part of the master plan. The details were hidden from him, but in that moment he realised it existed. The plan was all encompassing, constructed and orchestrated as it was by a higher intelligence. He staggered back in disgust as he caught the shortest of glimpses of the enormity of the ant hill.

What was worse, what engulfed him in the most horrifying sensation, was the feeling that this love he felt was not his own. It had been lived out before. It was repeated every century, over and over in different ways, between different protagonists. It was lived over and over again, retrodden, each time with a different outcome. He had been given a chance and this round he had failed. Irrevocably failed.

'Where did you go when you left?' he asked finally.

He thought perhaps she was asleep, but then she started to tell him her story...

She had left with Wijklawski on the spur of the moment. They had each taken only one bag and boarded a plane to the other side of the country. Once they arrived they had checked into a hotel. Wijklawski was a generous lover despite being so much older than her. It had been a relief for her to escape from her life in Sygeton.

From there they had moved down the coast. She didn't remember any of the names of the places they stayed. Always in nice hotels. It came back to μ how simple Alberta's vocabulary of place was. How she lived in a world largely uncluttered by names or concepts.

Wijklawski had some money, it seemed. They lived a lavish life but never flashy. They would eat in good restaurants but never the sort that charged too much. They would drink good wine but never had the need to order the most expensive champagne.

It got hotter as they moved further south. Beaches. Sand. Flesh.

Alberta remained faithful to Wijklawski. They were good together. She barely noticed the difference in age. Sometimes people thought they were father and daughter. This turned her on. Sometimes she would call him 'dad' in earshot of people and then let his hand slide up her skirt.

They had crossed the equator, travelling through an archipelago. She remembered they had stood on the equator line one night, under the stars. They had been on a beach. They were the only ones there that night. That was the high point of their journey, she said. Then they had been the furthest removed, the most separated from other concerns, the furthest from everyday things.

That is not to say things fell apart once they crossed into the Southern Hemisphere. There were plenty more months of happiness. The towns became more basic. They stopped staying in fancy hotels and got used to beach huts and simplicity. Wijklawski too started to change. He talked more about his old research. He missed having his books.

Alberta would have stayed there. It suited her, the life there. Tropical. Easy. Eventually the day arrived when they boarded a bus to the city. It was hot, suffocating, like living under a giant sweating sea, a grey iron mass that pushed down on their heads inexorably.

Wijklawski became more withdrawn. The city did not suit him, but he would not listen to Alberta's suggestions to leave. He started to become involved in research but there was something manic about the way he worked. He had none of the discipline that came from working in a regular job. He covered pages in scrawls and barely spoke to Alberta for hours.

She understandably grew bored waiting. She found lovers in the city. It was full of eligible men, it transpired. Muscular, dumb, not one of them spoke her language. They came to open her legs and then disappeared into the moisture laden streets.

One day Wijklawski announced he needed to travel inland to carry out some further research. He had made an important find, he believed. A rare book connected to his studies. A mathematician that he was researching had travelled in this region of the world apparently. This mathematician, a genius of some sort, had published five books of great significance. Wijklawski believed he had narrowed down the location of one of the final books. Alberta didn't remember the name of the mathematician.

With Wijklawski gone Alberta's disgust with the city grew. She waited weeks. A month passed. There was no word from Wijklawski. She started thinking of leaving again. One day a man appeared. Strange, tall, he claimed to have arrived from the jungle.

He had been so hypnotic, she remembered. So imposing. There was no way but to be drawn in by his character. He had been on a ship travelling upriver, he said, deep in Indian territory. He talked so beguilingly. Within the first 24 hours she was his. They set up together but they both knew he did not love her. That was how she met Ddunsel.

μ had listened to her tale passively. Images from far-off places, from another space entirely, filled his imagination. Now she drifted back into focus. Curiously there was no pang of jealousy when she talked of Wijklawski. She had finished her story and lay quiet now, his once again. He felt between her legs. She moved. It was nothing and she was wet. He slid inside her, erasing the past.

Alberta was dressed already. She stood over him, only half illuminated by the light from a gap in the curtain. Outside μ could again hear the hubbub from the other rooms of the tent. Muffled screams and moans. He beamed a smile of contentment. His body was released, he felt an energy without tension. Calmness.

Alberta did not return his smile immediately. When she did it was coldly, professionally.

'I have to go,' she spoke distinctly.

μ didn't know how to react. A panic started to climb up his neck, but the over-riding calmness prevailed for the moment.

'Where do you have to go? Why do you have to go?'

'I am still working.'

μ was uncomprehending for a moment. Alberta put out a palm and shifted her position to place her other hand on her hip.

'We need to settle up,' she said.

He tried to form a confused question.

'You're an imposter. You didn't think you would get it for free?'

'Free?'

'You have to pay. Of course you have to pay.' Alberta's stance hardened.

What was she thinking? Had she not told him that the clients here never paid? Twice he had been inside her. More than that, of course, over their whole history. What did it amount to? What did his feelings all this time count for?

Looking at her there, towering above him on the bed, he felt there must be some mistake, a miscommunication. Nothing more than that. How could it be that he felt such tenderness and she could feel nothing? 'Of course you have to pay.' The words rang in his head. Was he just a client? Was she trying to punish him?

'I don't have any money.'

At this Alberta became furious. She stormed around the bed, tightening her thin robe protectively, her blood almost visibly boiling.

'You. I knew I shouldn't have taken you.'

'Is that all this was? Business? And what about before...?'

'You think that entitles you to anything?'

'I'm not asking to be entitled to anything.'

'Well, you come in here expecting to get things for free – things that everyone else has to pay for. Salvador!'

The last word she shouted loudly.

'How was I to know that–'

'I don't care. You think anyone else is given any more head start than you? You think anyone else is given a rule book? Salvador!'

Sensing that their meeting was about to be cut short, μ started to dress hurriedly.

'Everyone has to work the rules out for themselves,' Alberta continued. 'They work them out and then they choose whether to follow them or break them. That was your problem – you weren't even bothered to try. You travelled around in your own little bubble and other people ultimately never meant anything to you.'

She shouted Salvador again, more loudly this time, and a burly man, presumably Salvador, appeared in the split of the curtain. He surveyed the room in an instant, evidently the sort of man used to checking for threats when first entering a room – concealed weapons, blind spots and the like. μ suddenly felt very naked.

'Problem?'

Salvador looked like he would delight in causing physical damage. No, beyond that he would delight in causing physical pain, suffering. Was it not St Anthony that had said only suffering was the gateway to the plane of the lord. He had gone mad, half-starved in the desert, had he not? The desert? Far off a bell seemed to chime.

Despite this first impression Salvador was surprisingly considered. μ had just enough time to slip on his pants and shirt before a thick hand grabbed him, propelling him through the dark interior of the tent at speed. Salvador's grip was vice-like.

A vicious pain travelled through μ's body from the points where Salvador's meaty hands locked on his neck and upper arm. And yet, there was something reassuring about Salvador. His violence was only for μ's own good. He flung μ like a paper doll but at the same time with a certain tenderness. He crushed μ's flesh to show him he was there beside him, taking him away.

They passed out of the tent into the hallway.

'Where are we going?'

Salvador merely squeezed μ's neck harder, reassuring, sending a wracking pain to the base of his skull. μ was thankful he was with someone who knew how to handle things. They marched down numerous corridors, away from the core of the party. μ was lost by now.

A swirling, foggy memory parted his thoughts. Who was St Anthony? Had he read of him in a book? Now he couldn't be sure.

St Anthony, temptation, a picture crystallised, St Anthony battling hallucinations in the desert. Why did it come into his mind now? It was nothing from his world. Perhaps it was a novel he had read, but then such a strange novel. What was the point of it? Man's struggle against the true nature of reality.

Who, after all, could accept the harsh nature of things as they really were? The frictionless movement of energy afforded little space for any soul. Frictionless energy had no need for concepts or ideals. Frictionless energy did not die, nor was it born. It was the ultimate horror and everyone would do anything to turn away from it – do anything to scramble madly away from it. There was really no such thing as hallucination; every human experience had, to some extent, the breath of illusion in it...

...and story and man and story and man the two are linked for all time. Man is the story and the story is only man. Literature is the current, and man the tide, that shape the face of this vast ocean. The one cannot exist without the other. Without literature, man is nothing but a collection of animals, eyeless, unthinking in the darkness. Without man, literature is nothing but a collection of dirty papers slowly turning into dust....

He searched for the source of his thoughts, but they ate themselves. Uroborus. The snake that eats itself. The serpent that devours its own tail. Eternally.

He had no idea where he was being taken. To be ejected from the party? To meet some superior? Perhaps Ddunsel himself? What part did Ddunsel play in all this? He had led him here. He had led Alberta here. Goodness only knew what stories there were behind the presence of all the other teeming guests in this never-ending house. Were they staying for one night? Had they been there for a fortnight already? Would they leave tomorrow? Were any of them ever allowed to leave?

μ thought back again on the various cryptic notes and manuscript he had received from Ddunsel. What connected them? What relation did any of it have to his own story? He needed to find answers and yet at the same time a weariness filled him. When would his life settle down? Settle down into something he was happy with – and if it did, would he survive that calm without boredom?

He should have taken better note of all the clues he had received. Could it be an elaborate trick? Now that he was close it occurred to μ that there might be no such person as Ddunsel. But someone had been sending him the material. He was so tired. How long could it carry on, how long could he keep going? Perhaps after all Salvador was leading him to Ddunsel and he could it end it all.

They were now back in that part of the house where the carpets were threadbare and the corridors were narrower. The light bulbs here too were cheap. It was the servant's house here. There was a shout from behind.

'You, release him.'

Salvador stopped instantly. His grip on μ did not loosen. He did not turn to face whoever it was that had shouted. He merely stood immobile and as a result μ was forced to face forward as well. Curiosity strained him.

'Let him go.'

Karl, that grumpy old salt. μ felt a surge of attachment towards the old man. He was not so bad – he was looking out for μ after all.

'What do you think you're doing with one of my employees like that?' Karl spoke sternly, leaving no room for argument, blocking the corridor to make no room for escape.

μ could feel the grip waver, but Salvador did not release him straight away. μ wasn't sure if Salvador could speak. Karl laid his hand on μ's arm possessively. It was enough. Salvador melted into the background and μ was left alone in the corridor with Karl staring strictly at him.

'What the hell was that?' Karl twitched with anger.

'I didn't ask for help.'

'You certainly are asking for something, wandering around like that.'

'Well, thank you,' μ spoke grudgingly, 'but I didn't ask for anything.'

'You have no idea what this could potentially cost me, do you? Saving your sorry hide from that thug. You think this whole thing is set up for your amusement? Someone goes out of their way to make things easier for you and what thanks do you show?'

'I said thank you.' μ's previous warm feelings were draining. He didn't need a lecture from this cantankerous old fool.

'You think that makes any difference? You think that things are only valid if you choose to ask for them? Did you ask for any of this? Where do you think you came from? What dream is this you are living? You believe that you are the master. None of us are masters. We are no different from the animals. We are simply puffed up with yarns.

'Not even I, with all the power I am given – I am no more a master, even with the countless staff under my command, all of them scurrying to do as I say, even then I am no master. We are all here only to play our part, we are only ever a part.

'There is no director. No, not even Ddunsel, that name you bandy about. Who do you imagine he might be? The lord of the manor, some minor deity behind the scenes pulling the strings? He does not exist. You must know this? There is only work.

'That is what I am here to ensure. That is our salvation. Once, perhaps, there was another option. Long ago perhaps it was possible to imagine a simple life without work, only desires, hunger, warmth, sex. Long ago in the first mists of history it may have been possible. I don't say this for certain, but there is a chance that in the beginning those simple necessities were all that was required for life. Well, if that time did exist it is long gone and can never return.

'Now we must accept the situation into which we are thrown. You may not like the idea, but you are the same as all the rest. You must work here amongst the filth and the sediment.

'You may rail against this idea. You have higher goals you say? You are not destined to work in the kitchens but on something purer, something more sublime? But then why have you not been working on it all this time? Why have you let your time slip away if you have this sacred mission? How long has it been since you completed anything towards this goal? You think I don't know? I would not be here if I did not know some things. Why do you not defend your labour if it is so precious?

'No, it is clear your work is to be here. You do not need to worry, we can find something quite suitable. That girl Alice, for instance, the one that brought you to me before, you liked her... but there is no need to be bashful, it was quite obvious. She is physically repugnant, it's true – I see you noticed the same – but that does not mean she cannot make a good workmate, and Emile, he is an energetic boy. I say that, of course, but you can see from my eye no doubt that I truly mean he is a little terror. The abuse he lays on poor Alice is atrocious, and believe me I do everything in my power to stop it, but, as I say, none of us are the masters we like to suppose we are.

'She puts up with the indecency of it well enough, though. You would do well to learn from her – and from Emile too. An empty mind,   that is what you need. To carry out this work successfully, you must appreciate we are nothing more than a collection of habits, you may think you are above the animals, that you are somehow fundamentally different from an egret or a lion. Your power of thought, your consciousness, perhaps, lifts you above these animals, but what are you really when you consider things more closely? What part of you can you truly say is you and you alone?

'That is why I say that an empty mind is the best approach, the only approach, if we are to live. Don't get me wrong, I do not venerate work as some great end, no, not at all. Far less, it is some step on the way to "progress". I only offer it as a poultice, a way to keep your mind empty, perhaps, empty that is of those destructive sorts of thoughts.

'But I can see you are a bright lad, you should have no problems – it may be difficult at first. Admittedly, there is some trouble already between Emile and Alice. They are so young, but I fear already he is corrupting her. I say corrupting – that is, he has his grubby hands over her, rustling about in her skirts. I've heard her shouting for help on several occasions, I'm not too proud to confess, but of course he has the right idea. She's not altogether an ugly looking creature, and he pleases himself certainly. I doubt the little devil stops for one moment to consider feeling guilty, but it is marvellous to behold, the young – so simple, so guilt free.

'What good can we do, stopping to consider every little thing? Building up some fantastic picture of our lives, of our "selves". Are we not essentially the same as the animals we so despise? The same as the machines, the dull inert nature all around us?

'Yes, I can see you are outraged at this sort of talk. You look like an enquiring sort, I imagine you would quite happily be a professor, or some such academic in another setting.'

The old man contemplated this notion for a moment.

'Professor, ha, yes that is what I'll call you,' he was evidently pleased with this name, 'but of course there is no space for academia in this house.'

Grabbing μ by the arm, the old man led him away down the corridor. μ, too taken back by the recent diatribe, simply followed behind, unsure of what to make of this latest twist. It seemed undeniable that this old man had given him some sort of reprieve. In a sense, saved him from Salvador and whatever lay after his heavy grip, but where did that leave him? A giant hole swallowed μ's thoughts making it difficult to think clearly. Where had he really wanted to go?

Now it seemed he was to have a job. Would that be such a bad thing? As Karl had said, 'an empty mind.' What good am I just floating about, purposeless, asking the wrong questions to the wrong people? Perhaps this was what he needed. He would be closer to the actual workings of this strange house, find out the real situation and meet the sort of people that could get things done. What if the old man was right and Ddunsel did not exist? No, he didn't need to think of that yet. He had time. He could watch, take things pragmatically.

After all, on reflection, this place was far more complex than he had initially imagined. It would take longer to find Ddunsel and get out of this place. It was a task that would take considerable ingenuity and planning – he had plenty of time. Would it not make sense to have a job, be working there on the inside, so to speak? and yet at the same time he couldn't shake the feeling that every step he took along the corridor he was trampling on his own dreams, slowly becoming less, a nothing. Would he eventually sink to the stage where he was indistinguishable from the rest of the servants?

They arrived at Karl's quarters by magic; µ recognised nothing in this house. He was given a uniform of sorts, a shabby shirt and trousers. Karl called for Alice and Emile to present themselves and sat in silence while they waited for µ's two co-workers to arrive. µ was comfortable in the uniform. It was pale green and white, a hard wearing fabric. Already he was more at ease in this place. He would not be an intruder, he would belong somewhere for a change.

Alice and Emile arrived in a flurry of activity. Emile was a fat, greasy little boy who managed to hover around Alice, tormenting her constantly. Even as Karl addressed them, to explain that they would have a new workmate, Emile poked and pinched at Alice, causing her to squirm and catch her breath, afraid of letting out a cry in front of Karl. Her discomfort delighted Emile and goaded him on to greater cruelty, groping and pinching her, prodding his hand between her thighs. Through all this Karl maintained an unequivocal tone.

Finally the interview was over and he sent the three of them away with instructions that Alice should teach µ the ropes. He would be subordinate to both of them as he was new to the position and his footing in the building was so uncertain. Alice would show him the basics to begin with and he would take his orders from Emile. He would present himself to Karl's office twice a day at the beginning and end of his shift and he would be given a mattress in the same dormitory as the others.

Was that it? Was it as easy as that? He should be destined to work as a dishwasher or whatever it was they did?

'There's been some mistake.' Now was the time to speak up, if ever.

'A mistake?' Karl had a broad grin on his face. 'Why, what sort of mistake do you imagine there has been?'

'Well to start with I am a guest in this house, I shouldn't be turning over bed sheets.'

At this, Karl, Emile and Alice all broke out laughing, although to be fair it did seem that Alice was only laughing out of politeness. To join in with the others, so to speak.

'In that case, perhaps I should call dear Salvador again. What do you say, Professor?' A look of mirth played on Karl's smooth face.

μ had no response.

Perhaps it was best to follow them for just now. He could work out a plan to leave later on. He felt a powerful desire to be with other people. On his own was he not in danger of becoming adrift in this place? He fell in step behind Alice, marching down the hall. As an act or rebellion he said nothing to Karl as they walked away.

'Is it not people in any case that you really need?' he thought, 'Nothing more or less than that will save me. All these theories, these grand ideas – but it is only people we can love, it is only people that are our kin. I am not a rock or plant or dolphin, after all, everything we think, or write or do is done as a human would do it. Every action, every breath is a human breath. Every love we can know is a human love. We cannot love the rocks, though there may be acres of poetry written about them. We cannot love the sea, or the sun, or the animals, the hills, the plants, or the forests, nor all the food, the mountains and buildings, cities and pathways – no, we cannot love any of those things if we cannot first love people. Isn't the word "people" simply another word for ourselves, our own nature? We are all people and all inseparably part of the people. That is what we are and all we can be.'

Lost in his thoughts, μ trudged a small distance behind his two new colleagues. He had a growing resentment for them already. His noble feelings of brotherly love disappeared when he looked at Emile's spotty little face. On what basis was that grotty little snot able to boss him around?

And what about Alberta? What had their encounter meant? Her briskness. Did she really do it for money? Or for some other need? To offer her openings for strangers to pierce, to be a slave, a master's toy?

μ knew he did not have the cruelty, the mien to be her master. And yet did he not love her even after that? Could he not expend his efforts chasing her, rather than some figment of his imagination such as Ddunsel?

All the elements of his life seemed almost to belong to some other story. They connected, vaguely. There was the definite suggestion that they were somehow unified, but how exactly it all connected was impossible to say. It was all tantalisingly close, yet so muddled. There were no easy answers. He had a feeling it might all take far, far longer to understand than he initially imagined. A lifetime even to unravel?

The work, once he got into it, was easy, stupefyingly so. Alice patiently showed him how to clean the tables, change filters on the machinery, re-stock consumables, position napkins or measure the detergent; all tasks he had no interest in learning, but which he followed dumbly nonetheless.

Throughout this Alice displayed a simple naivety that μ found inexplicably infuriating. From time to time she would clutch the small silver cross that she kept around her neck. The only time she became animated was if she was anxious that someone in authority might come and deliver a punishment, but otherwise she remained utterly vacant.

Emile was unbearable, but μ quickly learnt the best ways to avoid contact with him. Always keen to be seen strutting up and down in front of the guests, Emile was loath to venture too far into the bowels of the house and, by choosing the menial jobs furthest away from the main concourses, μ could spend a whole day without seeing him. Nobody cared about the work he did there. He could toil unbothered by any needless aggravation from the greasy boy.

The structure of the house also grew clearer in μ's mind. He started to understand how everything worked, but the knowledge brought him no satisfaction. The three of them – μ, Alice and Emile – were near the bottom of the pile. They truly had nothing.

They were fed, it was true, taking whatever scraps they pleased from the leftover dishes they cleared. Normally it was cold and slightly congealed, but they had little room to complain since the food, as they were regularly reminded, had been prepared by the finest chefs.

They slept well enough too, although it would have taken a miracle if any of them could have managed to stave off sleep by the end of each long tedious day. The space the three of them shared was a small room adjoining the kitchens, the air stained with grease, spice and noise at all hours. In reality it was little more than a storage cupboard, but at least they each had their own thin mattress to sleep on. Alice had even set about decorating the place, tirelessly carrying on after the long day to make the small space homely, hanging discarded cloths and towels she had collected, to brighten the place up.

And how long did μ work there? Did he stay a long time? It is hard to say. There were no clocks in that place, and even if there had been, what time would they have ticked to? Not the same time as that outside. How long can two clocks be expected to coincide in any case?

That he forgot a lot of details was only natural. There were few windows in that place and μ gradually forgot about the world outside. The hunt for Ddunsel, for Alberta, was never blunted, but rather buried, submerged so that it became hard to distinguish the desire from that of a distant story.

Once, he had a vision. A vision of Ddunsel. He was clearing a table in the library after the guests had left. He had assumed he was alone. He sensed a presence on the far side of the room. It was hard to make out the face. The stranger made no noise but it seemed to μ that he tipped his head toward him. They stared at each other across the green, limp space of the library and μ put down his cloth.

The figure stepped forward, a dark silhouette. Was there any forgiveness in him? μ was frozen. A sob rushed up his throat but no sound came. Before he knew it, the figure had left the room.

He wanted to tell Ddunsel that he was wrong. That some things were important. That you couldn't just claim that nothing mattered. The universe was impenetrable and beautiful and wonderful and there was a power in it, a power that you could not defile with impunity.

In that moment an overwhelming promise engulfed μ, an awesome wave of potential. There was more to life than thin cynicism, more than easy shots, more than all this rhetoric.

All this was in him, and in that moment μ felt a tremendous surge of passion, a terrifying vertigo, the impulse that he should do something – tear out of the room, run down the hallway, chase after Ddunsel, chase after Alberta – the moment for action was there and it was real and he was alive… but it passed. His thoughts dissipated. He crossed the room to stand by the sill and watch the green evening light fading.

INT. PUBLISHER'S OFFICE - DAY

UP enters from the reception area. The room has been transformed – it now has a sleek expensively minimal feel.

The books that lined one wall have gone, replaced by a smart glass shelving unit. Futuristic ebook devices and promotional material are on display. Along the top shelf a sign reads: THE FUTURE OF WORDS.

A woman, SAR, in her early forties and dressed in a power suit, sits behind the desk. Seeing UP she stands and offers her hand.

UP stops, startled, and looks around.

                    UP:
    It's been a while since I was here.

                    SAR:
    Please take a seat. I wasn't sure if you
    would make it after all today.

                    UP:
    You've got new chairs.

                    SAR:
    Yes, it was a difficult decision but in the
    end we went with a minimal look. I must
    say it feels a privilege to take on the
    mantle.

                    UP:
    I didn't know that you knew....

                    SAR:
    No, not personally, but you hear the buzz.

THE WAVE

It's such a tragedy.

                    UP:
The buzz?

                    SAR:
About the book. His book.

                    UP:
His book?

                    SAR:
They're saying it's shaping up to be a
publishing phenomenon.

UP looks uncertain and smiles politely.

                SAR: (CONT'D)
Digital pre-orders are unbelievable and
we are talking across multiple platforms.
All from a few posts online.

                    UP:
Sorry, what book are you talking about?
Tob's book?

                    SAR:
Well, I've only had a chance to read some
of it but they say it's a lot more than a
biography. It talks about suicide, life,
death, everything. It's the first digital
'novel of ideas'.

                    UP:
I didn't even know he'd finished it.

SAR looks at UP, confused for a moment.

                    SAR:
I thought the two of you were...?

                    UP:
I... We are ... I was. We haven't spoken
in a while.

SAR looks even more confused.

                    SAR:
Anyway, I'm glad I've got the chance to
finally meet you.

                    UP:
Likewise.

                    SAR:
I've heard so much. 'White Lilies' of
course is one of my all-time favourites.

                    UP:
Yes, it did do well.

                    SAR:
Sometimes, I think maybe there was a magic
about paper that you just don't get with
digital.

UP smiles wearily.

                    SAR: (CONT'D)
But then a book like this comes along.

                    UP:
I really didn't realise. You've bought
the rights?

                    SAR:
Oh no, not us. It went to Pommegrain Books.

THE WAVE

UP:
You know, I didn't think he would ever
finish it.

SAR:
No, indeed, it's been really moving the
way it has all happened so quickly.

UP considers SAR with a puzzled expression.

SAR:
We heard that parts were based on a
manuscript you initially took to him?

UP:
Ah, I can't help you I'm afraid. I'm no
longer representing that book. At the
request of the author.

SAR:
Really? And who is the new agent?

UP:
I don't know. To be honest I'm not sure
there is one. The last I heard the author
was starting a new project, a new direction
in life.

SAR:
But maybe you could let us have a peek at
the book that inspired Tob's so much?

UP:
It's not really my place - not if the
author no longer wants representation. I
couldn't. Why don't you ask Tob? He was in
contact with the author I believe.

SAR gives UP a worried look.

                    SAR:
Sorry.

                    UP:
Honestly he would probably know more than
me.

                    SAR:
But you don't know?

                    UP:
Know what?

                    SAR:
About Tob.

                    UP:
What about Tob?

                    SAR:
The cancer.

                    UP:
Yes, I knew about that, but it has gone
into remission.

                    SAR:
He told you that?

                    UP:
Yes.

                    SAR:
But that's impossible.

                    UP:
Why?

SAR looks hard at UP a sympathetic smile

THE WAVE

on her face.

> SAR:
> You don't know? His fight, these last few
> months?

SAR walks awkwardly around the table and stiffly
puts a hand on UP's shoulder.

> SAR:
> I'm sorry, you really didn't know?

UP smiles desperately at SAR looking for some
trace of a joke.

UP takes a few deep breaths.

> UP:
> I have to go. I'm sorry.

Curtly she turns and exits the room.

EPILOGUE

The gravel path led up a short incline to a point where it was possible to look down across the city. Today the clouds were only patches and the view from the graveyard was flawless. She walked unhurriedly, the wooden box clutched in her hand. She had been afraid to open it until then. Afraid of what she would find inside.

It had been an endless process: the preparations, the funeral and then the wake. She knew a lot of the people there but not one of them meant anything to her. All these acquaintances, colleagues, lovers, was it possible that they could mean so little?

She had been happy to let his family deal with most of the formalities. Margo had been a gem of course. They had talked at length those past few days and Margo had confided in her far more than ever. There was a deeper bond between them now and she felt she understood some of the reasons behind things she had long since assumed would remain a mystery.

She approached the brow of the hill and looked around at the gravestones. This was the grandest part of the cemetery and large stone tombs sat side by side imposing on the city skyline. What did any of it mean? When she looked back, it all seemed like nothing more than a streak of light. Like the jet trails left by an aeroplane on a clear blue day – sharp and rich for a moment, but almost instantly disappearing, wafting away. They had shared so much. She was sure of that and yet already she felt the connections loosening. How did it all tie up? Was it even possible to imagine that it could tie up?

She remembered the holiday they had shared in Arrecife. It had seemed so new then, she remembered, before they developed the place, destroyed it. They had seemed like adventurers.

She remembered the stolen lunches at Coram's Fields, half hiding in case they should be seen. The day he had told her he was leaving Margo. Their flat together and the furniture they had chosen together. The arguments and the reconciliations. And then the years apart. The cheating. The lies. The loneliness. Old age entering like an unwanted house guest.

What sort of story could she tell from all these parts? Was there any story to tell? It was quiet here. Was it not the silence after all that conquered everything? Was it not the gaps in between living that had held the gold?

How old age had sneaked up on her. At first it had taken the disguise of something benign, a friend staying over for a few nights while passing through town, nothing too serious. She had noticed a minor ache here and there or a moment of forgetfulness, but always accompanied by a comfortable excuse, a feeling that she had earned the right to unwind. Then, slowly, the realisation that this house guest was never leaving, that old age had pitched up camp in her life and would eventually inherit the house.

She walked off the path and sat out of view behind a large Victorian tomb. The grass was a little damp but she didn't mind. It would probably rain soon in any case.

Looking across the city she tried to make out some landmarks, but the perspective twisted the familiar streets. The city became a mysterious sculpture, a labyrinth of stone. From up here there were a lot of new buildings too. Modern, glass fronted skyscrapers – triangles, rectangles and domes that shouted that a new age was coming. All built by the 'invisible hand'.

Well, the 'invisible hand' had moved her as well and her life was not so bad. She had come a long way. Would she miss him? She didn't know. She had missed him violently before, when it had mattered, and now she was not sure she had the energy for feelings like those any more. She remembered the anger. The deep, indignant anger that had been her life for a long time. It had consumed her until finally the day had come when something clicked. She had decided it just wasn't worth it any more. She had let go of something valuable, but in actual fact all she lost was the need to shout.

It had been replaced with something new – a deeper, heavier ache. There was no wisdom in growing old. Only a whittling down of your responses. A gradual wearing away of your desire to shout back at the world.

When she had divorced, she remembered thinking that she was getting too old for romance, and yet her life had not been as deserted as she had feared after that. Perhaps there was room for surprises.

She placed the box on the ground beside her and pulled at a tuft of grass. How many lay dead here? How many more would she be around to bury, and one day join? Carefully she lifted the box onto her lap and felt the catch. It was a simple bronze latch that fastened with a short circular stud. The top of the box was varnished wood but the sides were merely sanded.

On the top were printed the words: 'Finest Hand Made Long Filler Cigars'. Supposing it really contained nothing more than a handful of cigars? She tried to picture what it was that he would choose to leave to her.

He had already been more than generous in terms of his worldly assets. She would not be short of money, according to the executor, but she had never asked for anything except the one thing he hadn't been willing to give.

Slowly, uncertainly she lifted the latch. What treasure lay inside? A wave of emotion flooded over her then. A whole lifetime of feeling descended from the sky above and pounced on her. Had she not been waiting for this? Was this not why she had delayed so long to open the box? A sadness ate at her as she felt the tears come. Why had he never listened? Why had it not been different? Why had she never listened?

On one side of the box packets of photographs were haphazardly stuffed away. There must have been hundreds of photos and films altogether. It was years since she had held an actual print in her hand.

The rest of the box was filled with trinkets, detritus, each one tugging at her heart. Hidden at the bottom was a gold ring, emblazoned with a green slash of emerald. She picked it out and held it up to the skyline.

A drop of rain fell, landing perfectly on the ring and rolled down the lip of the band. She looked upwards, her face red with tears.

Hidden under various papers was a small plastic souvenir. She recognised it with a shallow breath. It was a snow globe. Nothing but a tourist bauble. The sort of thing they sold at every airport.

It was over thirty years old, yet the crude plastic it was manufactured from showed no signs of age. Inside, three figures sat beside a frozen lake in a cosy winter scene. She remembered buying it on a whim as they ran to catch a flight.

Around the base it read: 'Alberta – A Lifetime of Memories'.

She shook it.

For a moment, it seemed like the whole world was contained inside.

.

THE WAVE

LOCHLAN BLOOM

A Note on Intellectual Property

The section of this book describing the events in Brazil includes a character variously referred to as Professor Bohm, Dr Bohm, and, in some places, simply David. It should be noted that while there are significant similarities between the character in this narrative and the real, although sadly deceased, theoretician David Bohm, the author wishes to state that this does not imply any material connection.

While it is true that David Bohm lived in Brazil during the 1950s, as a result of anti-communist fervour in the USA, the majority of the events in this book have been entirely fabricated. Several concepts mentioned in this story, such as his interest in holistic quantum philosophy and the concept of an implicate order or guiding wave at the foundations of reality are true, but the rest are heavily fictionalised. In short, a large amount of detail has been imagined by the author rather than proceeding from historical fact.

Having said this, however, it would be difficult to apply the standard disclaimer – All characters appearing in this work are fictitious. Any resemblance to real persons, living or dead is purely coincidental –- as, even from a brief reading, it is clear that the author has lifted certain sections almost verbatim from David Bohm's biography and clumsily worked them into the text.

This is a fictional tale. It is a description of certain distances: the distance between places, between real and fictional, between now and then, and, most importantly, the distance between people.

Just how far is it from Gotham City to Atlantis, or from London to Casterbridge, for that matter? What is the distance between Lady Chatterley and Raskolnikov? From Paul Auster to Pierre Menard? Or from me to you?

Some people may think these sorts of questions are idle and ultimately meaningless, but this book was not written for them.

Publishing the Underground

This book was published as part of Dead Ink's Publishing the Underground project and supported by Arts Council England. Publishing the Underground aims to bring readers closer to authors and enables them to support their work and bring them to publication.

Dead Ink and Lochlan Bloom would like to thank everybody who supported this project. Without your help the publication of this book would not have been possible. To thank you all for your dedication we have included your names in order to acknowedge the contribution that you made.

If you would like to support future Dead Ink titles and keep up to date with our authors then please stay in touch via our website.

WWW.DEADINKBOOKS.COM

Aaron Kneen
Akiho Schilz
Alex Shough
Alexa Radcliffe-Hart
Alison Ramsay
Anthony Finucane
Antony Scoulding
Ben Spiers
Bobby Gant
Catriona Ramsay
Christopher O'Brien
Claire Stephenson
Daniel Coxon
Daniel Grant
Darroch McNaught
Dave Bache
David Court
Douglas Streatfield
Eric Waring
Harry Gallon
Helena Blakemore
Ian Carrington
Ian Chung
Ian McMillan
J E Dalladay
J Ramsay
Jaimie Batchan
Jaimie Henderson
James Tawton
Jasmin Kate Kirkbride
Jayna Makwana
Jeanette Duncan

John Prebble
Jordan Philips
Joshua Beever
Joshua Crupi
Kathleen Bryson
Katy Woodward
Kelly Woollard
Ken Newlands
Lorna Riley
Lynn Earnshaw
Malcolm Smith
Michelle Ryles
Miss Leeming
Mr Earl
Nadine Fritz
Neale Long
Nicholas Dwyer
Nina Gryf
Nyle Connolly
Paolo Sedazzari
Patrissia Cuberos
Paul Kelso
Rebeca Delgado
Rebecca Reid
Rebecca Rosenthal
Rebekah Watson
Rupert Evans Harding
Rupert van den Broek
Sally Ashton
Sarah Bradley
Sarah Hunt

Simon Middleton
Sophie Offord
Steve Dearden
Thomas McColl
Tracey Connolly
Val Harvey
Vicky Pointing

NEW VOICES
2015

New Voices is Dead Ink's annual publication of new books from new authors. New Voices 2015 is...

The Shapes of Dogs' Eyes
by Harry Gallon
9780957698598

The Wave
by Lochlan Bloom
9780957698567

When Lights Are Bright
by Wes Brown
9780957698550

Available from deadinkbooks.com